RESISTANCE

Alex Cole

For everyone I love……

Copyright © Alex Cole 2008
ISBN: 978-0-9558558-0-1

RESISTANCE

- The act or an instance of resisting or the capacity to resist.
- A force that tends to oppose or retard motion.
- Resistance - an underground organization engaged in a struggle for national liberation in a country under military or totalitarian occupation.
- Psychology. A process in which the ego opposes the conscious recall of anxiety-producing experiences.

Biology
- The capacity of an organism to defend itself against a disease.
- The capacity of an organism or a tissue to withstand the effects of a harmful environmental agent.

INTRODUCTIONS

"Shit... I'm waiting for the sun to shine."
(Travis Bickle)

Hello, my name is David Marshall, welcome to the world through my eyes.

I have had enough of inconsiderate people. In fact that means I have had enough of almost everyone I come across in my life.

I am slowly losing my faith in the human race. Humans are a parasitic waste of time on this earth. There are probably lots of acts of kindness happening every day. But most of these happen so these 'helpful' people can feel good about themselves. These are not selfless acts. Human beings are programmed to be selfish. Darwin said that, not me. Charity work should be commended, but do you ever get the impression that the man who sits in a bath full of baked beans to raise money is more interested in the attention he is getting than the money he is raising?

An esteemed (but essentially stupid) Economist believes the opposite to me. He thinks that all people are fundamentally unselfish; I personally think he's talking rubbish. He cites road rage as an altruistic act, because there is nothing to gain for the 'road rager'. They are selflessly trying to make sure that other road users are upholding the laws of the road, and therefore benefiting other road users in future.

I think road rage is someone getting pissed off and wanting to vent their anger, thereby making themselves feel better. But maybe I am just too negative, and what do I know. The esteemed Economist should know more than me, he has studied it for many years, sat in a small office hidden away from real life in some university generating theories and never meeting ordinary people.

My personal experience of life has taught me that people are becoming less and less considerate. I much prefer Darwin's theory that natural selection makes people fundamentally selfish. People are constantly fighting to better their own interests at the expense of others. That's more in line with the people I see in everyday life.

Modern society has created a structure for people to get away with behaving more and more selfishly. Modern society creates freedom which encourages people to behave however they want. By allowing freedom, which is generally a good thing, you are providing an environment where people can police themselves. I see a lot of people abusing this freedom. A society that encourages freedom of behaviour is good, but on the other hand it creates an arrangement whereby there is too much trust placed in people. And people cannot be trusted.

This abuse of freedom is supported by the increasingly strange nature of human behaviour in the modern world. Serial killers, paedophiles, rapists. The modern world has created an environment where these people can exist a lot more easily than ever before. A German man met someone on the internet who wanted to be eaten, so they met up and he killed and ate him. I mean seriously, what the hell is that all about?

The fabric of society has morphed into something unpleasant and supportive of unpleasant people. Disgusting criminal behaviour will now only be punished by a suspended sentence, or a few months in an open prison. I know it's all about rehabilitation these days, but in reality it's about money. The politically correct and free loving nature of society means that everyone has gone soft, and this has left our societal system open to abuse.

It must sound like I am a bitter and twisted individual, but far from it. I actually lead what most people would consider a remarkably normal and rewarding life. It's underneath my layer of middle class normality that people and life are gradually driving me insane. No one around me can see it. I hide it well.

I have a large circle of friends, go on interesting holidays, enjoy sport, have a lovely girlfriend Laura, a pet Staffordshire bull terrier called Steve, and a well paid job doing something that bores me just like most people.

Every day I spend eight hours doing something I don't like with people I don't like. It's the same for most people. At least that is what I tell myself to rationalise each and every day of my working life.

I go through life watching people's behaviour with an anthropological interest. I view people around as David Attenborough might observe a group of chimps, and I have gradually been getting more and more annoyed with the selfish and inconsiderate tossers who inhabit this world. Life is wasted on too many people.

To make things worse it seems that the biggest culprits are actually some of the most successful people. So much for "Blessed are the meek: for they shall inherit the Earth", Jesus didn't quite get that right when he was preaching his Sermon from the Mount. From what I can see wankers are inheriting the Earth.

A great example of a complete tit in my office is the head of my department, Crispin Matthews. He is an odious man, universally disliked by everyone. However, he has his ass continually cleaned by the willing tongues of the brown nose brigade in my department. People swallowing their pride to advance their careers. He loves the power trip of it all. He loves watching these people subjugating themselves for his amusement.

Crispin Matthews is a weasel. He acts like a weasel, and he looks like a weasel. He is a short, thin man, with what looks like a normal hairstyle from the front, but at the back of his head is a monk-like bald patch. I sometimes wonder if he is even aware that he is bald. His fondness for pinstripe suits that are far too big for him, makes him look even smaller, and just adds to his weasel-like appearance with his little bald head poking out of his oversized suits. He spends most of the working day politicking around the office, being seen in the right places, and being smarmy with the right people.

He holds court in the department, telling some ridiculous anecdote about his painfully boring life. As he talks people from the brown nose brigade gather round him, hanging on every boring word and laughing maniacally at the right moment. Like a magnet he attracts the shameless sycophants around him.

When he finishes his witty anecdote, there is always an anxious pause as people look around for other's reactions. Someone quickly brings out their loud false laugh, and then the chorus of forced laughter booms out across the department. Crispin looks around to make sure other people are appreciating how amusing and brilliant he is. I find it pathetic. He once cornered me with a story about his love of making the local farmers hand deliver his vegetables. He loves the power trip he gets from making these 'simpletons', as he calls them, obey him.

The reality is, he's a tosser, everyone thinks he's a tosser, and the only person who doesn't know he's a tosser is him.

Behind his back he is the butt of many jokes from the two faced people who kiss his pinstriped ass one minute, and ridicule him the next. These two faced people are the ones who then get the promotions. They then promote in their own image, and so on, and so on. These promotions create a vicious circle, idiots promoting idiots, promoting idiots. It's a vicious circle; it's a circle of idiocy.

Crispin and one of his senior management pals came into the toilet the other day whilst I was at the urinal. They bowled into the toilets laughing and talking loudly over each other. They weren't saying anything particularly funny, and definitely weren't listening to each other. They were just talking loudly and laughing together as some strange form of bonding.

There were two spare urinals either side of me, and they approached me still jabbering away. Each took a urinal to the side of me, and to my surprise and horror, just carried on talking over me as they urinated. It was as if I wasn't there. I couldn't believe the rudeness, they didn't care about me, I was so insignificant that they could do as they wish. I quickly finished, shook, and left the urinal to wash my hands and escape the bizarre situation.

That is a good example of how some of the higher echelons of people behave. The 'superior' people looking down on everyone else. They are the pigs in animal farm, they are better than everyone else, so they assume control and do as they wish. All animals are equal, but some are more equal than others.

Crispin is married with two young children, but that doesn't stop him from abusing his position and taking advantage of the women in the department who are happy to sleep their way to the top. At the Christmas party five years ago he spent most of the night canoodling with a female member of staff, Jo Reed, who later went up to his hotel room and spent the night with him. It resulted in a brief fling (they were also seen having lunch together in a local pub a few weeks later). Jo Reed is also married and has children. And what do you think were the consequences of their outrageous infidelity? She was promoted fast tracked up the career ladder.

Both of these people deserve to be reprimanded for their behaviour. Instead they have both seen nothing but good times since their indiscretion, and for her the success is purely down to sleeping with someone and betraying her husband and children. I hate to see things like that, and I wish I had the balls to do something about it, but I just bitch and moan and do nothing.

It is common knowledge that at least four other married colleagues have been enjoying affairs. None of them seem to have any intention of leaving their wives/husbands/families. They are just enjoying themselves without a thought for their children or their partners. These selfish people fuck me right off. I hate them. I hate what they do, and I hate that they get away with it. And I hate myself for doing nothing about it.

IDIOTS

"I like long walks, especially when they are taken by people who annoy me."
(Oscar Wilde)

It never ceases to amaze me that there are so many annoying idiots in this world.

I am constantly surprised by the amount of people who I see and meet who are idiots. Not idiots in a stupid or slow sense. I am referring to people who are classed as normal, but who act like selfish, thoughtless, idiots. Idiots who should know better.

Everyday people who go about their business in a thoughtless way, only concerned with themselves, and lacking respect for other people. They just stroll through life in a little bubble, doing whatever they want, regardless of the consequences. They have no social conscience. I find these people really, really intensely annoying.

In the last few years I have begun to notice more and more of these people. I don't know whether this is heightened awareness on my part, or whether people in general are getting more annoying.

I see people happy to screw their colleagues for promotion. Swallow their pride and kiss ass. Reckless drivers who take other people's lives into their hands every time they get into their cars. Minor criminals who get let off with just a little slap on the wrist. The morals seem to have gone out of society. And the government's response? The ASBO (Antisocial Behaviour Order). I mean, what kind of bollocks is that. Ten years ago people would have laughed at the thought of an ASBO. Now they are being enforced all over the place to cope with the increasing levels of antisocial behaviour. People don't know how to behave themselves. People used to know what was, and wasn't, antisocial, they didn't need an ASBO to tell them.

The ASBO doesn't really cover what annoys me. I am more concerned with the everyday selfishness that I see exhibited all around me. Not the criminal selfishness.

Wherever you look you can see people doing selfish and annoying things. Take a look around you, observe people closely, and you will see more and more examples of people who are annoying. On any given day, if you observe the behaviour of people around you, I guarantee that you will see at least one example of someone doing something that is thoughtless or annoying.

It could be something minor. For example, an extra queue opens up at the supermarket; the people from the back of your queue immediately go straight to the front of the new queue. Everyone knows that isn't how it should work. You, and the people closer to the front of the original queue, have been queuing longer, so the new queue should rightfully be offered to you. Instead, you have to watch someone who only just joined your queue get served straight away, and walk out of the shop whilst you remain waiting patiently. I watch these people leave the shop, I follow them with my eyes, and sometimes I wish really hateful things on them for being so inconsiderate.

There is rarely anybody who offers the new queue to the people who have been waiting longer. Admit it, you have experienced this, and it has wound you up. Your impotence as you watch it happen, the disbelief that someone could be so ignorant, these must be familiar feelings.

Another example, which winds me up every time, happens in the rush hour traffic.

Firstly, I resent the fact that I have to sit in traffic for an hour just to get to and from a job I don't enjoy, but that isn't the point it just makes the situation worse.

Here is the scenario. You are sitting in rush hour traffic waiting patiently at a junction as the cars slowly crawl past. There is never going to be a space for you to get out, so you are reliant on someone else doing you a favour and letting you in. In an equal and righteous world the two queues would operate an alternate system, one car from each queue at a time. How often does that happen?

Instead you sit and watch as people in the main lane of traffic wait in their cars right in front of you. They know that common courtesy means they should let you out. Instead they sit there, avoiding eye contact, making sure they get that extra few metres further by not letting you out. It's just rudeness. They know they should let you out. That is why they avoid eye contact. Eventually someone will let you out, but not before the majority of selfish people have crawled by, happy to let you sit and wait.

If everyone shared that attitude, then there would be people stuck in that traffic for the rest of their lives. Also, I bet that when the selfish people, who make a conscious decision to let no one out, are in that situation themselves they expect to be let out straight away. They probably edge out until they are so far out of the junction that someone is forced to let them out. Everyday scum. I hate them.

Another traffic related example is the phenomenon of people hogging the outside lane on motorways.

When you are on a busy motorway you will notice that the outside lane, and the centre lane, fill up with traffic as people refuse to drive in the inside lane. Ultimately this slows everyone down. If everyone moved over one lane then the traffic would flow a lot better. Instead all the selfish drivers don't want to lose their place in the faster lanes, and the consequence is that everything slows down. Often the inside lane actually goes faster than the outside lane.

It is pure selfishness and individualism. If people actually thought about their actions, and were happy to move aside, then everyone would get to their destination a lot faster. Instead the selfishness slows everyone down. I fucking hate these drivers. I stare at them as I drive past, look into their souls, and try to understand what turned them into such a bellend.

The 'Supermarket Stand Off' is a further example of human selfishness. You find yourself in a busy shop, or supermarket, and as you work your way round the supermarket you encounter people who refuse to move out of your way. They just stand there with their trolleys, staring you down. They hate you for wanting them to move. I hate them back, a hundred times more than they hate me. Often they have moved in front of you, but still expect you to move out of their way. Sometimes there is literally no way past them, yet they still refuse to move. I hate them.

I wish I could be more outwardly expressive of my hatred for these people. Instead I step to the side and let them through so they can fill their trolleys with crisps, biscuits and ready meals, eat themselves to death with their obesity related diseases. Maybe that is why I move aside, so I can speed up their food shop and eating related deaths.

The worst examples of this kind of ignorant behaviour have been made illegal, and the people who cross those boundaries are classed as sociopaths. These are the kind of people you see on the news, murderers, rapists, muggers, etc, proper criminals. Everyone agrees that this criminal disregard for others is wrong and bad, but what I find myself more and more annoyed with are the every day selfish people. They get away with it too easily.

I believe that even the people who commit the minor acts should be classed as sociopaths. They lack empathy with other people; it is simply different levels of sociopathy.

IDIOTS AT WORK

"Employee of the month is a good example of how somebody can be both a winner and a loser at the same time."
(Demetri Martin)

You will probably find that work, or 'Idiotland' as I like to call it, is the richest source of idiotic people. You are forced to spend more time around your work colleagues, which makes it more difficult for them to keep their idiocy hidden. If someone is an idiot it always surfaces. Once it surfaces you become more aware of it, and it becomes even easier to spot these people when they are behaving like an idiot.

I only have to glance around my office and there are a dozen or so people that can be categorised as 'complete idiots' and then a good twenty or so more who fall into the 'bit of an idiot' category. There are only a hundred people in my department, so that means over a third are idiots. Here is an example of the mentality that I have to deal with every day.

A male member of staff wears a pink shirt to work. Then the rest of the men in my department immediately berate him for being gay, and this will go on for the entire day, no one ever gets tired of it. That is the kind of thing I have to sit and listen to all day. Every single day.

There are a lot of intelligent people in my department, but that doesn't stop them from being idiots. In fact, if anything, it makes me think that they are probably even bigger idiots. They should know better. They probably do know better, but make a deliberate decision to act in a certain way for their own good.

Every day I watch people striding round the office with their important looking struts. Moving at pace, shoulders back, making sure they are noticed as someone who is working so hard that they <u>have</u> to walk very fast through the office. Faster than the average worker who can afford to walk normally because he isn't pushing the agenda as hard.

My colleagues prance through the office saying stupid things like this;

(translations provided for people who don't work in the same corporate environment as me)

- "Is that fit for purpose in terms of the cohesion of the product spectrum?" - Is that any good?
- "Can we drive it through?" – Can we do that?
- "Can we talk high level in terms of the shape of the opportunity?" – let's talk about it.
- "Can I have a granular view of that?" - What are the details?
- "Can you refresh my thinking on that?" - Please tell me again?
- "Can I shoot the fox?" - Is it finished?
- "I have the bonnet up on that one", - I'm looking into it.
- "I'm in the van on that one", - I agree.
- "We need more impactful and sexy functionality", - It needs to be better.
- "We need to get together collectively to chew the cud and arrange alignment of our thinking" - We need to talk.
- "In terms of the landscape going forward" – This is what is going to happen.
- "Please can you clarify your thinking" – what the hell are you on about?

These insane quotes are all from just one day in my office, and examples of the utter rubbish I have to hear from the idiots around me.

Things in my office don't move, they 'migrate'. For example, we need to migrate that computer to the second floor, would mean that the computer needs to be moved to the second floor. Filing is no longer called filing, it is now given the more strategically important title of 'cupboard management'.

All day I am surrounded by these plebs. I just want to stand up and shout at everyone to stop talking utter bollocks and see their reaction. Instead I sit at my desk and say nothing. Some days it amuses me, some days it irritates me, and some days it drives me insane.

When I get to work every morning I zigzag my way through my trendy openplan office, past a barrage of idiocy, to get to my desk.

The first team I have to walk past contains 'The Welshman', Llewelyn Davies. He isn't actually Welsh. He was born, and grew up in,

Surrey. He was educated at a posh all boys school in Surrey. Married an English woman, and his two children were born, and have grown up in England. He also lives and works in England, as he has done his entire life. His only connection to Wales is his Welsh father, who moved to England years ago before Llewelyn was born.

Yet he is feverishly Welsh and proud. His favourite topic of conversation is rugby. Although when his new boss started, and it became apparent his new boss was interested in football he was quick to adopt a football team, and became almost as vocal about his love of football. He can often be heard mixing his rugby and newly acquired football banter, and sounding like a complete tit. My favourite example was when he referred to a footballer not returning the ball to the opposition from a line out instead of a throw in. He doesn't think before he speaks, and he speaks a lot, so he speaks a lot of crap.

He also tries to put on a Welsh accent, which doesn't work for two key reasons. One, he hasn't ever lived in Wales, and two, he is rubbish at accents. This combines to make him sound completely ridiculous. The only word he can say that sounds slightly Welsh is 'Boyo', so he calls everyone 'Boyo'. He thinks he sounds amazing, he actually sounds like a twat.

You can tell that being 'Welsh' is one of the pillars of his personality, and something that he would be lost without, but he isn't Welsh. It is just an office persona he has built for himself. He needs it to provide him with what he sees as an amusing niche within the office. The reality is that he comes across as a tosser.

I have witnessed him lie, and cheat, his way into a thoroughly unmerited senior position in our department, often at the expense of the people around him. He doesn't have one redeeming feature. He is one hundred percent annoying.

My granddad once said to me "Never trust a man with small eyebrows". I don't know how my granddad came to that conclusion. He was a prisoner of war with the Japanese, and I assumed this comment was down to his hatred of the Japanese, and perhaps he saw them as a small eye-browed race. Strangely, his insight was something I have observed to be true across all races. Llewelyn Davies' has such small eyebrows that in certain lights, he looks like he has no eyebrows at all. He can look like quite a freak, and he definitely cant be trusted.

I like to think that his rapidly balding head is a symptom of his inner knowledge, and the stress of knowing, that he is actually an idiot and that everyone thinks he is a twat. The office lighting glistening off his bald head acts as a 'twat beacon' warning everyone to steer clear of him. Like the 'bat signal', in that it warns you of danger.

I often think that the fuzzy pieces of hair that remain on his balding pate are reminiscent of a monkey's bum. There are a number of men with 'monkey's bum' hair in my department. All of them so stressed out by the pressures of being a 'corporate businessman' that their hair has given up on life and fallen out.

Llewelyn Davies also has another interesting facet to his personality. Although he his married with children, I am ninety nine point nine percent sure he is actually gay, and has been in the process of coming out of his closet for a number of years.

He keeps peaking through a crack in the closet door, but gets scared by the potential consequences, and has to close the closet door for another year.

There are a number of reasons for me to think this. Firstly, he enjoys nothing more than a girly chat. He is constantly trying to talk to the women in the office about their boyfriends, and their relationships. Secondly, he always makes comments about people's appearances and the clothes they wear. Not piss taking manly comments, but serious comments about how a certain blouse makes someone look really nice, or how well their skirt suits them. He will always notice if a man has a new pair of shoes, or a new shirt on, or has had their hair cut. It is very bizarre, and if it wasn't for spending so many working days trapped in an office with him, I probably would never have noticed his slightly camp approach to life.

The final, and most obvious expression of his homosexual tendencies, comes at the annual Christmas party. He dances like a woman. He is all spins, twirls, little thrusts, and sexual campness on the dance floor. He loves nothing more than to get in with a group of girls on the dance floor, and dance his little heart out all night.

As the party draws to an end, and he is drunk, he can usually be found chatting to some of the younger men in the office, testing the water.

He once sidled up to me on the dance floor and said, "You wouldn't think I was married with kids, would you."

I don't know if he was testing the water, but it was weird, and he could tell from the look of confusion on my face, that I wasn't hugely impressed.

He quickly back tracked, and said all he meant was I wouldn't think he was married with kids because he was partying so hard. I responded with "Yeah, you're a real party boy", and exited the dance floor quickly.

Llewelyn Davies is in his mid to late forties, so in his youth homosexuality was probably still illegal (homosexuality was only made legal in the UK in 1967). I believe that because he is from a generation when homosexuality was not accepted, he had to hide his homosexual tendencies. Society's pressures made him deny his natural urges, and forced him into a false marriage and the natural progression to fatherhood.

As he has aged, he has become more and more frustrated with denying these urges, it is also now more acceptable to be gay, so he feels more comfortable with 'letting himself go' from time to time. This means it has become more and more obvious that he might in fact be gay. It just takes a little alcohol to get him tapping at the closet door.

It's only a matter of time before he stops peaking out of the closet door, and comes charging out to the sound of 'It's raining men! Hallelujah!"

At some point in his life he has to decide it is time to come clean. Stop denying his urges, have some 'me time'and start his new life with someone called Jeremy he met at work, who is also married and they can come out of the closet together. That is how I envisage things panning out. It happens all the time; I have read about it in the magazines that Laura leaves on the coffee table at home.

If I can avoid any idiotic pro-Welsh, anti-English, comments on my way past Llewelyn's team then I have done well. The next obstacle is the 'Old School Daft Racist' (OSDR), Gerald Bennett.

The 'OSDR' is an interesting chap. He has worked at the company all his life, and now, in his mid fifties he is sitting on a big fat pension. He has given up on working life, and is effectively counting down until his retirement in ten years time. He can't leave as he needs his pension, he won't get promoted, but that doesn't matter as he doesn't want to be promoted. He is bored out of his brain, and spends most of the working day looking at the internet and planning what he is going to do when he retires.

This is a dynamite combination. It means he no longer cares what people think of him. If anything, he actually wants to upset people in order to progress the chances of redundancy and early retirement.

He is constantly experimenting to see what happens when he says, or does, something which isn't politically correct. He would love to be sacked and take a big redundancy package, and is more than happy to offend people, especially more senior people, if it means he gets closer to the redundancy he desires.

He has some favourite areas which he likes to exploit, especially in front of the more politically correct members of the department. These include immigration, in particular, the influx of Eastern Europeans into his town who are now taking all the jobs away from his children and other locals. Even though non of his children would ever have to do the kinds of jobs the immigrants are doing. Terrorism, and the role that Muslims play in British society, is another of his favourite subjects.

An Asian started at our work, he was obviously gay, and OSDR had to be reminded that he shouldn't use the term gaysian openly in the office as it didn't give out an appropriate impression of a professional workplace. Notice how he was just gently reminded, and told not to do it 'openly', he wasn't reprimanded in any way, and the message was clearly that it was ok to do it behind his back. That's because the senior team are a bunch of white upper class racists, who only employ minority groups to tick boxes in their diversity agendas.

OSDR knows how to be contentious, and he happily airs his right wing views just to get a reaction from his colleagues. His colleagues, all of whom would never want to be associated with that kind of thing (but only in case it affects their careers), feel compelled to argue against his old school views and often get very irate. This is exactly the reaction he wants, so he winds them up even more.

I find his impact on the department quite amusing, but only from a distance. I have spoken to him on a few occasions and he is actually quite a scary person who is best avoided. I wouldn't be surprised if we found out he has people buried under his patio, or has spent the last twenty years murdering prostitutes.

If I can successfully negotiate the first two office pitfalls, without being drawn in, then the third hazard is the 'Male Predator', Ian Morris. This is the most difficult obstacle on the route to my desk. This man is a danger, mainly to women, but also to men who he tries to use to look popular. He is dangerous to me because he thinks that looking sociable and humorous is a powerful aphrodisiac for the ladies. He tries to be everyone's best friend.

Someone being friendly is normally a good thing, except you can tell he isn't interested in anything you have to say, and is using you to send out a positive impression to the women in the department. This makes him intensely boring and frustrating to talk to.

I often see him stood brazenly in the office, scratching his armpit like a chimp asserting himself amongst his troop. Using the armpit scratching to spread his pheromones, sending love signals to the females, and territory signals to other males.

Ian Morris is a man who wants women, he wants women badly. He is informally known as the department's 'New Starter Liaison Officer', for the way he immediately pounces on any new girls who come into the office. He doesn't know this, but new women to the department always tell everyone about his advances. He thinks that surreptitious emails keep his attempted womanising a secret, but they always eventually get forwarded round the department. He won't leave women alone until they get angry and threatening with him. He is a classic sex pest. If he was at a less senior level then he would have been sacked for sexual harassment a long time ago. Instead, because of his influence on their career's, the women humour, and even encourage, him.

He never gets anywhere with women because he is an oily, slippery, greasy, middle aged man, who has never grown up. He dresses in tight t-shirts and tight jeans, and still wears trainers. He hangs out with the younger members of the office on his cigarette breaks, and walks with an Afro-American style swagger that looks like he is wafting a fart from his ass.

He is a ridiculous specimen. He must have a severe case of denial, because no matter how many times he gets blown out, he keeps going back for more. Like a boxer who never knows when he's beaten. His ego is unshakable.

Ian always tries to spark up a conversation with a witty remark shouted at people as they pass his desk. These remarks are never funny, and always make me feel awkward. They are purely to make him look good. They aren't conversation starters, just awkward comments that have no real response, and are aimed at making everyone look at Ian, and think that he is a witty man. The kind of man that a woman needs to sleep with. A powerful man.

Usually his comments make people hover around his desk feeling awkward and then slowly move away when the conversation fails. It has got to the point where I just ignore him. I know he hates it when I ignore him. It makes him look unpopular and an idiot. I don't care anymore. It's easier, and feels better, when I ignore the idiots, rather than try to tolerate them. I gave up tolerating these fools a long time ago.

I watch Ian working his mojo at the printer. Waiting for the attractive women in the office to print something and then printing any old rubbish so he can head them off at the printer for a 'printer chat'. He sees women as a war of attrition. He lives in a fantasy land where he eventually breaks the woman down and she falls madly in love with him, and his irresistible charms.

Ian Morris goes jogging on his lunch break to keep his slightly flabby middle aged body, and man boobs, in a bit of shape. His jogging outfit is tremendous. Tight lycra cycling shorts and a loose running vest that rides around his abdomen so you can clearly see his package. I think he likes the idea that he is on display, why else would you dress like that? It's not like he's trying to set any running world records. He returns to the office from his lunchtime run, dressed like that, with sweat pouring off him. He looks a mess, but always pauses to catch his breath in the reception area, making sure women see him in his full lycra glory. Women want nothing to do with him.

I really want to confront him and put him out of the misery, he is so delusional that he doesn't perceive his own idiocy. I want to tell him what he looks like, what everyone thinks about him. I want to shatter his fantasy. It sounds really harsh, but he needs to get back to reality. Watching him every day makes me cringe. His smug self importance. His massively misplaced self belief. But most of all his sweaty, lycra encased package. He needs to get a grip.

The most visually obvious idiot in my department is 'Military Man'. He prowls the office like a ball of furious, business focused, energy. I have nicknamed 'Military Man' because of his flat top haircut, regimented dress code (everything is thoroughly ironed, even after a hard day at the office there is not a crease in sight), his booming Northern accent, and his 'dynamic' competitive approach to work. He sees work as a war, he wants to win at all costs.

I often see him standing proudly in the office like a field marshal surveying his troops in battle. He has an amusing stance, with his hands on his hips, elbows out, and his crotch pushed forward aggressively. He is the alpha male. The office is his jungle. He comes to your desk and dominates you. He will fight any man to maintain his place in the hierarchy. It wouldn't surprise me to find him staying late in the office to rub his scent on the filing cabinets, and taking a crap by the photocopiers, to mark his territory.

When he wants something, he is on you, all over you like a rash, dominating your personal space. If he needs something from you, he needs it yesterday. You are scum, you are slowing down his ideas, and vis-à-vis his career. He will fight any man, or woman, who threatens his career. He is hyper-competitive; he would rather die than lose. He's a businessman, it's what he does. It is his raison d'etre.

I don't even escape these buffoons when I get to my desk. There are a couple more within earshot of my desk. All day long they blather on about their boring lives, kiss the arses of the senior managers at every opportunity, do very little work, and try to involve me in boring conversations about their cars and their lives. I don't know how I struggle through this daily drudgery.

Steve 'Midlife Crisis Man' (which sounds like a bizarre super hero) Clark, sits near to me. I don't know what powers he would have as a super hero, maybe the power to regress adults and make them act like teenagers again. Or the power to make people wear an inappropriate leather jacket well into their forties.

I can see his computer screen from where I sit, and he does little in the way of work. He spends most of the day on motorbike websites, chatting on forums to other sad middle aged men about the power of their bikes, and the routes they will be travelling at the weekends. I do sympathise with him a little bit. I know that his wife left him recently, but the midlife crisis started before then, so she probably left him because of the midlife weirdness rather than being the cause of it.

A midlife crisis is a strange phenomenon. People talk about it as if it is some kind of medical condition like the menopause, but it is basically just men getting old, and scared, and acting like idiots. Maybe when I get to that age I will understand it better, but I am pretty sure my old chap never had a midlife crisis, and when I look around my office there are plenty of middle aged men who seem perfectly happy with the lives they have chosen for themselves. After all, your life is a series of choices that you make. So if you are annoyed with the way things have turned out, then the only person you can blame is the one that looks at you in the mirror every morning.

I hate it when Steve squeaks into the office every morning in his motorbike leathers. You can hear him as soon as the door opens. He lumbers over like a big leather robot. The awful leathery smell gets more and more pungent as he gets closer to his desk. Then he strips it off revealing a sweaty, but clearly very proud, middle aged man in a creased suit. He could get changed somewhere else and arrive in the office looking normal, but he thinks he looks cool when he arrives in his leathers. He even thought it was cool when he broke his clavicle in an accident. It was all we heard about in the office during the week after he returned.

I wonder what would happen if I told him to get a grip and sort himself out. Would it make a difference.

Another office 'favourite' of mine is 'The Pervert', David Lester, who is best known for his habit of speaking to women's breasts rather than their faces. After a few drinks at the office parties he is a borderline deviant. At times, if he was in a public, rather than a work setting, he would probably be reported for his lecherous behaviour. Luckily for him, the office is a male oriented environment, and the other men laugh along, which leaves the women having to do the same, or risk their careers by speaking out.

There are a group of middle aged men who I like to refer to as the 'Weird Urinators', for obvious reasons. One of them will always take the middle urinal of the three in the male toilets. It is as if he wants other men to stand next to him when he pisses.

Another of the 'Weird Urinators' always drops his trousers to his ankles when he urinates. He uses his shirt to cover his bum cheeks and brazenly goes about his business. This is so strange that it has become the talk of the office. Everyone, even the women, know that he uses this strange technique. Most men grew out of the full trouser drop when they were at junior school, but not this guy. Surely there must have come a time when he thought to himself, "Hang on a minute, no one else is dropping their trousers like I do. As I am in the minority, perhaps it is I who has the incorrect procedure."

The final member of this illustrious group is the vigorous shaker. At the end of his session he stands there shaking, and milking himself for a good minute to make sure there are no drops left. I don't know if he has a urinary problem, or whether he just enjoys it in a semi-masturbatory way, but it is very weird.

There are plenty of people in my office with bizarre and irritating toilet habits. Then there are the shadowy group who simply have no sense of manners. When they are alone in the confines of a toilet cubicle, they turn into animals. These people will urinate on toilet seats, not bother flushing the toilet, etc. I guarantee you that they wouldn't treat their toilets at home in the same despicable way as they do at work, but they are another example of the inconsiderate bastards I have to deal with every day at work. Someone else will clear up their mess.

My office contains all kinds of strange people. Some of them are slightly unstable, some are annoying, some are just plain depressed, and others who are really peculiar.

'Moustache Man' is bitter and dysfunctional. He is short and angry. Unpredictable and volatile. I can see his moustache twitching like an angry little mouse, impotent, but wanting to express power. Eyes darting around looking for somewhere to express the anger that eats away inside him. Anger at not being promoted, anger at not being taken seriously, anger at being insignificant.

I can sense latent anger across all types of people in the office, very few people are happy here. On the face of it there is a lot of happiness in the office. Jokes and forced laughter often ring out across the office, but it is the minority who are genuinely happy. Almost everyone else is just making do. They would rather be somewhere else with other people. People they genuinely like, instead of tolerating, and in some cases hating the people they spend their day to day lives with. Boring people, sat in a boring office, doing boring things all day long.

One of the most peculiar is our heath and safety expert, Peter Danson. 'Danson Dares' or 'Dangerous Danson', as he is ironically known. He is perfectly suited to the role of health and safety guru, as he has never taken a risk in his entire life, and always sees the worst possible outcome of every situation. He is forty five, and has lived alone for ten years, probably because he sees other people as too much of a risk. Before that he lived with his mum and dad until he was forty. He is very bald (too much worrying), quite thin (too much worrying) and dresses very smart. Every item of clothing is a bland colour and thoroughly ironed. Not surprisingly, he is an obsessive compulsive, but he takes it to a whole new level.

In the canteen he obsessively checks his cutlery until he finds a set he likes. He then goes to the staff kitchen and cleans the plate and cutlery he has chosen before he can eventually go and select some food to put on it.

Myself and 'Dangerous Danson' have an uneasy relationship. I once caught him weirdly caressing one of the health and safety dummy busts. He was in the stationary cupboard, where the dummy is kept. He hadn't properly shut the door behind him, and when I opened it, he didn't hear me. I saw him running his fingers sensually over the dummy's rubber mouth, and caressing its head. I froze, completely unaware of how to handle the bizarre situation. When he turned and saw me, there was a look of horrified guilt on his face. He knew, that I knew, that he was having 'a moment' with the dummy. From that day on he could never look me in the eye, or talk to me, ever again. This is why we have an uneasy relationship.

If I think about it I could probably come up with monikers for most of the people in my department. They are all striving to achieve a niche in the office environment. They are desperate to stand out, and see a 'unique' personality as a way to achieve that. These people are willing to do anything to get to that next level and earn that extra cash, that extra two hundred pounds a month that means the world to them. They will sell out their colleagues, lie and cheat at any opportunity.

They all come into work with their 'Vitellino Nappato' briefcases, wearing their 'North Face' jackets, writing with their 'Mont Blanc' pens, with their bald patches and receding hairlines glistening in the office lighting. It is the school ground syndrome. Everyone wants to be like the most popular kid at school. The top man gets a 'North Face' jacket and a 'Vitellino Nappato' briefcase, and his minions follow. They know, and he knows, that imitation is the sincerest form of flattery, and they know that by pandering to his ego they are currying favour and have a greater chance of promotion. Its makes them look like they all come off a senior management production line. It's another form of swallowing your pride. Another fringe benefit to imitating your boss is that they have something in common with their 'leader' and have a conversation starter, a route into his ass.

It's survival of the fittest (lying, cheating, ass kissers) in the office habitat. Darwin's theory again. I see them all, they are like frenzied pigeons feeding in a park, fighting over the scraps of gravy on the gravy train.

In an office with so many idiots, there are lots of annoying things going on. They are thoughtless, selfish and annoying.

I used to be able to laugh at these kinds of people, but after a few years of work, and the day in day out exposure, it is grinding me down. I can feel myself getting more and more irritated by things each day. It drives me crazy. Every day at work makes me feel like I haven't lived a day, I've just died one more day. I am ticking away the hours that make up the dull day. One day closer to death as Pink Floyd might say......

The mannerisms of people around me are becoming more and more irritating. I can't go a single day without finding another person who irritates the life out of me.

A woman in the lift who laughs after everything she says. Each sentence is followed by a fake laugh. I don't know why she does it, nerves possibly. I stare at these irritating people with contempt without even knowing I am doing it. Sometimes the irritating people catch me staring and get bemused at the hatred in my eyes. I enjoy their bemusement and concern; it is payback for being so irritating.

The lift woman is particularly annoying. She laughs on cue as soon as anyone she even remotely knows gets in the lift. How can seeing someone you know in a lift make you laugh out loud? I see people I know all the time. I don't laugh in their face the moment I see them. I don't burst into fits of

22

laughter when I see a colleague in the toilets. If anything it is rude. The lift laugher is a fat woman in her forties. She has lost nine pounds in last month (she tells everyone she ever meets in the lift). She is still huge, and has a massive eighties poodle perm (in a Jon Bon Jovi style). When she laughs her little blonde moustache wobbles around on her top lip. It's horrible. She makes me feel claustrophobic. I end up having to leave the lift before my floor just to stop me freaking out.

I feel imprisoned in this office. I sit at my desk looking at my stationary made by 'Niceday', and I wonder what kind of sarcastic bastard came up with that name.

As the years have passed the wheels on my chair have gradually made a circle of slightly worn carpet, the circle has become more and more worn until the carpet has frayed and been rubbed away. I am actually starting to grind a hole in the floor. I am subconsciously trying to dig my way out of this life. Like 'The Great Escape'. I sometimes catch myself humming 'The Great Escape' theme tune. Am I subconsciously geeing myself up to escape the idiots, and the monotony of the office world.

I spend my days pondering mundane issues. Should a used tissue be put in the normal waste bin, or the paper recycling bin? I train my eyes to stop me becoming short sighted from staring at the computer screen all day. I look at things at varying distances out of the window, a tree, a house, a hill, and back in to the computer screen again. So bored that I 'train' my eyes.

I daydream a lot, and think about the people in my office, and my life. It occurred to me that I very rarely meet any genuine people. These days everyone seems to have an agenda or a fake personality, people are suspicious of other people. They have an act, a persona, that they see as the person they should be. They constantly act out this ideal person instead of being themselves. It is refreshing when you do meet a genuine person, but it doesn't happen very often.

As I gaze around the office hear Jack Johnson's song 'Good People' in my head. Where did all the good people go? I don't see them. All I see is rubbishness, and it's contagious.

People can't be trusted to drive, they need speed bumps, speed cameras and traffic calming measures just to stop them from killing themselves and others. It's crazy. Where did the social conscience go?

People need reminders to 'Keep Britain Tidy'. Surely it's obvious that rubbish goes in the bin, not on the floor, but no, people need to be constantly policed to stop them being idiots.

People can't even be trusted to eat properly. They need to get their stomachs stapled. They need warnings on food. A red sticker means it will make you fat, amber only a little bit fat and green means you won't get fat. How obvious do you need to make these things?

We can't be trusted to discipline our children correctly. Employers cannot trust their employees.

People moan about the nanny state and the government becoming 'Big Brother', but this is happening because of people no longer have any respect for anything. The dumming down of society has forced these things on people. They can only blame themselves, but they never will.

You can't trust your partner. You can't trust your neighbours. No one trusts anyone. The trust has gone and no one seems to care.

I see these people around me. Every day I see them. And I see all these phones, and all this stuff on their desks. It means nothing. They mean nothing.

INFIDEL

"Try not to become a man of success, but rather try to become a man of value."
(Albert Einstein)

Every Thursday after work I play football across the road from my work. It's a good way of winding down after a frustrating day in the office.

Near the pitch there is a car park and a nature area. The car park is surrounded by trees, and very secluded. Someone driving casually past my work would never notice there was a car park or even a football pitch. It is a very pleasant area, and combined with the seclusion, it has become something of a lover's meeting place for couples from my work who are carrying on extramarital affairs.

As you drive into the car park the main road branches to the left and takes you along a short wood lined road to the football pitch. If you take the less obvious route, along the road which branches to the right, then you are in a secluded parking area. Everything is surrounded by trees, and cars can park there without being seen from any angle.

Quite often when we are playing football the ball gets kicked over the trees and ends up in the secluded area. This gives you an opportunity to the see the unfaithful couples conducting their unfaithful work affairs. At 5:30pm there are normally at least a couple of cars with people from the company rubbing each other's hair, nibbling each others ears and sneaking a quick thrill before returning home to play happy families.

Before I just laughed about them, and enjoyed spotting them around the office and knowing that they were hiding a dirty little secret. But now, the more I think about it, the more disappointed and annoyed I become. And now, whenever I go over to the car park to collect the ball I am looking out to see who is doing what and taking a mental note. When I see them there it pisses me off that they are being unfaithful, and it pisses me off that they get away with it. In the office I look at them with disdain, and my amusement has turned into hatred.

My heightened awareness of other people's behaviour, and increasing annoyance seems to be spiralling out of control.

I get more and more disappointed with the things I see around me. I feel impotent watching the behaviour of people, unable to say or do anything about it. I sometimes rant about the behaviour and injustices I see, but I never actually do anything. I feel ashamed of myself. It's the 'none of my business' syndrome, which is something which suits the people who are acting like tossers and no one else. I want to make these people my business.

TURNING POINT

"There is only one way to achieve happiness on this terrestrial ball, and that is to have either a clear conscience or none at all."
(Ogden Nash)

Then something happened, I believe it is called an epiphany. An acquaintance of mine from work, Mark Cunningham, was involved in a car crash and suffered serious trauma to his brain.

I wouldn't say he was a close friend, but I liked him. We met on a project at work and hit it off straight away. Now we chatted from time to time when we bumped into each other around the building. He was a good guy, we had a similar sense of humour, and if we had met earlier in life we might have been good friends. As it was, we were work acquaintances. I enjoyed bumping into him at work, and occasionally when we were out socially, but we were both at an age where men have decided that they can't make new close friends. It takes up too much time, and can result in 'Cable Guy' syndrome, when you end up getting stalked by someone who seemed ok, but turns out to be a bit of a weirdo and a little bit annoying and embarrassing.

I found out from another colleague that Mark had been in a crash and was in a coma for a few weeks in intensive care. He was ok now, but was still recovering, and wouldn't be back at work for a few months.

He had been hit by van when he pulled out onto a dual carriageway. Apparently the grass on the verge at the junction hadn't been cut for a long time due to council cut backs, and the long grass had kept the van obscured from Mark's view when he pulled out.

The van had hit the driver's side of Mark's car and carried him over two hundred metres down the dual carriageway before the car and van had eventually come to a standstill. It sounded nasty.

I don't know if the story had been embellished over time and repetition, but the details weren't good. His wife, who was on the passenger side, had suffered a collapsed lung, and the top of her ear had been severed off. She also suffered a few broken ribs, and was still in hospital, but was, generally speaking, ok.

Mark, being on the side of impact, had come off a lot worse. He had broken both legs, a broken arm, broken ribs, broken collarbone, but the most serious injuries were caused by the head impact. He was in a coma, and they weren't sure that he would make a full recovery. As with a lot of head injuries, no one can say for sure what the long term effects will be.

It turned out that his head injuries had some very bizarre long term effects. Effects that would prove to be the turning point I needed to start sorting out the wankers in my world.

Mark appeared to have fully recovered, but people close to him noticed that he seemed to become a lot less tolerant of everything. They just assumed that the crash had been a life changing experience, and this new attitude was part of that life change.

A few months after the accident I bumped into him at work, and he seemed like his old self. However, I did notice that he seemed very quick to criticise people. Before he was charming about everyone, with occasional jokes, but nothing harsh. Now, when he was criticising people he didn't show any of the usual traits. He didn't lower his voice, or check around him to see if anyone was within earshot. It was as if he couldn't care less what other people heard, or what they thought.

It was quite funny that he was so open about his dislike of certain people. Although initially taken aback, his candour amused me. I would later find out that his head injuries had caused him to lose all his inhibitions.

He no longer cared about what people thought of him. He had no internal check before saying anything that popped into his head, and no concern for the fact that some people might be upset or offended. He had lost any concept that some things are better left unsaid. The part of his brain that says "hold on, let's think about this before we say anything" had been damaged and no longer worked.

It didn't sound like such a bad thing. I was a little bit jealous that he could be so open about his thoughts and feelings. I assumed that if people were aware of his condition, then they would be fine with it. I was wrong. Honesty is definitely not the best policy in today's world, and so it proved.

It seems that a lot of people really can't handle the truth. A female employee wore a short skirt on the day of her appraisal, knowing full well that her pervert manager would give her a better score as a result. Mark openly told her, and everyone else in his team, that this was an obvious ploy. It was true, she knew it was true, everyone in the office knew it was true, but hearing it out loud was another matter entirely. He was reported, but because of his condition he wasn't given any kind of formal warning.

Informally it was a different matter. His colleagues were always wary around him. They all knew they were operating in a false manner in the office, and didn't want to run the risk of being exposed. He had become a liability.

On another occasion, when asked, in passing, how things were by his Director, he opened up about all the mistakes the department had made.

People in his department had spent months hiding the truth and sweeping these incidences under the carpet. Now, in the space of five minutes he had told their Director everything. He even outlined the costs to the company of all these mistakes, and who was responsible. The Director was delighted with his honesty, but the colleagues, who he had to work with on a day to day basis, were less than impressed. For some people a few years worth of ass kissing had been destroyed in just a few moments, and they were back to square one. Mark had highlighted the ineptitude that had been so cleverly hidden, and done the company a favour, but he would not be rewarded.

I imagine there were similar scenarios in his home life. When my girlfriend asks me how she looks, I always say things like 'amazing', 'great' and 'stunning'. When the reality is that I am thinking the colour looks a bit funny, or I prefer something else.

Mark would be too honest, and say things like, "it makes you look a bit fat". He wouldn't think twice about saying one of her friends looked attractive, or that he disliked his mother-in-law. He is living proof that honesty is rarely the best policy. I don't know why, and it is sad, but it is true.

People's empathy with his condition, which was probably insincere anyway, didn't last long. Within a year of returning to work he ended up losing his job, his wife and his family, and all because he was unable to lie. This is the sad state of affairs in modern society, it is the liars, the cheats, the false people, and those with no conscience, these are the people who flourish and succeed.

These thoughts were fresh in my mind the following week when I was having car trouble. I was pissed off as I walked up to the local garage after a hard day at work to collect my car.

All the way there it rained hard. Knowing I was about to spend a fortune on my car only made the walk to the garage twice as annoying. I was cursing the weather. Why did it rain on the one day I didn't have my car. I was also frustrated at how stupidly expensive it is to have a car in this country. Everyone from the government down to the mechanic were pissing me off.

When I got to the garage I was met by your typical car mechanic. Covered in grease, wearing blue overalls and unbelievably chirpy. I am sure that it is an act, purely designed to make you think that there is no way he could ever rip you off. Meanwhile, as soon as you leave the garage, usually a few hundred quid down, he is laughing at you. He thinks you are an imbecile for knowing nothing about cars, he thinks you aren't a proper man. Or maybe that is what I think, and I am just being paranoid.

The mechanic listed all the problems with my car, baffling me with technical terms, knowing full well that it goes in one ear and out the other.

Whilst I nodded along in a manly way, pretending to understand what he was saying, there was only one thing I was thinking about. The only thing I cared about was the cost to me.

He blathered on and my mind wandered, I gazed around the garage and noticed a familiar looking car. A silver Peugeot 405 estate, the classic family man car. I was sure it belonged to one of the men I had seen enjoying an extramarital affair in the car park opposite work. In fact I was positive. He had an 'amusing' car sticker which stated that his 'other car was a Ferrari'.

This type of estate car is very useful for a car park relationship for obvious reasons (you can lay your lady down in the back), and is also practical for the family duties.

As I was thinking about the times I had seen the car, I became aware that the mechanic had finished talking about the numerous problems with my own car. He was looking disheartened by the fact that he was about to hit me the final cost. Outwardly he looked disheartened, inwardly he was delighted that he had another customer who knew nothing about cars. Another mug who could be milked for virtually any amount of money, within certain obscene limits.

I trudged into the office to pay the bill. I had forgotten about Peugeot man's infidelities, and was now more concerned with thoughts of the money I was about to hand over. A weeks wages, earned by a week of boredom and frustration.

Five hundred quid is a lot of money to spend on something which essentially takes you to work to do a job you hate.

I entered the office, which was covered in oil and grease and stunk of sweaty men. There was the obligatory topless women calendar on the wall. Although I have to admit I liked that touch of authenticity. I got my credit card out ready to add to my debt, and began thinking of what I would now have to sacrifice in order to pay for my latest expense. People always say that life is about sacrifices, but it shouldn't be, that's such a negative way to look at life.

The mechanic placed the invoice on the counter. I didn't understand it. Paranoia told me that the majority was unnecessary.

I looked down at the invoice, and noticed that the invoice for the Peugeot was also on the counter, awaiting 'Mr Unfaithful'. He also required a lot of work, which made me feel better. It appeared that there was a bit of karma at play. But I then noticed that his bill was significantly less than mine. That definitely wasn't karma. I was surely a much better person than him. He was clearly a wanker, but my bill was much more. What kind of justice is that?

His invoice contained a number of details which were of interest to me. His name, so now I could look him up on the systems at work. Even more interestingly, his address, which happened to be particularly close to my own house in the rabbit warren that is a modern English housing estate.

As I scanned the invoice I made a mental note that he, John Simmonds, lived at number 22 Cagney Road. This was only two streets away from my own house, but far enough away to mean that I had never seen him, and he had probably never seen me…..

At that moment something inside me changed. It was then that I first begin to think about influencing this karma process myself.

John Simmonds was being unfaithful to his wife and family, living a lie, and he was getting away with it. As I drove home from the garage through the rain and the gridlocked traffic, my mind turned to ways in which I could expose him and what the consequences might be. The journey home that day wasn't as slow and frustrating as usual.

By the time I got home I had convinced myself it was simply my annoyance with the garage bill that had prompted my thoughts of revenge. Reality took over, and the feelings of futility returned.

However, the idea remained with me, and it would return at a later date.

BACK TO LIFE

"Life is pleasant. Death is peaceful. It's the transition that's troublesome."
(Isaac Asimov)

I slipped back into the monotony of reality and luckily the following few days at work were actually some of my most rewarding and amusing.

I was at the urinals talking to a colleague who is an idiot and an ass kisser. He has stooped to all levels to impress the senior management team. He has taken their cars in for MOTs when they can't be bothered, help them sort out their car insurance. He will do anything for them, absolutely anything. They have influence over his career so he is basically their servant. It had served him well (no pun intended). His subservience was obviously viewed as an endearing quality. In England we would call him a dogsbody, and in America he would be referred to as a 'grunt'. 'Grunt' fits him well. He is a short, slightly chubby, pig-like man with an annoying face. A grunt.

At the urinals he was telling me all about his weekend, and how brilliant it had been. As per usual with him, it was purely a one way conversation. He was completely self absorbed, and this became very apparent. He was so engrossed in what he was saying about himself, that he failed to notice he was actually urinating on his own feet.

I was stood next to him, and not really paying attention to what he was saying, which meant that I heard the pitter patter noise immediately. I was trying to stop myself laughing. I had to look away. I wanted to see how long he would go before he noticed what he was doing. It took him a lot longer than I thought to realise what was happening. Maybe ten seconds. By then there were splash marks almost up to his knees. This was more like it, a bit of karma at work. Perhaps I didn't need to interfere.

Most people in that situation would have to laugh at the sheer stupidity of their actions. He takes himself far too seriously. He flew into a rage at himself and demanded that his mistake went no further than the two of us.

I was still laughing uncontrollably as he placed his feet in the sink to wash them under the tap, and began vigorously scrubbing at the stains with a paper towel. Unfortunately this made the wet patch even bigger, and made me laugh even more.

I struggled to compose myself as we walked back into the office. He was still demanding that the incident went no further. I had already decided that this was far too good to keep to myself, especially as the evidence was still fresh. Karma demanded that I tell as many people as possible.

Within seconds of returning to my desk it was obvious to everyone around me that I had been laughing at something. My face was red, and my eyes watering. Genuine laughter is rare in my office, so everyone knew something was up. The levels of boredom in my office, mean people picked up on it straight away. I cracked (quite easily) and told them exactly what happened. The secret was out, so I sent an email to a few other people for good measure.

I viewed this as karma offering me a sign. This was a good start to the working week. I was in a good mood, and all thoughts of the injustices around me were pushed to the back of my mind.

The working week then got even better, and I was starting to think that maybe I should let karma get on with its own work without any help from me.

The second instance of someone being 'rewarded' for their behaviour happened at one of the most important meetings of the year.

Jane Davids, a girl in my office, and another serious ass kisser of the year contender. She is amazing at it and very sneaky as well. I know this because I have access to Crispin's inbox.

It's a long story. He used me like a bitch when I first started. He was in love with power, and saw me as someone he could exert his power over to make himself feel good. He gave me access to his inbox so I could print out meeting agendas and minutes. Mainly because he couldn't be bothered, but also because he loved that his status meant he could order people around. I was young and did what I was told.

Being a technological imbecile he asked me to set myself up with access to his inbox, which I did. Like an idiot, he never asked me to remove my access, and now I am privy to all kinds of information. Information that frustrates and annoys me, but I like knowing.

I know all the information that only Crispin is supposed to know. I can never say anything, as this would expose me, and it is an enjoyable feeling to know information that others don't, or that they don't think you know. You can test them and make them lie. It's quite funny at times. For example, I know when people are going for promotion. The promotion process at my work means that Crispin has the final say. He loves that process. He likes to make people sweat. It is all part of the power trip. No one likes to look like they are pushing to get ahead of their peers, and pretend that it happens as a result of work and not being a creep. So I openly ask people if they are going for promotion (when I know they are), and watch them lie. It's interesting to see people openly lie, and know they are. You get an insight into people and their lying behaviours. I use it to develop my ability to read people. It passes the time.

The most intriguing bits of information are the grovelling emails which he receives from his minions. They are all oblivious to the fact that he isn't the only person reading these emails.

So that is how I came to have access to his emails, and how I saw Jane's campaign of disgusting sycophant emails. Sadly it yielded positive results, she got promoted and is now quite senior, and I can categorically state that it isn't related to her ability.

I'm sure it goes on everywhere, in all walks of life, but when you witness it first hand it is much more irritating. That is the downside to having access to all this information.

For three months, I read through almost daily emails from Jane to Crispin, congratulating him on what a splendid job he was doing as head of department. My personal favourite was the request that he give himself a huge pat on the back for having a team which loved (yes, loved!) and respected him so much.

In reality everyone apart from Jane (and probably her too) think he is a twat, and he is a twat.

Other emails have involved inviting Crispin to her house for dinner at the weekend, telling him how much she loves her job, and generally telling him what a wonderful and special person he is.

Hopefully that provides some insight into Jane Davids as a person, and sets the scene for the next amusing work incident.

It was a hugely important meeting, which had been put in everyone's diaries a month in advance, and there were some very 'important' (I use that in the loosest possible sense) people attending. By important, what I mean is they earn a lot of money. I leave it up to you to decide if you think that makes them important.

Jane had organised this meeting as a starting point for her new project. She was trying to convince everyone her project was going to revolutionise the way our company operated.

[In reality it was a pointless exercise, and that is what it ended up being, a pointless waste of time and money for everyone involved. The project died on it's arse, achieved nothing, and was quietly forgotten about.]

Everyone had arrived early for this meeting, which was being hosted in the very austere boardroom. About thirty people were attending. The presence of so many important people had given everyone the false impression that something important was going to happen.

Helping Jane, as joint leader of the project, was a strangely dressed, new age type woman. She had straggly hair, and looked like she didn't have much regard for well groomed bodily hair. She was not the typical business person everyone had expected (including Jane, but she had been too lazy to meet with the woman beforehand).

She began the meeting by requesting that everyone stand up and close their eyes. I glanced around the room and could see a few looks of indignation and confusion. These were serious businessmen, not a bunch of hippies.

Once everyone was standing with their eyes closed, she requested that we all go to a 'happy place'. It was at this point someone let out a large sigh, and the screech of a chair being shoved backwards woke everyone from their 'happy place'.

One of the more 'important' attendees, was clearly disgusted by this approach, and stormed to the door of the board room before turning round to everyone and declaring that "this was hippy bullshit". Brilliant.

The look on Jane's face was priceless. The project dragged on for ages, achieved nothing, and Jane was promoted shortly afterwards.

Her promotion left me with a feeling that life, if left to run its own course, is just not fair. Karma was once again at the forefront of my mind.

It was then that I decided it was time to reveal some of the emails that Jane had been sending to Crispin. It was time to uncover the real reason why people get promoted in my office.

These emails, which I mentioned earlier, were the ones which had gained Jane a couple of promotions. They were vomit inducing, pride swallowing emails. I had kept these for a long time, but had not felt able to do anything with them. It would have been a breach of information security. Now I was so annoyed that information security could go and fuck itself.

I had a simple plan. I printed a couple of the emails out, checked that there was no way of tracing the print outs back to me and left one copy of each email near the printer. Their names were clearly marked in the 'To' and 'From' fields, so the arse kisser and arse kissee were easily identifiable.

It didn't take long for a bored colleague to take an interest in the printout. From there it didn't take long for them to start discussing the contents. Shortly afterwards someone came over to me to check if I had heard about the emails. I acted surprised and shocked, and gladly joined in the amusement at Jane's expense. I knew no one would have the balls to approach Jane or Crispin about the emails. This one was going to do the rounds on the informal communications network and show Jane up for what she is. It felt good.

THE INTERVENTION

"Physical infidelity is the signal, the notice given, that all fidelities are undermined."
(Katherine Anne Porter)

It was around this time that I returned to thinking about John Simmonds again. The success, and satisfaction, of exposing Jane had given me the confidence to try someone else.

John Simmonds was still having his secret rendezvous in the car park. I had seen him on a couple of occasions nibbling and caressing in his Peugeot 405 estate. I had also seen him on our housing estate with his wife/girlfriend, walking to the shops hand in hand, living a lie. Having his cake and eating it.

Seeing him with his partner was the final straw. He was a bad person, and it was time he faced the consequences of his actions.

I love technology. The internet, television, the mobile phone, all of these things have made life much better.

Some people still see these developments as evil, and something to be avoided to maintain the simple life. And that is what it is, simple.

I am the opposite. I love technology. I love the fact that it has made my life better in so many ways. I shop online and get my groceries delivered. I organise car insurance online. I bank online. I use online encyclopaedias. I read the news online. I keep in touch with friends and family online. I share photos online. If something can be done online, I will do it.

The mobile phone has revolutionised people's lives. Ten years ago a minority had mobile phones, now we all do. My phone is also my camera and my music player, it's amazing. I can take a photo on my phone and have it printed and ready for framing within a minute.

When you think back to only ten years ago when there were no mobile phones or email, how did people cope? How difficult it was to keep in touch. Offices didn't have email. That would have been bizarre. How did anyone manage to organise anything without email. Phoning people individually and tell them the same thing over and over again, that would have been awful.

By embracing these developments, I was now in a position to record exactly what John Simmonds was up to, and gather irrefutable evidence. It wasn't even going to be that difficult. It took a bit of patience, but that was all.

Every time I played football on the pitches opposite my work I would run off to collect the ball when it was kicked over into the adjacent car park. After a couple of weeks I had my opportunity. The ball bounced into one of the bushes in front of John Simmonds' car. He was in there with the same woman he was always with, I recognised her from work as well.

Whilst in the bush retrieving the ball I was able to take a couple of very compromising photographs on my phone. Some nibbling, some stroking and some kissing. I even managed to get his number plate in the frame as further proof. Neither of them noticed. I now had the ammunition, and just needed to have the courage to put the next stage of my plan into action.

In the weeks I had spent waiting to get the photo opportunity I had experimented with a couple of minor payback incidents. I was practicing, confirming to myself that I was ready.

There is a cup recycling unit at work. It consists of four tubes which people put their empties into for recycling. Every day people put disused tea bags in the tubes. The tubes are specifically designed for the cups, so the tea bags block up the tubes. This is made worse by the fact that there are bins right next to tubes. Some people seem to have a problem with lifting the bin lid, and instead toss their tea bags into the recycling tubes. This laziness pisses me off on a daily basis, and now I had decided enough was enough. Something could easily be done to teach someone a lesson.

One particular lady in my office was a consistent offender. Every time she had a cup of tea (and she seemed to spend most of her day drinking tea) she would drop the empty bag into the chute and block it up for everyone else. She was too lazy to lift the bin lid next to the disposal unit and drop the bag in there. So I prepared a little surprise for her.

I got myself a cup of tea, and left the bag in the cup stewing on my desk. I watched her from across the office as she surfed the internet looking at clothes and reading gossip columns. When her boss looked like he might be wandering over, she would click onto a spreadsheet and look like she was actually doing some work. I believe it's called a 'boss-spasm' when someone sparks into life in the presence of their boss.

Generally, she spent most of the day drinking tea and surfing the internet. After half an hour of this, she was clearly so over worked that she would often need a tea break to help her relax and get ready for some more internet surfing. It was when she was on one of these numerous tea breaks that I spotted my opportunity.

Luckily for me, and unluckily for her, she sits in part of the office which is a natural walkway through to the toilet. I casually picked up my cup of tea, which had been stewing on my desk for about ten minutes, and made my way towards the toilet. Her handbag was on the floor by her desk. As I strolled past her desk, in one smooth motion, I dropped the used tea bag into her handbag, and carried on towards the toilet. No one had spotted a thing. I casually disposed of the cup of tea in a nearby bin and carried on to the toilet.

Once inside the toilet I had to get myself inside a cubicle ASAP. Mainly because I wanted to laugh at how stupid and juvenile I had just been, but also because I didn't actually need the toilet and it would have looked a bit strange walking into the toilet, doing nothing and then walking back out again. That kind of behaviour would be the talk of the office in no time. That's how bored people are, they notice crap like that.

I took the long route back to my desk, down the stairs, through a separate department and back up again on the other side of the office. I wanted to make sure that if the tea bag had been discovered, I wouldn't be quizzed on the way back to my desk.

As it happened I had no reason to worry, she hadn't noticed the teabag. It was over an hour later that I was alerted to the commotion by her desk.

You would have thought that someone had died with all the noise and histrionics. A crowd of women were gathered by her desk, all of them looking accusingly around the office. They were all totally amazed and bewildered by the rogue tea bag. They were also looking for a bit of office drama to brighten up their boring day and their boring lives. The tea bag was about to become the focal point of everyone's day. I was going to have to play along.

An immediate informal investigation was initiated by the women in the office. Partly to find out how it had happened, but mainly so that the female gossips in the office had an excuse to wander round all day talking rubbish and doing no work. Their detective work consisted of asking people if they knew who did it, and everyone saying that they had no idea (me included). They canvassed opinion on the event, and acted shocked and horrified that anyone could be so cruel and stupid. Inside I was laughing at the trauma. That woman was hurting. She knew the teabag was symbolic. A symbol that someone in the office hated her, and everyone else knew that someone hated her. She looked like a prick and it served her right.

The rest of the day was remarkably good. The swift justice, and being able to see the instant rewards, had made me feel pretty good. I wanted her to know the reason the tea bag was in her handbag. I wanted her to know that she had been consistently inconsiderate, and this was her retribution.

At the moment she just thought it was bizarre, and cruel. I couldn't explain the reason to her. But she had been annoyed, and that was payback for the amount of times she had annoyed me by blocking up the drinks tube. It was trivial, but immensely satisfying nonetheless.

The act had a sinister edge, which I liked. I knew it would freak her out, and I took pleasure in that. I didn't care. I liked her being freaked out.

That initial success left me feeling that I was doing the right thing. This could be rewarding, and also amusing. The feeling of satisfaction which I had at work that day was awesome, and left me wanting to repeat that success. It wouldn't be long until another opportunity presented itself, and I was more than ready.

POSTAL DELIGHT

"Revenge is a confession of pain."
(Latin Proverb)

It was a lovely English summers evening. One of those midweek evenings when you have been working all day, but the sun is still shining and will be for hours. It almost feels like you have another day to enjoy after the working day has finished.

I was home fairly promptly after work, as per normal, and decided that I would take Steve over to the park for a walk before Laura got back from work.

My local park is huge, and there is plenty of space for everyone; dog walkers, children and footballers. I always walked Steve around the edges of the park, careful to keep him away from other dogs and the children's play area (because he can be a bit savage and likes to crap a lot).

The sunshine was putting me in a good mood, and I was happy. I didn't even mind pooper scooping, which was the worst part of walking Steve, but a necessary evil.

My mind turned to the teabag incident and I chuckled to myself about how juvenile I had been. At this point I suddenly became aware of a giant Rottweiler. I was normally aware of Rottweilers because Steve wanted to fight them. He loved to fight the bigger dogs, and he was a bastard to control once he got going. I noticed this particular Rottweiler because he was crapping a huge turd just metres away from the children's play area. It was disgusting and seemed like it would never end. To make it worse the owner was not bothering with pooper scooping. He just strolled away and left it there. A huge pile of steaming turd on a hot summers day next to children playing. I felt something switch in my brain. This man was a twat, and I was pissed off. He had ruined my happiness.

I knew this guy. I didn't know him well, but I knew that he lived not far away from me. I had seen him come out of his house to walk his dog. So I knew exactly where he lived. He was a nasty looking skinhead, who would probably smash my face in without even thinking. Another opportunity had presented itself, and even with the risks associated with skinheads, this was too good to turn down.

I took Steve on another circuit of the park to kill some time until the skinhead and Rottweiler left the park.

The park was emptying as everyone disappeared home for their tea. The skinhead left, and I was ready to do some pooper scooping.

When I got to the steaming pile of dog turd I almost decided that it was a stupid idea. Then I thought about it. This guy had allowed his dog to do this right next to a playground full of children, he deserved some recompense, and even if it was a mucky job I felt compelled to do it.

Remembering how good it had felt at work that day spurred me on. I scooped up the massive pile, gagging slightly, and my pooper scooper was full. I now had to hurry home before Steve decided he might need another one.

It was too early to go straight over to the skinhead's house. It was still broad daylight. I emptied the pooper scooper into a plastic bag, and left the offensive bag in the garage.

I went inside to wash my hands. Later that evening I would make up an excuse to go out, and do the deed under the cover of darkness.

Laura was waiting for me in the lounge. She had eaten already. I could tell that she was annoyed as soon as I walked in through the front door. There was a definite air of annoyance in the room that was almost tangible. The kind of tangible annoyance that only a woman can create.

I was confused, but then I remembered that we were supposed to be eating together tonight. We hadn't had a chance to eat together all week because of commitments. Tonight had been earmarked for the special occasion. Oh shit. When a woman assigns importance to something you had better assign equal importance or you are fucked.

I wasn't particularly fussed about eating together. It was nice, but not the end of the world. Laura saw eating together as a way of bonding, its weird, but women do things differently.

I tried to explain that as the weather was so nice I had decided to go and give Steve a nice long walk in the park. I stupidly thought she would sympathise with me. No chance. I was informed that my dinner was in the microwave, and she was going upstairs for a bath. I knew I was about to endure an evening of indifference and silence.

In order to get back into her good books I spent the evening watching awful programs like 'You Are What You Eat' and '10 Years Younger'. Feigning an interest in someone who has eaten themselves to the point of near death, and who now requires a TV program to sort their life out, and to stop them from dying in their thirties.

I am of the opinion that before you reach 17 stone you should begin to think that your lifestyle might need to change. Getting up to 22 stone is just carelessness. Luckily Gillian McKeith can sort you out by looking at your crap, and showing you what an idiot you are.

I actually find it disgusting that someone can get that huge. It's a poor reflection on our society that people are able to become like that. Especially when you consider people are starving to death all over the world, and yet here people are eating themselves to death, and blaming it on genes and metabolism. Not a lot of fat people in Darfur so how can it be genes.

I was shocked to read that the NHS recently had to invest millions of pounds upgrading beds and mortuary slabs to cope with the increasing weight of people in the UK. It annoys me that money is being spent on reinforcing beds instead of being spent on treatment of proper illnesses. Do you know the reason these changes are required? Because there are an increasing number of patients who weigh more than forty stone. Unbelievable.

On a similar note, there is a crematorium in Norfolk that has been forced to turn some obese people away as the coffins are too big to fit into the facilities at the crematorium. Instead they need to be transported 120 miles to Watford to be cremated. What is the world coming to?

The hours of banal TV slowly passed, and eventually it was time to make an excuse to leave the house for a bit.

"Right, I'm going for a jog", I announced as I stood up from the sofa.

Laura looked surprised, but was still trying to be annoyed and indifferent.

"A jog? You have never been for a jog. I've been with you for five years, and you have never been for a jog." She emphasised the word 'jog' like it was a dirty word.

She was right though, jogging should have stayed in the 1980s, and calling it 'running' doesn't make it any more acceptable.

"Watching all these fat, unhealthy people on TV, has motivated me to get fit". It was lame, but she bought it, and I went to get changed.

I left the house, and after a quick detour via the garage, was on my way to post my delivery.

The house I was looking for was only a couple of minutes away. I got there and quickly scanned the surrounding houses to check that no one was doing their Neighbourhood Watch duties. It was dark, and most of the houses had their curtains drawn.

I sprinted up the drive, and returned the dog turd to its rightful owner, emptying the contents of the plastic bag through his letterbox. I sprinted back down the short drive, round the corner and slowed to a jog to make myself look less suspicious. I jogged for a minute or so, and disposed of the plastic bag in one of those random bins attached to lampposts. I jogged for a couple more minutes to get a bit further away, realised that jogging was crap, and walked home.

I arrived at my front door, I wasn't really sweating, and I hadn't been gone for very long. But I couldn't be arsed to run, there was a reason why I hadn't been for a run in over 10 years, it's shit. I knew Laura would quiz me when I got in the front door. She was still in an awkward mood from earlier. I had an excuse ready.

Laura looked up from the television, looked me up and down, and looked back at the TV, "you weren't gone very long….."

I informed her that running was boring, and that I didn't think I would bother with it again.

"What is that funny smell?" She asked, looking confused. Oh shit, I hadn't even thought of that.

"I can't smell anything. I'm going for a shower". I was upstairs in a shot.

I enjoyed annoying another idiot. I was now looking forward to annoying even more idiots in future. I felt like a big kid playing practical jokes, but these jokes were for people that really deserved it.

As I showered I wondered whether what I was doing was stupid. Was I a moral guardian, or was I just being an idiot like the people I hated. Acting like a stupid student, trying to make my own life more interesting. Everything I had done so far could be classed as stupid, but had been immensely satisfying.

By the time I had finished showering I was up on my high horse and determined to undertake more challenging and rewarding schemes.

I still managed to find time for one more juvenile prank, before I would move on to more serious matters, and my life would begin to change forever.

I went through to the bedroom and saw Laura lying in bed. Laura was in a mood with me. I knew that. But I also knew that this was a silly mood, not one that would last. One that would be forgotten soon enough.

It was also a mood that sometimes led to a good time. We had been together long enough for me to know that I might be able to turn Laura's mood into sexual energy.

We lay in bed that night. Laura had deliberately got into bed and faced away from me to continue her demonstration of annoyance. I

deliberately faced towards her, lying on my side, close enough for her to feel my
presence without actually touching. As the duvet started to warm up I made my move. I ran my fingers along her thigh, she slapped them away. It was petulant, but not aggressive. I waited a few seconds, and tried again. This time Laura let me run my fingers all the way down to her knee and back up again. I was in. I took things up a notch, spurred onby playing Barry White songs in my mind. I ran my finger nails across the small of Laura's back, she wriggled a little bit and I ran my fingers downwards across her buttocks. She wriggled some more, and let out a little moan. Barry White sang louder in my head, he was excited too. Missing the meal was well and truly forgotten and it was business time. I loved Laura.

FAKE BOOBS AND VANITY

"We are so vain that we even care for the opinions of those we don't care for."
(Marie Von Ebner-Eschenbach)

I was stuck in traffic the next morning, as I am every day of my working life, waiting in a queue for a roundabout. One of those huge roundabouts that splits into three lanes, one to go right, one for straight on and one to go left. There was the usual endless stream of traffic crossing the roundabout. This meant that one car per minute would be able to get across the roundabout. The lanes to go right and left were always rammed full of traffic, and took about ten minutes of patient waiting to get to the front. The middle lane was always quite clear as it leads to a small industrial estate which is a dead end.

All of a sudden I saw a woman in a Renault Clio accelerating down the middle lane, as if going straight on to the industrial estate and past everyone who was sat in their cars patiently queuing. To my shock and amazement, she forced her way into the front of my queue, and into the inside lane to turn right.

I couldn't believe it. I was turning the air blue with my language, and had my palms turned up to an imaginary Lord. I caught the eyes of the person in front in their rear view mirror. They looked terrified and I held my hand up to apologise.

My lane had been at a virtual standstill, like it was every morning. She had obviously decided that she wasn't going to wait like everyone else, she would just push in. She clearly thought she was a special case.

I knew that her choice of lanes wasn't a genuine error, I recognised her from work. I had definitely seen her around the building. She must be familiar with the roads. She had no excuse for pushing in.

I was annoyed to say the least. I sat in my car and watched her as she pulled out onto the roundabout and headed off on the route which I was waiting to travel. I was furious. I hadn't felt this furious for a long time.

The following day the same thing happened again. Then it happened again on the Friday morning, and again, and again, and again. I had never noticed this travesty before. She must either moved house, or had a change in her work shift. This meant she was now commuting to work along the same route as me, and she was pissing me off on a daily basis.

As each day passed, she kept on doing it.

After a week of watching her, it got to the point where I was getting absolutely furious, and that is putting it mildly. I could feel my blood pressure rising. I would see her around the office, and she would rekindle the same feelings of annoyance as I felt in my car. I wanted to shout at her and tell her that I saw her every morning. I wanted her to know that every morning I saw her and thought "What kind of twat does that? What kind of wanker are you?"

My perception of her had become so distorted by her behaviour, that I was now convinced she had an annoying walk, and an annoying face. She had become annoyance personified for me.

They say that people become their faces, or they get the faces they deserve, so grumpy people will have grumpy looking faces and grumpy mannerisms, and happy people will look naturally happy. Well, she was an annoying person, and I found everything about her annoying. Her walk was annoying. It was a really upright walk with her head held high like everyone was beneath her, and her boobs pushed out like a dog's nose sniffing for a scent. Her dress sense was also really annoying, the clothes she wore were clearly chosen to make her look younger, but instead it made her look like mutton dressed as lamb. She would wear short skirts, and low cut tops, but was far too old for them. Her face was annoying, it was difficult to pinpoint exactly what was so annoying about her face, but she definitely had a really annoying face. I couldn't let this carry on. I needed to cure my annoyance.

About a year earlier I had been in a meeting, and some of the men in the meeting had been joking about her. One of the managers was showing off to the 'guys' and had mentioned that she had breast implants. He obviously thought that knowing this made him cool in front of all the other guys. He seemed like a bit of tit, but had provided me with some valuable information.

I already knew that this lady was slightly obnoxious. One of my friends worked in her department, and had told me a few stories about her.

Her name is Alison Loveday, she is a team manager in the callcentre, she is ridiculously thin for her age (mid to late forties I would guess), and was thought to have had a boob job. The best way to describe her would be as looking like a man caked in make up with massive fake breasts. Like the weird amateur dramatics men who seem to really enjoy dressing up as a woman. Picture that, and you have Alison Loveday.

She was also well known for flirting with the teenage boys in the callcentre. Even though she was supposedly happily married with children. She loved the attention of the young boys, and they loved big breasts. It's a win-win scenario.

I knew she was married with children, she had appeared in our silly staff magazine on numerous occasions, doing all kinds of stupid things, and loving the attention.

She was interviewed in the 'Me and My Car' section, where people explain why their car is like them, and why they are so inseparable, and how much they love their car, and it's like the car is one of the family. And she shares some of her greatest memories of the car.

She was also in the 'CDs of My Life' section, where people explain why certain CDs mean the world to them, why they are inseparable from their CDs, how much they love their CDs, and how the CDs are like part of the family. And finally, she was in the 'Pets Are People Too' section. Her poodle was like one of the family, they were inseparable and she was in love with the dog. Alison Loveday is a stupidly self-centred and self-absorbed person

She must absolutely insane to think that anyone would be remotely interested in her car, CDs and pets. She thinks everyone should be very interested in her, and every aspect of her life. I'm sure if there was a section called 'Me And My Toilet' she would happily parade in front of her toilet for photos, and explain how much she loved her toilet, how the toilet is like one of the family, inseparable, etc. Anything to be the centre of attention.

The staff magazine is not a riveting read. Only people bored out of their brains at work would even consider reading it. Other great sections include 'How I Spend My Time' where someone explains how they spend their time at work. They make up a load of rubbish; 10% strategising, 15% personal development, 75% in meetings. It should be 10% drinking coffee, 40% surfing the internet, 10% talking rubbish at meetings, 25% trying to look busy, 15% ass kissing.

As Alison Loveday was such a vain person, I decided that the most appropriate method of payback would be embarrassment and humiliation. Now I needed to think of something suitably embarrassing.

She obviously valued the happy family life, but also wanted to be the centre of attention with the young boys in the callcentre. So it would be one of these areas that would provide the greatest opportunity for embarrassment. As her actions weren't in the same league as John Simmonds, I decided that the work option presented the easiest and least harmful opportunity, and set about finding some more details about her.

I wasn't sure that the information about her breast implants was common knowledge. It was probably something that she thought was a well kept secret. This was the thing I could use to embarrass her.

At work we have a loudspeaker system which is used for announcements such as fire alarm tests, minute silences, etc. This system provides instant, and anonymous, access to the three thousand people who work in my building. The loudspeaker system is located in the basement of the building and is very rarely used. Surprisingly the room in which the system is kept is never locked. It might be so that alarms can be raised quickly. I know it is unlocked because I got lost in the basement looking for a meeting room, and stumbled upon the loudspeaker room.

My plan was simple. I was going to expose her secret over the loudspeaker and make sure everyone in the company knew about her vain secret.

All computers have a facility to type in a sentence, and then a computer generated voice (which sounds a lot like Stephen Hawking) reads out exactly what has been typed. I borrowed a Dictaphone from work, and typed in the following sentence into my pc to record the computer generated voice;

"Callcentre manager Alison Loveday's breasts are not real. Alison Loveday paid for them to be enlarged. Alison Loveday is vain. Alison Loveday uses her breasts to titillate teenage boys in the callcentre. Alison Loveday has strangely large, and very fake, breasts (and she looks a bit like a man)". I liked the last bit, it made me laugh.

I recorded this on a loop onto the Dictaphone, being careful to leave a good minute of silence at the start of the recording to allow me time to get back to my desk.

The following day I went down to the basement area, checked that the coast was clear, and sneaked into the loudspeaker room. The microphone was standing in the centre of the table in front of the system. I lay the microphone on its side on the table and placed the Dictaphone next to the microphone. I started the Dictaphone and turned on the speaker system. It made a slight 'click' noise, which set my heart racing, but not enough to stop me.

I crept out of the room, flipped the latch on the inside of the door so it would lock shut from the inside, and eased the door closed behind me.

I now had about forty five seconds to get back to my desk. I walked quickly up the stairs, trying not to draw attention to myself by walking too fast, and was back at my desk with about ten seconds to spare.

Once at my desk I logged back in, and put on my serious work face. It was a struggle.

Then the tirade against Alison Loveday started up. It was even louder and clearer than I could have hoped for. Everyone else in the office was looking surprised, but finding it extremely amusing. People were asking who 'Alison Loveday' was, I shrugged, but there were plenty of people who did know her, and they were more than happy to fill everyone in.

In my mind I pictured Alison Loveday in the middle of the busy callcentre with everyone looking at her, and her breasts. She was going to be horrified. Her stupid false little life humiliated in front of everyone. She wanted to be the centre of attention, well now she was.

I went outside for a cigarette to celebrate. Within moments of lighting up I saw Alison Loveday scurry out of the building, and hurry past me looking absolutely furious. I guessed she must be leaving for the day. I took a long and satisfying drag on my cigarette, and watched her scuttle off into the car park.

As soon as she was out of sight my enjoyment dissipated. This wasn't enough. Like a drug addict I needed more. I needed something more worthwhile. These people were twats and deserved what they got, but there were bigger twats than Alison Loveday in this world.

At work the next day, I still couldn't shake the feeling that everything I had done so far was stupid.

I needed to do something that meant a bit more, something bigger than just a minor inconvenience. I really wanted to make someone face some serious consequences. I decided it was time to use the photos of the adulterer John Simmonds.

COMPLETING THE INTERVENTION

"The days go on and on... they don't end. All my life needed was a sense of someplace to go. I don't believe that one should devote his life to morbid self-attention, I believe that one should become a person like other people."

Travis Bickle (Taxi Driver, 1976 – Paul Schrader))

They weren't the best photos in the world, but you could clearly see who was in the picture, and what they were doing. That was all that mattered. They weren't pornographic, but they were incriminating.

John Simmonds was leaning across from the driver's seat and passionately kissing his mystery woman. You could see that his hand was caressing her breast as he leant over. Another photo clearly showed the same two people, not in a clinch this time so you could clearly see their faces. The second photograph included the car registration number as additional proof.

I had transferred the photos from my phone to my pc and stored them in a hidden file. They had been there for the last few months. Now the recent events had given me the conviction to use them. All I needed was the photo paper for my printer and I was ready.

This was the first 'intervention' with potentially very serious consequences. There were privacy and ethical issues of photographing someone unawares. Not to mention revenge issues if John Simmonds ever found out that I was behind it. This made me overly cautious with my preparations. I was acting like some kind of espionage specialist. The confidence would come with time, and doing more and more of these interventions.

I decided to get the most common photo paper available, and to buy it using cash to make it untraceable. I had no idea whether I could be traced using the type of paper, but as it was the only evidence which could be linked to me it was a good idea to make it as generic as possible. I was also sure I had seen something on the 'Discovery' channel that showed criminals being caught by tracing products they had purchased using credit cards. I was even slightly concerned that my printer might leave a unique reference number imprinted on the photos. I decided that I wasn't committing the crime of the century, so would let that one slip.

If the police were going to make that much effort to catch me then fair enough, well done. It's a fair cop. My previous experience of the police involved them mainly sitting in their police station drinking tea, reluctant to perform any kind of police work. Or handing out crime reference numbers after telling you they didn't have a chance in hell of solving the crime. The police might as well be a callcentre these days so I figured I would probably be ok.

Two days later I was sitting in my lounge with the two prints in my hands. Admiring my handy work, and considering life as a private investigator. It would be an interesting life, but I was being more of a maverick, motivated by doing the right thing, rather than money. Or so I told myself. Being motivated by morals sounded a lot more glamorous. Travis Bickle didn't kill the pimps and the drug dealers for money, he did it because he felt he had to.

I slipped the photos into an anonymous looking brown A4 envelope. I wasn't sure how to address the envelope (handwritten or typed), typed probably, or when was the best time to make the delivery.

I wasn't entirely sure he was married, only ninety five percent sure. He still needed to be exposed, but it was definitely more appropriate if he was married. I actually hoped he wasn't, and that he wasn't as bad as I was imagining him.

I checked b4usearch.com. This website enables you to find anyone who is listed on the electoral role, and get their address and telephone number. I don't know if this is legal, but it is there, and I was about to make use of it. They were listed as Mr & Mrs Simmonds, that confirmed it. Now I needed to decide whether to hand deliver the photos, post them from a local address, or post them from another town. This whole business was a lot more effort than I had first anticipated.

In the end I decided the best option would be to post the letter locally, but in a post box away from where I lived. I wasn't sure if they could trace letters back to specific post boxes, but I believed that if the letter had originated locally it would put more suspects in the frame and take attention away from an outsider. I just hoped that John Simmonds didn't think to link the photos to us playing football. Loads of people played football there, and it had been months since I took the photos, so the chances were very slim.

So it was done. A slight detour on my way home from work and the letter was posted. There was no turning back now. I had paused before letting the photos drop, and had an initial pang of fear and change of heart once I had let go, but it was too late. As I drove home I became more and more comfortable with what I had done.

Later that night I was relaxing at home, contemplating the consequences of my actions. I wanted to see the fruits of my labour, but knew that I would have to keep my distance, and would probably never know the outcome.

I was getting occasional feelings of guilt for meddling in other people's lives, but quickly rationalised these with the fact that John Simmonds was a liar and a cheat. His type of deceit deserved to be exposed, and he deserved to take some responsibility for his actions.

A few days passed without any incidence. Another boring day at work, was followed by an evening at home. Then another boring day at work.

In one of my projects, for a new application form, I had to spend two hours listening to people talking passionately about the importance of making some 'tick boxes' on an application form one millimetre wider. Apparently some people might have difficulty keeping a tick inside the current box. There was 'powerful' feedback that suggested people wanted bigger boxes to tick. Is this what my life had come to.

It was interesting to see how excited and motivated people can become about a form. More interesting than the actual form. There are a lot of forms in the world, so there must be a lot of people out there putting a hell of a lot of thought and passion into their forms. No doubt they all have dreams of making the perfect form. They work hard all their lives to achieve the Holy Grail of forms. When they retire they must look back at some of their greatest forms and feel such pride. What a load of bollocks. What a bollocks life.

Two hours seemed like a long time to discuss forms, but my project team managed it. We actually over ran. I was amazed. By the end of the meeting we had all agreed that the tick boxes needed to be bigger, we should rework a few options with different fonts, and see how the form looked with a logo that had the harsh edges 'smoothed' to make it more circular. What a pointless waste of time.

I spent most of the two hours daydreaming and nodding. I was too concerned with John Simmonds. Since I posted the letter I hadn't even seen him at work. I was itching to find out what had happened. I hoped that he was off work, begging and pleading to save his marriage, and I hoped that his wife was having none of it.

A week passed, and the initial rush of adrenaline from posting the photos had well and truly subsided. Now I was feeling frustrated that I wasn't able to know what was going on. I had even driven past their house looking for clues, but nothing.

I saw John Simmonds at work, in the canteen a few weeks later, but he looked and acted the same. He didn't seem upset or emotional in any way. Maybe he was incapable of feelings, after all, he had carried on his affair completely oblivious to the feelings of his wife. Maybe I had got the wrong address, or maybe he had found the photos, not her……

Then, nearly two weeks after I had posted the letter, there was a breakthrough. I was in the work shop, scanning the magazines, when I saw John Simmonds come into the shop. He was looking very sombre, and in deep discussion with a male colleague.

I delayed the magazine decision. John and the other man had paused by the drinks fridge, clearly engrossed in their conversation, they hadn't noticed me listening in.

I strolled casually over to the crisps section, which was near the drinks fridge, and began pretending that I was in turmoil about which crisps to choose. It required some rubbish acting to make crisp selection seem like a complicated process. I listened closely as the two men discussed marital issues. John was in a bit of a state. I felt the excitement rise up inside me.

Apparently his wife was leaving him because he was having an affair with Jayne (a secretary in his department). Jayne now thought he was going to leave his wife for her, but he had no intentions of doing so. John had obviously been using Jayne. Now his wife was leaving him. His life was falling apart (his words, not mine). I felt a perverse pleasure, and I liked it.

He didn't want to get together with Jayne, but because his wife was leaving him Jayne now expected him to move in with her. She lived in Parkhill, a shitty part of town, and he was never moving there. Everything was a mess, and it was all the fault of some twat who had posted some compromising pictures to his wife. He suspected that it was Jayne's boyfriend, who was some 'chav' from Parkhill.

This was brilliant news. The fact that he was annoyed more than upset made it even better. It had confirmed my suspicions that he was not a nice person. This made me feel good about betraying him to his wife. She had thrown him out, I was pleased she was doing the right thing. Taking him back would have meant he had escaped without being punished. If anything it would have been punishing her. I hadn't thought of that before. I had always assumed she would leave him, but if she hadn't then I could have harmed an innocent person. That thought stayed with me for some time. I needed to think more about the consequences.

This resolution was about the best I could have hoped for. In fact, I was so pleased that I felt like telling Laura. I knew I couldn't. If you have a secret you can't tell anyone. The only safe secret is one that you keep to yourself.

I had also been proved correct with my prediction that someone close to them would be the main suspect. Jayne's 'chav' boyfriend was in the frame. I felt a bit sorry for him, but at least he also knew what she was like now. I appreciated for the first time that this was having twice as much influence as I had planned. Which was a good thing.

I returned to my desk, unable to concentrate on the future of the application form and the size of the tick boxes. My mind raced with ideas of what to do next. This opportunity had pretty much presented itself to me. It had required very little work. I felt a surge of motivation go right through me, I needed to hold on to that feeling. This was much better than the juvenile pranks I had been playing recently. John Simmonds was fucked.

My mind was a blank. Having been irritated by almost anything all the time, I was now in a good mood. I was being less observant of all the irritating things that were going on around me. I needed to re-find my annoyance so I could begin to plan my next 'intervention'.

Whilst I was mulling over my next move I received further news that John Simmonds was being kicked out. Laura, being interested (some would say nosey) in neighbourhood issues, had noticed that a couple round the corner had obviously split up. She had seen a removals van moving someone out. A few days later she had noticed that the wife was still in the house.

John was starting to look a bit of a mess at work. I would see him from time to time in the canteen, or pass by him in a corridor. He was looking unshaven, and carrying himself in a forlorn way. He also had a huge black eye for a week or so. It must have been from Jayne's boyfriend.

Karma just needed a little prod and now it was carrying on my good work. I didn't feel sorry for John at all. He was no longer meeting up in the car park with Jayne, that must have ended too.

Something inside me wanted to know how John's story ended, but I knew it would be too risky to try and keep up to date with his life. I had to let it go. Hopefully the occasional update would present itself.

The last 'intervention' had convinced me that the juvenile pranks were not the way forward. There was much more satisfaction to be gained from long term bigger plans.

WORK PROJECTS

"Work is the refuge of people who have nothing better to do."
(Oscar Wilde)

After a few days considering my next project, I realised that this wasn't the way it was meant to be. Something needed to happen to trigger it. That was the only way to find the motivation I needed.

I settled back into everyday life. Working nine to five. What a way to make a living.

Dolly Parton once said "if you don't like the road you're walking, start paving another one", wise words from Dolly. She's a lot smarter than people think.

I think I might be paving a new road for myself right now. Or at least paving a road parallel to the one I am walking, to make the one I am supposed to be walking a bit more interesting. Maybe you can walk two roads, or is that some kind of schizophrenia?

My work was to provide the next project, and proved to be a very high profile affair.

I work for a mutual building society, which essentially means that we do not have any shareholders, and are owned by the 'members' of the society (known as customers in most forms of business, but referred to as members in the socialist ideals of a mutual society). This means we do not have to pay dividends to shareholders, so all the money which is made can be reinvested in the society. Fundamentally it is a good idea, but in practice it has a few problems.

It's all very nice and sweet, and a thoroughly decent philosophy. However, this form of corporate governance also has a very amateurish side to it. A society like this doesn't answer to anyone, there are no investment banks who have an interest in monitoring the performance of their investment. A public limited company needs to answer to these investment banks. The banks want to make money and police their investments very closely. In a mutual the directors are free to act as they see fit, there is very little in the way of administration of their behaviour, they have virtually no one to answer to. There is an executive directorship, but they just pop in and say hello once a year, collect their hundred grand and go off on their merry way.

This type of organisational culture enables people to hide. By that I mean that they can get away with doing very little, and because the hard decisions can be procrastinated on you get something which I think is called 'corporate drift'. The organisation just drifts along doing the same things, making the same mistakes and not adapting. It also means that people can do well in this culture without necessarily being particularly good at their job. There is a serious lack of accountability. I was about to make someone accountable.

The best example of this hidden ineptitude comes from one of our directors, Brian Cockburn-Emery. He currently occupies the role of Customer Retention Executive. I'm not quite sure what that involves, but that is true for most of the titles for people where I work. It sounds like his job is to go round asking customers, sorry members, to please not leave. Brian is not very bright, but is one of the most important people in the organisation. His journey to the top is typical of the upper class nepotism which, contrary to what the upper classes would like everyone to think, is still prevalent in British society. Meritocracies my arse.

His father was high up in the company many years ago, and by all accounts a very competent and intelligent man, who oversaw a glorious period in our history. Prior to his retirement a touch of nepotism kicked in, and he fast tracked his buffoon of a son up through the organisation. He must have known he was incompetent, but that didn't stop him.

Brian came in at a relatively high level, and within a few years had progressed quicker than anyone in the history of the organisation. Quite impressive, especially when you consider that he was, and is, a complete buffoon. He is now the third highest paid person in the organisation earning nearly one million pounds a year, and that doesn't even include bonuses, pension and other benefits.

His meteoric rise would have been questioned at any other type of organisation. Investors would want to know why someone had been fast tracked so quickly. Exactly what had he achieved to justify this, and could he be trusted with this power and influence. After all, he would have influence over the future of the company, and vis-à-vis the future of their investment.

No questions were asked where I work. The prevailing attitude amongst senior management was that for the sake of their own careers, bearing in mind the authority his father still carried, questioning his string of promotions was not a wise career move.

After his father retired Brian was left in a very lofty position. His dad had set him up for the rest of his life. There was one small problem, his complete inability to do the job. This left the remaining directors with a difficult dilemma. How could he remain in such a powerful position, without having any responsibility for anything? At the same time he had to be perceived as integral to the future of the business? Otherwise all of the previous decisions would be questioned. Tricky, but definitely achievable. As was proved.

The strategy they decided upon was one of limited responsibility, but massive visibility. He became the face of the company. Providing quotes for the press at every opportunity. Quotes that someone else had written for him. He was never allowed to do any proper interviews. That would have been too dangerous. Foot in mouth opportunities in actual interviews meant they were seen as far too risky. He was always available for photographs with the media doing various tasks. He cut the ribbon at opening ceremonies, flipped burgers at the staff barbecue every summer, flirted with the middle aged ladies at work, appeared in all the corporate videos, and generally did anything that wasn't considered important, but was highly visible. It seemed to work. I remember reading an article in a national paper which described him as 'media savvy'. I laughed out loud when I read that.

Unfortunately, after a number of years within this role, someone made an error and trusted him with a task that had some importance. Although the task had some importance, it was a very simple task. Once a week he had to check some numbers in a spreadsheet, and make sure they matched with some other numbers in another spreadsheet. These numbers affected pricing, and as long as they maintained the same level of difference, it meant we were pricing correctly to maintain a healthy level of profit. There weren't a great deal of numbers to check, probably a dozen, or so. Simple you would think, especially for someone earning in excess of a million pounds every year.

A number of months went by without any problems, but then he became lackadaisical with the task. So far he hadn't spotted a single error, ever. This meant it wasn't worth checking properly most of the time, maybe once a month from now on was good enough. For three consecutive weeks he only cast a cursory glance over the numbers without properly checking the differentials. Regrettably, he chose to stop checking, at the same time as our Finance department chose to handover the responsibility for producing the spreadsheets to someone else. And there were some errors, not immediately noticeable, but noticeable if the final check in the process was carried out correctly.

The three weeks passed, and then another director noticed that something didn't look right with the monthly profit figures, they were way down on the planned profit figures, about twenty five million pounds down.

An emergency meeting was called. Brian Cockburn-Emery's secretary was called to inform him he was required immediately.

It was a lovely summers day, and Brian had decided that it wasn't a good day for work, it was a day for golf. However, he had also decided that it wasn't worth taking the day as holiday, and had gone to play golf with his chauffeur. He had informed his secretary that on the slight off chance he was needed, she should inform people that he was working from home that day.

The other directors didn't care if he was working from home, he needed to get on the phone for a conference call without delay.

After twenty minutes of desperately trying to get hold of Brian without success, the Chairman lost patience, and came down to Brian's office to quiz his secretary as to what exactly was going on. Her guilty face was immediately apparent to everyone, and it didn't take long to get Brian's exact whereabouts.

The Manor Golf & Country Club were surprised by the intensity of the director on the other end of the phone.

"Are you sure this cannot wait until he has finished his round?" enquired the receptionist, "We wouldn't want to have to disturb everyone on the course in order to find one person." She was informed that this could not wait.

Brian was putting on the 13th green, and was surprised to see a golf buggy being driven up to all the golfers playing on the previous holes. This wasn't golf protocol. One by one they were approached and spoken to.

He sensed something was wrong, and instinct told him they were looking for him. Deep down he was aware of his own shortcomings. It was only his confident approach that managed to gloss over his ineptitude on most occasions. He knew his father was the only reason he was a director of a large company, and suspected that they were looking for him because he had buggered something up. Oh well, he had cocked up plenty of things before and had always weaselled his way out of it.

Brian Cockburn-Emery waited with knowing inevitability as the buggy approached him. He wanted it to hurry so he could refocus on his putt.

Luckily for Brian, his mistake also reflected extremely badly on all of the other directors. Feeling that this error would undermine them, and destroy confidence in their ability as a team, it was decided that this problem required one very big carpet, and one very big brush.

The directors controlled all the official channels of communication, and there was no way this story was ever getting out. Some creative accounting would cover the twenty five million pound loss. The Proles could pay for it from the employee bonus.

However, the directors didn't control the informal communications network, which was far more powerful. Brian's secretary had not been able to control herself. This gossip was far too good to keep a secret. She had to share it with someone. She told another secretary, who told her sister at a family barbecue, who mentioned it to her husband, who joked about it in the changing rooms at football. His mate told his friends at the pub, and one of them worked at our company. He told a friend, who emailed a few friends, and eventually a few months later pretty much everyone in the company knew.

Most people laughed at the stupidity of the mistake, some were annoyed that the money was taken directly out of their staff bonus. Initially I wasn't that fussed, I found it amusing that someone so incompetent was holding down such a prestigious and highly paid job.

But now, in my current frame of mind, I was becoming a little outraged at the injustice of it all.

Being a whistleblower sounded quite cool. However, I didn't really want to be known. I just wanted the story in the public domain, and for Brian Cockburn-Emery to face up to his actions and ineptitude. Anonymous whistleblower was the way forward.

It was easy enough to get email addresses for financial journalists from the daily national newspapers, they were printed at the foot of all their articles. Now all I needed was to set up a fake email account with hotmail, which takes five minutes, write the email, and send it from an internet café to make extra sure that there was no way of tracing the email to a specific computer.

I really enjoyed drafting the email, I felt like I was doing something important. The customers, sorry members, of our company had a right to know. I also knew full well the mayhem it would cause. I was looking forward to being in prime position to enjoy the impact of the information, and that made this project even more exciting than the John Simmonds experience.

"To whom it may concern,

I have some information which you might be interested in....."

I then went on to outline exactly what had happened, naming names, and possible dates (I wasn't sure of the exact dates). I even decided it was appropriate to add some context around how such a buffoon had made it so far within the company.

I made sure that all the other journalists could see who had been copied in. I wanted them to get this thing up and running as soon as possible. It would be a race to see who could break the exclusive first. I wouldn't be surprised if the story was in the papers the following morning.

Pressing send caused me a few nerves. This was a career-ender if it was ever traced back to me. I paused for a moment to confirm with myself that this was the right thing to do.

Even though my job was boring, and I spent the day surrounded by people I didn't really like that much, it was still the thing that kept a roof over my head and food on the table. Without it I was struggling. Perhaps, being caught wouldn't be such a bad thing. I had been cowardly and lazy about my job so far, constantly complaining, but never actually doing anything about it. Being caught could be the kick up the ass I needed, and not being caught meant another project/person had been completed. This project had a lot more impact, a lot more visibility, and a lot more satisfaction.

I have to admit that I hadn't expected it to have such a big impact. I could tell something was different as soon as I entered the office the following day. There was an eerie silence in the office. People were talking very quietly to each other in small groups. There were none of the usual loud, raucous, group discussions which were normally so commonplace in my office.

Everywhere I looked I could see and feel people looking at me. But luckily it wasn't just me. I could tell that everyone was looking at everyone. They were searching people's faces and actions for clues. Looking for the slightest change in behaviour, trying to be the one to catch the culprit, and use the associated kudos to further their careers.

I could see that this was going to become another McCarthyist witch hunt, which didn't bother me. I had thought it would be funny to see the fallout of my actions, and I was right. The hype and overreaction from everyone in the office was amusing. I joined in, casting suspicious glances around the office to fit in with all the other people. My co-workers were clearly revelling in the scandal. This had bought a bit of excitement into their mundane lives.

From my desk I can look over into the exclusive part of the building where the Directors have their plush offices. Working here reminds me of George Orwell's Animal Farm. We are supposed to be a pluralist organisation (society) all working for the good of each other. Yet the directors get more money, their own parking spaces, and a shoe shining machine in their toilet. Every day I am constantly reminded that all animals are equal, but some are more equal than others.

This morning I could see that all of the offices were empty. They were hopefully having an emergency meeting in the boardroom, discussing the issue of the day, and panicking. How the hell could they explain the twenty five million pound loss, but not only that, their shameful cover up would also require some deft public relations. This was bad.

I liked the fact that they were squirming. I felt like I was making them earn their ridiculously high salaries. If they had all been honest in the first place this would never have happened. If anyone had been brave enough to suggest that Brian Cockburn-Emery's promotions were perhaps not based on merit. If they hadn't swept his mistakes under the carpet. Then this would all have been avoided. That cowardice was now being punished.

The office gossip machine was in full force. People were accusing all kinds of different people of being the whistleblower. Names were being thrown into the hat left, right and centre. The favourites were anyone who had recently left the company, who had done it as a parting shot. There were also a few people using this opportunity to dirty other people's names behind their backs. I noted who they were for later.

Throughout the morning I pieced together the consequences of my actions. It appeared that virtually every paper had run the story. Some had made it fairly big news. There weren't any front page headlines, but it was the lead story in the business section of some of the major papers.

Looking across from my desk into the directors area, it was like watching fish in a fish tank. They were hurrying between each others offices, looking perplexed. A usual day would have been, in at 10:30ish, some coffee and gossiping, a meeting, a two hour lunch, then off to the gym. Back to the office for a meeting and then off home at around half three. Today was going to be a day of hard work. At last. I watched with interest as they panicked.

The hours ticked by and there was still no official response. I was scanning the internet, keeping an eye on my emails. I had even heard a rumour that the lunch time news on BBC News 24 had picked up on the story. There were a couple of reporters, and a cameramen, outside our offices waiting for a comment.

Finally the official response came. Brian Cockburn-Emery was being suspended on full pay, pending an investigation. The classic response. It might as well read, "Here is a short term media friendly response. By the time the investigation has finished please can you no longer be interested in this and we will sweep it back underneath the carpet again. Thank you".

At least I had achieved something. Although suspended on full pay felt like I had provided him with a free holiday to play some more golf. I was angry that an investigation was required. I had made it quite clear in my email that everyone was aware of the error, so why was an investigation required. I would have been disappointed in any journalist who allowed the story to end there. Fortunately no one was prepared to leave the story there.

There is an added detail to this story which made it even more amusing for me. The head of our press office is a middle aged man who has a lot of love for himself. His hair looks like it belongs on a teenager, all spiked and trendy. He dresses in sharp clothes, and drives a turquoise convertible MG. He is a classic example of a middle aged poser.

As head of the press office his recruitment policy consists of employing pretty young girls, regardless of ability, to work in his department. He spends most of the day flirting with the attractive young ladies he recruits, wishing that the flirting will one day come to something. Today, his recruitment policy was going to come back to haunt him.

He needed to somehow turn this fiasco around with the resources at his disposal. Resources which had been carefully picked, but not for situations like these.

If only I could be a fly on the wall. This was knock-on karma again. I hadn't even thought about this aspect until I had seen him on the news that evening.

I watched with delight as he was pushed in front of the cameras, and grilled by journalists on the local evening news. The journalist was enjoying this. They had all the ammunition they needed. Every sound bite that came out of his mouth was shot down. He was asked to speak in plain English, and continuously told that he was avoiding the point. He was visibly shaken the whole time, and it served him right. I loved watching him trying to wriggle out of it, and failing. Perhaps if his recruitment policy involved recruiting able people, then he would have been properly briefed going into the interview.

I wondered if there were other consequences to my actions, of which I was completely oblivious. I thought again about John Simmonds, and reflected on what might have become of his life since my intervention. I hadn't seen him at work for a long time.

The following day I sat at my desk and scanned all the reports of the Cockburn-Emery affair (as it was being called). I began to realise that this was going to be big. I couldn't wait to see the official response.

The press attention continued relentlessly. Normally an internal investigation would take months, years even. I had known internal investigations to just disappear into the ether, never to be heard of again. Thanks to the media attention, this investigation was concluded in two weeks, and Brian Cockburn-Emery was eventually relieved of his position.

The directors knew that this drastic action was required to stop the issue snowballing out of control. I felt it was a satisfactory outcome. He had lost the company twenty five million pounds, and was being paid over a million pounds a year for constant buffoonery. It would take him twenty five years of working for free to cover his debt. Instead he was gone, probably to enjoy a nice fat pension and retirement on the Costa del Sol, but at least he was shamed and he was gone.

This latest mission had been more high profile, more exciting, and more rewarding. I felt brilliant. There was a thrill to be had by influencing the retribution on these people. As soon as one person was finished my mind raced with ideas for who should be next.

It was then, through being extra vigilant, that I noticed another work project might be available to me. Llewelyn Davies. Remember him? The 'Welshman', who I suspected of being gay. Over the last few months I had noticed him leaving work at 3pm every Thursday. Apparently he needed to pick his children up from school, and his wife was otherwise engaged on a Thursday. This seemed innocuous enough at first. He got some abuse about being a part timer, but everyone else with children did the same thing from time to time, and the abuse died away.

Then half term week came. I know it was half term because it was taking me forty five minutes less to get to work in the mornings. Strangely, Llewelyn left at 3pm during the half term week as well. Schoolboy error, he clearly hadn't thought that one through. It appeared to go unnoticed, but my suspicions had been aroused. He was obviously up to something on a Thursday that he didn't want people knowing about.

The next week I decided to follow him from work, to find out what he was up to. I made the usual excuse of dentist appointment (with the amount of 'dentist appointments' people in my department have, we should have the best teeth in Europe), and followed Llewelyn out into the car park. He didn't see me. I ran to my car and quickly drove round to the car park exit so I could be there before him.

A couple of minutes later his car emerged. I started my car, pulled out, and followed from a safe distance as he made his way through Bristol and out to the M4. It was raining quite hard, which made visibility difficult, but that was also true for Llewelyn. There was no way he could see me in his rear view mirror through the driving rain. He travelled a couple of junctions down the M4 and came off at the Bath and Stroud junction. He headed north up the A46 and turned west towards Chipping Sodbury.

At the beginning, following had been quite exciting, I felt like Jason Bourne on a secret mission. Now it was boring. I was getting concerned that it was going to end as a wild goose chase, and a waste of time and petrol.

Then Llewelyn turned off into a housing estate on the edge of Chipping Sodbury. It was obvious that the journey was coming to a climax. I became excited again at the thought of what he might be hiding. There was no school round here. I hoped it would mean I had something on him. I couldn't wait to make him squirm.

He pulled up outside a normal looking newly built house. I drove past, turned round at the end of the street and sat observing his movements from a safe distance. I hoped for something scandalous.

It was still raining quite hard, and I had to leave my wipers going so I could see exactly what was going on. It was risky, but Llewelyn didn't notice. He had a few furtive glances around as he scampered up to the front door to avoid getting wet.

He rang the doorbell, continuing to look around nervously. It was blatantly obvious he was up to something.

Another man answered the door. He was about five foot seven inches, bald the same as Llewelyn. He wore a pair of square glasses with thick black rims, not nerdy glasses, painfully trendy ones that probably cost a fortune. He was wearing a tight black vest and a pair of tight black cycling shorts. The look was completed by a neatly trimmed goatee, a perfectly coiffured strip of hair that travelled from the middle of his bottom lip all the way down his chin. He looked like a prat.

I was chuckling about the bizarre man who had answered the door, the chuckling quickly turned to a gasp of shock when the man leaned in and French kissed Llewelyn Davies on his doorstep. This was the scandal I was after. I wrestled with my pocket to get my phone out and just managed to get a photo in time.

They went inside. I noted the address and drove home. All the way I was shaking my ahead, and smiling about the shocking double life he was leading. My suspicions had been confirmed.

A quick check on b4usearch.com revealed the name of the mystery goatee man. Mr Paul Stephens. The name rang a bell. He worked in another department in my company. I was used to seeing him in a suit and tie, so the vest and cycling shorts had briefly thrown me off the scent.

I was feeling creative, and decided that a good way to bust Llewelyn was to scrawl something on the inside of a toilet door at the office. I would let the office rumour mill take care of the 'outing', and then he could deal with the consequences of his actions.

The next day I worked quite late, until there were only a few people left in the office. Once the coast was clear, I went to the gents and scrawled a brief message inside the cubicle at the far end of the toilets.

"Llewelyn Davies, in Marketing, who is married, is having an affair with Paul Stephens from Personnel."

I had scrawled it left handed and in capital letters in a completely different style to my normal handwriting, and stood back to admire my work. It was impersonal and to the point. I liked it.

It took less than a morning for everyone in the department to find out. Not long after lunch one of Llewelyn's colleagues let him in on the rumour.

He was furious. Vehemently denying this most 'vicious' of rumours. He started proceedings to find out who was responsible. Contacting our Personnel department (Paul Stephens probably) to see what could be done.

I had pre-empted this response. I had printed out a photo of their clinch, and placed it in an envelope with 'Llewelyn Davies' printed on it along with a note suggesting it was time he owned up to his family. I put it in the internal post, making sure there was no way of tracing it back to me.

I didn't know whether he would own up to his family, or whether he would break up with Paul. I wasn't that bothered. I had already decided that I was going to expose him at work whether he came clean or not.

Eventually, after he thought he had squirmed his way out of it, I would leave copies of the photo around the building until he was embarrassed enough to leave. I wanted to see him shamed. I wanted to witness him face the consequences of his years of lying, cheating, and walking over people to achieve his status at work. I wanted to see his pain. This was payback for all the people he backstabbed, all the lies he told and all the ass he kissed. I wanted to enjoy it for a few weeks before finally finishing him off.

He managed two weeks of denial, but once I sensed that the rumour was losing its momentum I was ready with the photos of his indiscretion. Mainly I scattered them around the department, but a couple of special copies were left in the staff canteen, the whole company would see those. It didn't take long for the confirmation of the rumours to spread across the department, and probably the company.

Llewelyn Davies managed a few more days at work, then he was signed off with stress, and I never saw him again.

Work was proving to be an excellent source of assignments, but then 'Idiotland' was always full of idiots. Thinking about these people and my projects made the working day bearable. I was using the planning and thinking as a form of therapy to stop the banality of work, and the buffoons around me, from getting me down.

SUE YOU

"All the honesty in the world ain't legal tender for one loaf of bread"
(Josh Billings)

One of the most annoying buffoons in my department had recently stepped up their annoyance to a new level. Her name was Joleen Bingham, and in case the name doesn't give it away, she is an American. Like a lot of Americans I meet in the UK, she was actually a lot more American than she needs to be. I think she felt threatened by English people, and needed to assert her American-ness a lot more than normal. I can hear her voice booming across the office every day, because of her brashness everyone else knows everything about her life, and she lives a very annoying life.

She is only in England because she married an English man, otherwise she would be back in the great US of A. She misses the US so much it hurts. She hates the English weather, she hates how small England is, she hates how dark it is in the winter, she hates soccer, she hates cricket. England is just so awful (so why not go back?).

The most annoying of her American traits is her reflex action to sue anyone who ever annoys her. She should be sued every day for the annoyance she causes me. So far I know of three people she has sued.

Someone who drove into the back of her was sued for causing her 'extensive' whiplash injuries, even though I have heard her admit that the crash was probably her fault. Apparently she went to pull out at a roundabout, there was nothing coming, but then she caught a glimpse of her hair in the rear view mirror and decided it needed sorting. She braked suddenly, and the person behind her crashed into her. It was blatantly her fault, but the rules clearly state that the person crashing into the back is the one at fault. Obviously she didn't own up to braking suddenly, she exaggerated the injuries, and was now £8,000 richer as a result. She has since pulled off that trick once more. When she thought her car might fail its MOT she decided to get someone to crash into the back of her, claim whiplash, and get a new car out of it as well. She was annoyingly proud of herself for being a cheating idiot. I listened from across the office, and wished her nothing but misfortune.

The third person she sued was by far the most unlucky, and it was her next door neighbour. She moved into a new house. I heard her telling everyone about it at work, how wonderful it was, and how everyone must come and see it. Not that it mattered as she had photographed it from every angle and was forcing people to see her photographs if they came within a few metres of her desk. She was also delighted with how nice her neighbours were. Although I am not so sure they would have been so delighted with their new neighbour.

About six months after she moved into her new house she was scanning through the reports they received during the move, and noticed that one of her neighbour's fences was probably six inches further across than it should have been. The garden was twenty feet long, so they were stealing ten feet of her garden space. She immediately set the legal wheels in motion and within a few months had reclaimed the six inches, bartered a further six inches of their garden, and claimed £3,000 in damages for lost time she could have spent utilising her garden space. It was ridiculous, and so frustrating. I think I actually hated her. She definitely needed to be sorted out.

Once I had decided upon Joleen as the target and identified the problem, it didn't take too much imagination to come up with an appropriate solution. I needed to sue her. I would have to lure her into a situation that would provide me with good reason to sue her, and make sure I had either a witness or evidence to support my case.

I didn't mind the lack of anonymity on this particular occasion. I was sure I would have people's support if I provided her with a taste of her own medicine. I sensed that there were others who felt morally offended by her attitude, and who felt that the American claim culture needed to stop.

There are a lot of terrible things coming over here from America, obesity, rap music, the claim culture, the war in Iraq. They sit in their big skyscrapers, thinking up their protectionist economic policies, and disastrous foreign policies, and bully the rest of the world into doing as they say. Harassment of Joleen was a small victory in the war against the Americanisation of the world. I was striking a blow against Team America.

Anyway, I deviate from my plan. It was a simple plan, I would make sure I left work around the same time as her every day, and drive in front of her until the opportunity arose to make her slam into the back of me. Not too hard, I didn't fancy any pain, just enough of an impact to write off my car and claim a healthy amount of whiplash compensation. That was the least she deserved, and depending on how this incident went, I might not even be finished there.

It took a couple of weeks for the opportunity to arise. She was actually quite a careful driver. I was getting concerned she would notice I was always the person in front of her when she left work.

No matter what time she left, I was always right there, but she didn't say anything, she was too self-absorbed to notice, so I carried on.

Over the two weeks I had plenty of time to think about the best sections of the route to get her. There were a few roundabouts, but the visibility was really good, and they were always quite busy, so had to be approached with caution. With the roundabouts ruled out, that left a couple of traffic lights on route that provided good opportunities for stopping quickly. One of these sets of lights was on a busy dual carriageway. The dual carriageway went past the hospital, and there were lights stopping traffic to allow the hospital traffic to join the dual carriageway. The lights consisted of the normal set, and then an elevated set, about twenty feet above the normal set of lights. On a dual carriageway cars approach them at about sixty mph, and I had noticed that, even though they gave plenty of warning when changing, it was quite difficult to stop in time when the road was wet. I thought this provided the best opportunity to lure Joleen into crashing. I was slightly concerned about the speed of the impact, but decided to try it nonetheless. Cars were safe enough these days.

A few days later, after a heavy downpour, I was driving along, as per usual, with Joleen about fifty feet behind me. I was travelling at sixty mph, and was about a hundred feet from the lights when they changed to amber. Normally at that speed I would continue through before they changed to red, and the car behind would usually go through with me. But, on this occasion, I slammed on my breaks and skidded to a halt just in front of the white line.

I looked in my rear view mirror. Everything went into slow motion as I watched Joleen's car approaching me. She didn't seem to be slowing at all, and I even had time to think that this was a bad idea. It was going to be a nasty collision. Then she slowed, not much at first, but I could see her car wobble a little bit at the force of slowing so quickly. Then the impact happened. Even though I saw it coming, and had braced myself, it was still an almighty bang. My car shot forward about ten feet, and I genuinely had the wind knocked out of me. The seatbelt snapped into my collarbone. I felt it break. There was no pain, just a crunching noise. The impact was intense, and I took a few moments to compose myself. I was ok. A little shaken, but fundamentally I was ok. Whiplash takes twenty four hours to emerge, but there was no whiplash. There rarely was in these types of cases. In my rear view mirror I could see Joleen's car behind me. Steam was rising through a large gap in the front of her bonnet.

Through the steam I could see Joleen sat in the driver's seat, she looked shocked and shaken, but I had no sympathy for her. I didn't wish her any physical injury, just financial injury.

Other drivers had left their cars and started to check on myself and Joleen. After a few moments I was composed enough to start my 'act'. I wound down the window, and in a shaken voice, explained to one of the concerned drivers that I thought I was ok, but could they phone an ambulance and the police. I wanted to make sure everything was done by the book. I didn't want Joleen weaselling her way out of it on some technicality.

The man told me to stay still until the ambulance arrived. He didn't think it would be a good idea to move around after such a heavy collision. I pretended to try and nod, and grasped my neck in feigned pain.

The man informed me that the driver behind me was going far too fast as she approached the lights, and that he was prepared to vouch for that. This was all going too well. I had come out of the impact relatively unscathed, and I had a willing witness. I hadn't even left my car and the plan was going like a dream.

I glanced back in the rear view mirror to see what was happening with Joleen. She was also waiting in the car for the ambulance to arrive. I wondered if she knew it was me she had crashed into.

Having crashed next to the hospital was also a stroke of genius. The ambulance arrived within minutes and after a few checks for paralysis, they deemed myself and Joleen fit to get out of our cars and into the ambulance. They wanted to take us both in for some scans and overnight observation. This was the worst bit of my plan, I was going to have to spend the night in hospital.

Joleen recognised me immediately, and was kissing my ass within seconds. I knew that she was in a financial predicament, and I knew that it was purely for this reason that she was showing so much concern.

"David! Are you ok?" she didn't really care, I knew her well enough to know that.

"I'm not so sure, I think I need to get to hospital to get checked out" I was acting feeble and stunned. My collarbone was starting to hurt a bit, but I didn't care. I felt happy. Elated.

On the short ambulance ride back to the hospital she tried to curry favour with me. Offering to 'sort' everything out with my car. She was subtly trying to check what my stance on suing her might be, without losing any of her fake concern. It didn't work. I saw straight through her.

Once in the hospital we wished each other well and went our separate ways for the various scans and tests. Bitch.

The police were sorting out the crash scene, my insurance company were sorting out my car. Laura had been informed and was on her way down to the hospital to keep me company. All I had to do now was sit through a few scans and milk the whiplash and collarbone. I would even get a few days off work, which was an additional bonus I hadn't even considered.

Laura arrived with my mum and dad. They were all extremely concerned, it was written all over their faces. I wished I could tell them that I was fine, and that I had meant to do it, but I couldn't tell anyone. They thought that they could have lost me forever. I hadn't even considered their pain. I felt awful. My parents were being overly caring, in a way that only devastating incidents, births and weddings allow. I felt worse, so I focused on Joleen's financial pain to get me through it.

When I did return to work Joleen had been back for a few days already, and had planted the seeds of doubt that the accident was her fault. Her lawyer had told her never to admit guilt, and she was trying bless her, but if you crash into the back of someone then it is your fault. That's the law. She pretended to be concerned again, asking how I was, and more importantly, what I was planning to do. It was awkward, and she was making it deliberately awkward so I could see the kind of thing I could expect should I pursue a legal case. I didn't care. I don't think she grasped the irony of the situation, and she definitely didn't grasp my hatred of her. If only she could be more self aware, maybe she could change.

I suggested that it was probably best not to discuss it, and to let our insurance companies sort things out between them. I made sure she was clear that was the end of the conversation. I had never really spoken to her in the office before the accident, and I didn't want to start now. She thought she was holding out an olive branch, well she could take her olive branch and piss off.

In the end I got four thousand pounds for my car, and five thousand pounds for my non-existent whiplash and clavicle. It was a welcome financial bonus, but I didn't feel like keeping my ill gotten gains. The pleasure I got from seeing Joleen around the office was worth a lot more than that. I would even say priceless. On a daily basis I was able to see her annoyance. The dirty looks across the office just made me feel even better.

I bought a new car with the four thousand pounds, and gave the whiplash money to Cancer Research UK. Cancer had claimed both my grandfathers before I had a chance to know them. I always regretted that.

My next, and as it turned out final, work project was my favourite. It would also leave me slightly exposed, and made me realise that shitting on your own doorstep with work associates was getting too risky, and a little bit boring.

XMAS TIME, MISTLETOE & FLIRTING & INFIDELITY

"I wasn't kissing her, I was whispering in her mouth"
(Chico Marx)

Another thing that annoys me about work are the Christmas party prats.

There are a few different types of prats. The over drinkers, people don't get out much, and don't know how to let their hair down properly. They end up getting smashed out of their brains, behaving out of character, dancing like absolute idiots, being sick and passing out early. They are amusing prats, but the prats I really cant stomach are the twenty something women, who dress like sluts to catch the attention of the sad middle aged men who can influence their careers. These women see the Christmas party as a career advancement tool. They use their breasts to create positive associations amongst the senior managers, and hope that these positive associations continue into the workplace and lead to promotion. Sometimes they even go as far as snogging them to create that extra special bond. These women have boyfriends, fiancés, etc, which is all shamelessly forgotten in the pursuit of their career.

It was our latest Christmas party which gave me a brilliant opportunity to get back at another idiot from my workplace. A girl called Faye Axleby. She was an incredibly posh twenty something who believed she was far more important than everyone else at her level. She rarely spoke to her peers, reserving her attention and energy for the senior management team, and anyone she felt had some influence over her career.

She was engaged to a guy who was also incredibly posh, and incredibly loaded, and was due to be married. How did I know this? Well, as luck would have it, her and Laura used the same hairdresser's, and, as girls do, had struck up a friendship during the many hours spent together in the salon. Even though it was simply a hair salon based friendship, Faye was keen to show off about her impending wedding, and keen to show as many people as possible her perfect life, and her perfect wedding, so she had invited Laura and partner (me) to the lavish affair.

She knew I was with Laura, and this granted me an occasional 'hello' in the office, but other than that she didn't really want to be associated with me. I was at the losers level, and had nothing to offer her career. At first I had tried to insist that we didn't have to attend the wedding, but Laura loves a good wedding, and she had put her foot down. So now we were going, and Laura insisted I was going to enjoy it.

As luck would have it our Christmas party that year provided me with a brilliant reason to go to her wedding.

It was a black tie affair. Faye was drunk and wearing a dress that was so low cut that she might as well have taken her breasts out and put them on a plinth for the senior managers to look at and talk to. She knew what she was doing, and she shamelessly worked the room, starting with Crispin and gradually working her way down through the ranks of seniority. She was making sure they all got a good look down her top, and flirted with them enough to make them think that they just might have a chance with her if they played their cards right. In return they plied her with free drinks, and slipped in an extra shot with every drink to try and loosen her up a little bit.

After a while she was really drunk, and had lowered her guard. The flirting was bordering on obscene. At one point I overheard her jokingly (but with a hint of seriousness) say to Crispin, "If I show you my pussy will you promote me?" The senior managers gathered around her like a pack of hyenas waiting for the final moment of weakness. They didn't have to wait long, and suddenly, she was tonguing away with a middle aged married man. And all this only a few months before the 'dream' wedding.

Later on that evening she was spotted outside the venue tonguing a different senior manager. Faye was so hammered she didn't know what she was doing. Both of these men are married with children, so they needed to be ashamed of themselves as well. My trusty mobile phone was out again. Held up, as though writing a text, but actually taking photos. They were all too drunk to notice. It was terrible, but in January she achieved the promotion she had desired. The rumours and gossiping eventually stopped, and it was back to business as usual.

Behind the scenes I had started plotting, she needed to be exposed, and what better opportunity than the "Wedding of the Year". I could I sit in the church and 'forever hold my peace', or I could ruin everything.

The day of the wedding came around. I had prepared one hundred copies of the photos and placed them all in fancy envelopes with "Open during the bridal procession" printed on the front. People loved these little treats at weddings……

The ceremony was to be held in a small village outside Bristol, at a picturesque church situated in the village centre, opposite the village green and with a small stream running alongside the bottom of the cemetery. It was all very picturesque. The weather was lovely, especially for this time of year. The sun was shining and it was a lovely Spring day. She didn't deserve the weather to be this good.

I persuaded Laura to get there early so we could enjoy a romantic walk through the village.

As soon as we arrived I jumped out of the car, and pretended to fiddle about in the boot for something. Actually I was taking the envelopes out of a box and sticking them up the back of my shirt. I tucked my shirt back into my trousers and pulled my jacket over the top. I announced my desperate need for the toilet and ran into the church, telling Laura to wait for me outside.

Once inside I hurriedly put small piles at the end of each pew. My heart was beating like a drum, and very slight noise startled me. It didn't take long and I was back outside again. Taking a deep breath to calm myself, before heading back down the church path to Laura.

We had a quick stroll round the village, and I could barely keep a smirk from my face. We headed back to the church.

Laura and I had our invite checked by the ushers, our names were checked against the register, and we went inside. I had a quick look through the order of service and was gutted that we would miss one of the readings. Faye's sister was going to read the lyrics of Boyz 2 Men's "I'll Make Love To You" as a genuine reading. It was so awful it was amazing. I was disappointed that my actions were probably going to deny people that special treat.

The church gradually filled with people and the murmur of conversation. Then everyone was alerted by a slight creaking of the church doors and the church fell silent. The church doors opened majestically, the organist started playing 'Here Comes The Bride', and Faye entered the church holding her dad's arm. She looked nice, and I was about to ruin it all. I had orchestrated the ruining of her special day. I focused on her behaviour at the Christmas party in an attempt to justify what was about to happen.

As she moved slowly past loving and milking every moment, people opened their envelopes and gasped. It was awesome.

This wedding was all about putting on a big show for the people. Faye wanted people to envy her, to envy her lifestyle and envy everything about her. She wanted to be seen as perfect.

The murmuring and gasps confused Faye. This wasn't the perfect joyous procession she had expected. She sensed something was wrong. I could see the confusion on her face and I loved it. I loved every second of it.

The Minister started his speech;

"Dearly Beloved, we are gathered together here in the sign of God - and in the face of this company - to join together this man and this woman in holy matrimony, which is commended to be honourable among all men; and therefore - is not by any - to be entered into unadvisedly or lightly - but reverently, discreetly, advisedly and solemnly. Into this holy estate these two persons present now come to be joined. If any person can show just cause why they may not be joined together - let them speak now or forever hold their peace."

The minister stopped. The murmuring was too obvious to continue. The groom's side of the church looked furious. Faye's side looked ashamed and upset. The minister tried to repeat himself, "Let them forever….." He tailed off. The murmuring was worse now.

Someone stepped forward and handed a photo to Faye. Then someone stepped forward and handed the groom a photo.

Even Faye was too stunned to cry immediately. She just stared at everyone in the congregation, more concerned with their reaction than her fiancé's. It was only when he made his move to leave that she became aware of him again. She grabbed his arm and tried to pull him back up to the altar. He shrugged her off. Faye looked down at the floor. Her fiancé left, all eyes followed him as he stormed out of the church closely followed by his best man. It was at this point that Faye began to cry. I sensed she wasn't crying for her husband, she was crying out of embarrassment. Crying because the day had not been the perfect spectacle. Her dad put a comforting arm around her, and everyone in the church took this as their cue to leave.

Laura was stunned.

"I wonder who did that?" I asked.

Laura just shook her head, looked and me and said, "Well, I guess you reap what you sow"

Brilliant. I got away with it.

So that was the end of my work projects. It was time to take this thing to the next level……

COMA TEXT

"Have you ever noticed that anybody driving slower than you is an idiot, and anyone going faster than you is a maniac?"
(George Carlin)

My mum phoned me at work, which she never did. I knew immediately that something was wrong. She sounded terrible on the phone. I could tell she had been crying. I spent the first few moments trying to calm her down, before I could find out what was bothering her. Eventually, through her tears, she was able to tell me the story.

My cousin had been cycling into work this morning when he had been hit by a car. I was beginning to think that I was cursing people. So many people I knew were getting involved in car crashes. Maybe they are just too common.

The police hadn't disclosed too much about the cause of the accident. My mum understood from her sister that originally the driver had admitted to writing a text message on her mobile phone when the accident happened. Now, having received legal advice from her insurance company, she had changed her story, and was claiming that she hadn't been using her phone at the time of the accident. Even though she had admitted it to begin with, it didn't matter. It sounded crazy to me. It meant she was probably going to avoid any serious trouble as there were no witnesses to the accident. Most of the witnesses had just carried on driving, probably too worried about being late for work, or getting involved in something that might inconvenience their own lives. My cousin was now in Bristol Royal Infirmary, on a life support machine, and it was touch and go whether he would pull through.

I wasn't particularly close to my cousin. We were very different people, who enjoyed very different things. He was into jogging, cycling, rock climbing and any other sport that seemed to involve wearing a lot of lycra. I preferred football, drinking, golf and watching TV.

We had been fairly close as children, forced together by our mums, and I had some happy childhood memories of the times we spent together. Once we reached our teenage years we drifted apart, but we still got on ok at family occasions. He wasn't the kind of person I naturally gravitated to, but we could chat quite amicably for a while and then move on. He certainly didn't deserve to be knocked down, and put in hospital, so that someone could send a text, and then lie about it. I didn't know this woman, but I already felt so much hatred towards her.

When our family went to visit that evening he was still in a bad way, and we were only allowed to see him through the glass windows that looked into intensive care.

My auntie and uncle were understandably mortified. Fluctuating between all kinds of emotions, from despair to anger. I could tell they were glad that we had made the effort to come, but confused as to how to act. Wanting to be hospitable to us, but not feeling in the mood to do so. We stayed for about half an hour, my mum had wanted to be there for her sister, but sensed, as we all did, that her and my uncle were best left alone to deal with this.

Leaving the hospital that night I knew I had to do something, give something back. Every day I saw people driving whilst texting or talking on their mobile phones. Especially the annoying white van men. Cutting people up at roundabouts whilst smoking, eating pies and talking on their mobile phones.

I decided that I would catch people using their mobile phones. I wasn't going to change the world, but maybe I could stop someone else from causing an accident.

A quick internet search revealed that someone using a mobile phone was four times more likely to have a crash. That meant if I could catch and punish four people using their mobile phones, then I would stop one accident. I also read that in 2002 there were 302,605 crashes, of which 3,431 were fatal, meaning 1.1% of crashes are fatal. So I would need to catch four hundred people to save one life. It wasn't the best logic, but in my anger, it made sense to me. I didn't have the resources to catch four hundred people, so I set myself the target of trying to catch one hundred people.

This seemed like quite an interesting project, but also one that would involve a lot of time, and would be better if I had company. I mentioned my plan to Laura, she thought I was insane, but that it might be an fun experiment, so decided to join me.

We set up 'camp' by a bush, out of sight from the road, on a dual carriageway not far from our house. We both had camping seats, my camera was set up on a tripod, and we sheltered from the heavy rain underneath a large umbrella. Laura was enjoying herself. She thought it was nice and cosy snuggling up under the umbrella watching the traffic go by. I was taking it a little more seriously. I had a set of binoculars, and could spot the mobile phone offenders well before they were within distance to be photographed. My digital camera was quite good, and after a few practice shots, some adjustments in position and camera settings, I was able to clearly show the driver, the fact they were on the phone, and their number plate.

I was shocked and appalled to see the number of people using their mobile phones whilst driving, and within an hour I had snapped 40 offenders, nearly one every minute. Laura was getting bored, it had been cosy under the umbrella, now she was cold and bored.

I knew I only needed another hour and a half and I would have the hundred I needed to satisfy my silly target. There was no way I was going now, and I told her so. The rage inside me would only be sated by achieving my target. If I gave up the feelings of futility would stay with me, and eat away at me.

Laura left and walked home. She clearly thought I was an idiot. As it happens the traffic slowed up and it looked like I was going to be there for days.

In the end I was only there for another hour due to circumstances beyond my control.

Someone had seen the flash of my camera and complained to the police that I was distracting drivers (I'm not exactly sure how a speed camera flash is any different). So the police came, gave me a telling off and asked me to move on. They weren't even interested in what I was doing. I tried to explain, but Dixon of Dock Green and PC Plod were too busy trying to be officious to take any notice. Where do the police recruit these wankers from?

So I trudged home with my tail between my legs, cursing the police and feeling hungry.

Laura was a little annoyed to say the least. I had missed dinner again, and she had been home alone all evening. She no longer saw my experiment as interesting, she thought it was dumb. I wasn't that bothered, I had achieved something. I decided to leave out the bit about the police. I didn't want to give her the ammunition for another argument.

I may not have reached my target, but I had over fifty photos of reckless drivers using their phones. I printed out all the pictures. The next day I went to the local police station on my lunch break and handed the photos to the police. I explained why I had done it, how I had been ignored by the police last night, and requested that I be informed of their progress in catching and fining these people.

He thanked me for taking the time to collect the evidence and assured me that they would be investigating each case. I could tell that he wasn't pleased I had gone to all this trouble. He actually seemed annoyed with me. Maybe he thought I was undermining his role as a policeman, but given the inability of the police to do anything these days, he should have been grateful for any help he received. I wouldn't be surprised if he filed my photos in the bin, but I felt a bit better about my cousin.

I never heard anything back from the police.

I felt like I had been fobbed off at the time, and I was right. I was impotent to do anything about it. That didn't stop me feeling like I had done something for my cousin, and in a strange way that helped me come to terms with what had happened to him.

A week after the accident my cousin came out of his coma, and whilst he was still not brilliant, the doctors felt that there was going to be no long term damage. He would eventually get back to the life he had enjoyed before the accident. Whereas my life was about to change forever.

OLD SCHOOL

"Be an opener of doors for such as come after thee."
(Ralph Waldo Emerson)

The next person to feel my brand of karma was someone who had mistreated me in my youth. One man had been the bane of my life. As I am sure is true for a lot of people the man I hated was a teacher.

A man called Mr Peter Rimmer, an unfortunate name for those of you who are aware of rimming. He was a teacher who had taken a dislike to me, and bullied me at school. His bullying had lasted for three years, and whilst I tried to laugh it off at the time, as I reached adulthood I became more and more aware of his mistreatment of me. He had probably bullied children before me, and carried on bullying children after me.

Mr Rimmer saw himself as a bit of a ladies man, flirting with the secretaries and female teachers, but in reality he was a short, chubby, power crazed little man, who was a bit of a joke amongst the rest of the staff.

Mr Rimmer was an awful man. He ended up having an affair and his wife threw him out. He now lived alone in a council house in a small village on the outskirts of Bristol. This gave me some pleasure, but he was still a teacher in the same school, probably bullying other children in the same way he had bullied me. He needed to be taught a lesson. No pun intended.

He needed to be taught this lesson in front of his pupils. He was a bully, who felt power over children, this power then fed his ego, and his ego was the most important part of him. I needed to embarrass him in front of his pupils so he would lose any respect, or fear, that he held over them. I wanted to expose him as the loser he was and break down the myth that teachers are all powerful. Children learn quickly, and it would only take one incident to set the ball rolling for his demise. I just needed to work out what that incident would be.

I cast my mind back to my school days and tried to remember what annoyed him (apart from me), what he liked and what he hated. The memories were hazy, and had become glorified over the years, so much so that I had glossed over my memories of Mr Rimmer and what an arse he had been. I struggled to think of his weakness.

It came to me out of the blue. One night when I had given up wracking my brain, and was watching tv with Laura. 'Watchdog' was on and I was, as usual, stunned by the idiocy of some of the people on the program. If someone turns up at your door offering you something, don't believe everything they say. I felt like shouting it at the tv screen. These people just needed to do some research, but they were too lazy, and now their laziness had caught up with them and they were bitching and moaning. It was in the middle of a feature on solar heating that I had my eureka moment.

Someone on 'Watchdog' had paid five thousand pounds to a door-to-door salesman to have solar panels fitted, and subsequently found out that they could have had it done for three thousand, they thought they had been ripped off, but they had just been lazy. However, they felt that they needed compensation, and the facetious Nicky Campbell agreed. He was all over the solar panel company like a cheap suit.

It was during his interview/harassment of the solar panel company's director that it came to me. Mr Rimmer was a narcissistic man. He was an ugly man, but he was a narcissistic man. He loved himself a lot, and he thought he was a bit of a ladies man. He made you wonder whether he actually had any mirrors in his house. He was also a very brown man, too brown. It was obvious he visited tanning parlours, even twenty years ago when they weren't very common, he must have used them. He had an orange, David Dickinson, complexion throughout the year. His permatan, and his vanity, were his weakness. I needed a picture of him, and it needed to be as unflattering as possible.

Moving my train of thought on a bit, I reasoned that he must also be a lover of natural sunbathing. It was summer and I fully expected him to lie in his back garden in some German style swimming trunk briefs, holding a reflective sunbathing fan to make sure he was brown under his chin and eyebrows. That was the ideal scene that I had in my mind. That was the picture I wanted. The reality was to be much better.

As usual I found his latest abode using the internet. If I was him I would have my name and address taken out of the directory, but as I alluded to earlier, he is so egocentric that he would never believe that anyone could have anything against him. I chose a sunny Saturday to travel over to the village of Swineford (how ironic) to scope out the scene and begin planning my embarrassment of Mr Rimmer.

He lived on the end of a row of 1960s terraced houses at the edge of the village. They weren't very impressive, and you could see that they didn't fit in with the rest of the wealthy rural abodes in the village. They were hidden away from the main village down a winding, hedge lined, country lane. Probably to avoid any negative affect on the house prices of the wealthier villagers.

The location meant that Mr Rimmer lived in a relatively secluded area, especially as he was on the end terrace. I walked along the lane, trying to look inconspicuous as I counted down the house numbers to Mr Rimmer's.

His house was heavily protected by six feet high hedgerows, which added to the seclusion. I hopped over a stile and into the field of wheat that surrounded the row of houses. I skirted round the edge of the property to find a position for spying on Mr Rimmer.

I peered through the hedgerow into his back garden, which was empty. My heart sank. I don't know what I had expected, but it was a bright sunny day and I was sure he would be in his garden sunbathing.

I sat down in the wheat that surrounded me. No one could see me as the wheat came up well above my head. It was very relaxing. I lay down and looked up to the clear blue sky. It was warm. The wheat swayed in the breeze and I found myself drifting off.

I was awoken by the sound of a lawn mower starting up. I was startled and annoyed that someone had woken me up, but I soon realised that the sound of the lawn mower was coming from Mr Rimmer's garden. I couldn't believe I had fallen asleep, and was relieved that I hadn't snored and alerted Rimmer to my presence in the field on the other side of his hedge.

I slowly got to my feet, remaining in a hunched position so I could stay below the line of the wheat. I edged closer to his hedge and peered through a gap.

It was shocking, repulsive and disgusting. But it was exactly what I was after.

He was mowing the lawn completely naked except for a pair of black socks, which he had pulled up so high that they almost touched his knees. It was a ridiculous sight. His huge pot belly hung over his penis and saved me the repugnant sight of his manhood. The noise of the mower gave me an added level of security against being caught. I pulled out my mobile phone and snapped a couple of delightful shots. The full frontal, and a cheeky shot from behind as his saggy buttocks wobbled with the motion of the lawn mower.

Still slightly dazed from my snooze, I gathered myself, returned to the lane, and the short walk back to my car.

On the journey home I daydreamed about how I would distribute the photos. Ideally I would like to march into my old school and leave a pile in the staff room, and piles in each of the assembly rooms, and then present Mr

Rimmer with a framed copy of the two snaps. In reality I was going to have to distribute them anonymously, and quickly, before the staff managed to nip them in the bud. The quickest way to get the photos distributed would be the children. The entire school would know within a few hours if I could somehow provide them with access. I needed to do this without being seen as distributing pornography to minors.

    I knew the layout of my old school well. I had spent seven years of my life there. I remembered that there were three access points through which the entire school had to pass. I would simply leave copies at the entrances at an opportune moment. The teachers all drove through the main entrance, so I could leave piles scattered at the other two entrances. Kids were naturally inquisitive, it wouldn't take long for them to notice piles of photos and investigate.

    And so it was. Another plan completed. More satisfaction, and on to the next idea.

    This was all too easy. I had continuously been planning or carrying out a scheme for months. It had been awesome. Some parts of my life had been sacrificed. I didn't see Laura as much anymore, and I rarely saw my family and friends, but they weren't as important at this moment in my life. I didn't care.

MY FATHER

"He wants to live on through something-and in his case, his masterpiece is his son. All of us want that, and it gets more poignant as we get more anonymous in this world".
(Arthur Miller)

It happened on July 25th 2003. That was the day that my father died.
    I know it sounds like stating the obvious, but when people close to you die it is the worst time in your life. You reflect on the person's life and how it developed along with yours. You begin to really appreciate what you had. You think about the good times you spent together, and even the bad times become nostalgic. It becomes depressing when you realise that you probably never properly appreciated what you had. Life is strange like that. As Joni Mitchell said, you don't know what you've got til it's gone.
    My relationship with my father was sometimes tense, but always a very loving one. When I was growing up we fell out a lot, but always loved each other. That was an unspoken fact that we both just knew, but rarely acknowledged. As I grew up and matured I begrudgingly accepted that we were too alike, something that was very difficult for me to admit. But something that was the reason behind a lot of our early difficulties. I was also forced to acknowledge that he only ever had my best interests at heart. All the lectures, all the grief, everything he ever did was for me, for my own good and because he loved me. When I matured and accepted that fact our relationship became very close.
    He once told me that he would never be able to describe the unconditional love a father has for his child. And as I watched him slowly

slip away in that hospital room it felt like something inside of me was dying with him. I felt like I was losing that unconditional love before I had even had a chance to properly appreciate it.

All the times we had spent together would now be memories that we would never share again. We would never laugh together again, and it was the finality that made me the saddest. The times we had, that chapter of our lives was closed. He would never see me get married, become a father, see his grandchildren. He would never share in that joy.

My earliest memories of my dad were of a huge strong man, probably the same as most people. At that age your dad seems like a giant. On holidays he would carry me on his shoulders for hours. I used to love being carried on his shoulders. I remember constantly nagging him to carry me. He always gave in.

My most recent memories of my father are of him taking me to one side and telling me how proud I made him feel. How proud he was of the man I had become. Even though I was a grown man, I felt like a child again, a child who had sought and received the praise of its parents. It was a strange feeling to have as an adult, but it felt good.

I could see in his eyes that, of all his achievements in life, he classed raising a child as his greatest. Seeing and knowing this made me feel good. I had never said anything at the time, and wished I had.

In those last few weeks in the hospital I was grateful for the opportunity to really talk with my father. Even though he was weak, and knew he was dying, I could tell that our time together now was as precious as any we had spent together in the last twenty eight years, and I would do anything to make the last few weeks of his life more valuable.

Spending the last few weeks together as the stomach cancer quickly took control of his body was heart wrenching. Especially towards the end as he became thin and weak. He barely resembled the man who had carried me on his shoulders all those years ago. Only his deep and caring eyes seemed familiar.

If this terrible tragedy wasn't enough, it was combined with the heartache of my mum. She was now watching her life partner slowly, and painfully, slip away. She had the knowing inevitability that after so many years, these were their last moments together. Fifty years had come down to just a few more weeks.

If someone dies suddenly in a car crash you get to move on to grieving immediately. A long term illness is a much more painful experience. It disturbed me to think that this was something which would happen more and more as I got older. I would now see friends and loved ones die on a much more regular basis. I thought about my granddad, he lived to a good age, but he watched everyone around him die.

The innocence of youth dies with the death of a parent, replaced with the knowledge that there is more pain to come.

I had experienced a couple of deaths a long time ago, but I was too young to understand what they meant. At that age you don't really appreciate what is going on, which makes things easier. As an adult you have all the memories, and the realisation of what this type of loss means. This is what makes losing someone so hard to take.

My mum was putting on a brave face, but I could tell she was dying inside. I knew life for her without my dad would be bad. I saw the sorrow in her eyes. A massive part of her was dying too. It would be a long time until she would experience proper happiness again.

In modern society everyone thinks about themselves. They divorce each other as soon as they find something better, or get a little bit bored. I was immensely proud of my parents for staying together and being so in love to the very end.

Growing up it had seemed that every month another one of my friend's parents split up. I witnessed the effects of divorce on a lot of friends, and it isn't very nice. I valued the stability of my home life.

One of my friends lived through the middle of his parents divorcing when he was twenty one. His mum had an affair, and although his dad took her back, and they tried to make it work, it was always doomed. I remember going round there to watch tv after a night at the pub. We found his dad fast asleep in the armchair with the tv still blaring. Apparently his dad watched tv until he passed out, and then slept in the armchair. He couldn't face sharing the same bed as his mum.

My friend tried to laugh it off, but I could see in his face that having to watch his parent's marriage fall apart was killing him. This lasted about a year, and then she moved out and went back to the guy she had been having the affair with.

My friend went completely off the rails for a bit. He couldn't stand being at home, and was constantly trying to find people to go to the pub with him. Any excuse to drink away his feelings. He became a regular at the Tuesday night pub quiz, watched the Monday and Wednesday night football at the pub. Went clubbing on Thursdays, Fridays and Saturdays, and had a roast in the pub on Sundays, which was invariably followed by a bit of a drinking session.

It was sad to see. He was previously a happy and relaxed person. Now he just wanted to drink. The last time I saw him was the night before he went travelling around Australia. We lost touch after a couple of months, and I imagine he is probably still drinking his way round Australia.

I have seen plenty of friends lose their way as a result of their home life breaking down. I will always be grateful to my parents for the stability they provided.

Now their bond was coming to an end, and it was too painful to witness.

For just over four weeks we spent every evening in the hospital, at my dad's bedside. The first two weeks weren't so bad. They were still bad (he had just been informed there was nothing they could do for him, and that he only had three to six weeks to live), but he was still the same person we all knew. He was putting on a brave face during visits, and was outwardly in relatively good spirits. It was remarkable to see the inner strength people have at times like these. Once the inevitable is accepted they seem at peace.

Every evening after work I would drive over to the hospital. Sometimes I would pick Laura up on the way. Laura was finding it all very distressing, so I spared her some visits by insisting that I needed to go alone. To be honest some of the time it was nice to have her there, and some of the time I just wanted to be alone. I liked to be alone with my dad in the hospital.

Those two weeks gave me the chance to end things with my father in the way I would have wanted. We both found an openness with each other which would never have happened in our every day lives.

Although this was a horrible experience to go through, it had changed my opinion about sudden, versus prolonged, deaths. If someone you love dies in a car crash you don't get the opportunity to say many of the things that I was doing now. I had the chance to genuinely open up to my father about everything. We talked about our strained relationship when I was growing up, how it had made me feel, but how as an adult I came to understand why he had been so hard with me. I was honest with him about everything. I had made mistakes, but so had he, now he was proud of me, and I was proud of him.

Reviewing our lives together proved to be an amazingly cathartic experience for us both. But then he took a turn for the worst, and the final two weeks of his life proved to be the most dreadful experience of my life.

Having spent so much time talking and laughing, I was feeling closer than ever to my dad, and then I had to watch him slip away.

It was amazing how quickly he deteriorated. One day we were talking and laughing, the next day I arrived at the hospital to find my mum sat in a chair in the corridor outside his room crying. She told me that he was in a bad way that day. I looked through the pane of glass in the door and saw him lying on the bed with catheters in his nostrils and arms. His eyes were open, but there was only a blank expression on his face. He was in another (morphine induced) world, and he didn't really ever come back.

My mum told me that he was in a lot of pain that afternoon, and had been given morphine to ease the pain. He was now awake, but so spaced out that he didn't really know what was going on. My mum wanted me to wait with her outside. This was the worst we had seen him, and I could see how scared she was. Yesterday she didn't seem too bad. Today she seemed full of fear. I waited outside the hospital room, holding my mum. I could feel her gently sobbing. I knew this was the beginning of the end.

His condition never recovered from that point. We never properly spoke again, he was always either in too much pain, or pumped full of morphine. The two weeks of decline seemed like the longest two weeks of my life, and, although it sounds awful, it was actually a relief when he finally passed away at 2am on 25th July 2003. My mum and I were at his bedside. My mum was holding his hand. The only noises in the room were the sounds of the machines, and his occasional gasps for breath.

The gasps were horrible. They didn't even sound like a human noise. Hearing someone take their last breaths is the most disturbing thing I have ever witnessed. It will haunt me for the rest of my life. There is a strange presence in the room when someone passes away. You can tell immediately when they pass from life into death. I can't put my finger on the feeling, it is just there.

My mum held his hand and looked at me. She was in shock. Lost and desperate. I moved round to the other side of the bed to comfort her.

She didn't want to say goodbye. I don't think she could ever properly say goodbye. To this day she still holds him closer to her heart than anyone else, and in some ways she cannot wait to be with him again.

After a few minutes a nurse cautiously entered the room. She had been alerted by the machine, and stood by the door for a few moments to let us acknowledge that she was there before saying anything.

I found myself being strong for my mum, and asked the nurse what we had to do next.

She quietly informed us that the body would be removed and taken to the morgue as soon as we were ready. The body would remain there until the funeral arrangements were complete. I thanked her and requested that we have a few more minutes alone.

I said my final goodbyes to my father, thanked him, and left the room. I waited outside in the corridor for my mum. She needed more time than me. After fifty years together it would take her a long time to say goodbye.

THE END FOR LAURA

"No matter how good she looks - no matter how sweet she talks - somebody, somewhere is sick and tired of putting up with her shit."

Another tragedy beset our family at this time. My mum's parents, who are both in their seventies, suffered a terrible accident.

It was a cold and frosty evening, and my gran had gone outside to put the rubbish at the end of the drive for collection the following morning. She had done this on countless occasions before. On her way down the drive she slipped on the frosty tarmac and landed heavily on her hip. She was in agony, and my granddad heard her screams. When he looked out of the window and saw her slumped on the floor he knew immediately what had happened. He had warned her about the possibility of slipping on numerous occasions. Knowing that he shouldn't move her, he went to get some blankets to keep her warm, before heading back inside to phone for an ambulance.

After covering her with the blankets he turned and began to walk back up the drive to the house. The cold weather again took its toll, and my granddad's heart gave out. He collapsed and died just a few metres from the front door. They live in a remote village in Wiltshire, and no one heard her screams. All night she lay in the blankets, gradually losing hope, staring at my granddad. The postman found them both the following morning. My gran was still alive, but later died from hyperthermia. It was devastating news, and such a horrible and unexpected accident. Coming so soon after my father's death it was terrible timing. My mum was devastated, and I was left feeling that life just wasn't fair.

Life was really pissing me off. The twats at work, combined with all the family stuff was getting me down.

My father's death hit me hard. I had previously been annoyed by all the selfish people I saw. Now things were increasingly going beyond annoyance, and making me more and more frustrated. I was becoming noticeably more irritable with everything and everyone. I was arguing with Laura a lot more. Arguing over stupid things, like why she always left the landing light on. That particular argument escalated so badly that I ended up sleeping in the spare room. I also lost it when she wanted to watch 'You Are What You Eat'. I fumed about what a disgraceful program it was, and how the people on it were complete wankers, and so were the people who watched it.

Deep down I knew there was something going wrong with me, but I no longer gave a shit. There were lots of things that wouldn't have annoyed me before, but they were now driving me insane. I was gradually becoming more and more intolerant of anything and anyone that disagreed with my philosophy on life.

My attitude had not gone unnoticed by Laura. She had been having the occasional dig about me for a few months. Each night I seemed to return home from work with a new rant about someone or something which had upset me that day. Something, or someone, was constantly doing something that annoyed me.

Laura told me that I was never in a good mood anymore. I was letting things annoy me so much, that I wasn't able to get on with enjoying my own life.

Maybe it was a coping strategy following the death of my father. That's certainly what Laura thought. She kept bringing it up all the time, which didn't help. I didn't like to think about it. I did accept that getting annoyed with people was a good way of keeping me occupied, but it had nothing to do with my dad's death.

This all culminated, (as these things often do), after a night out drinking. Laura thought that all the pent up frustration with life was turning me into a different person. Apparently, I was no longer the person she had met and fallen in love with. She needed me to let all the frustration and annoyance go.

I had apparently become hyperactive and fanatical about everything, and I now seemed to enjoy being annoyed more than I enjoyed being happy. Laura felt it was like I actually wanted everything to annoy me, and in a perverse way that was now what made me happy. She wasn't sure she could live with me being like this.

I wasn't sure I could live with her nagging and moaning.

If I had been thinking rationally I would have realised that when you live with someone they know you better than anyone else, and that you should probably listen to their opinions. I wasn't in the mood for listening. Laura was becoming just another annoyance like everything else in my life. If she couldn't live with me I didn't really care. There were more important things in life than relationships. I needed to do something about the idiots I was seeing day in, day out. I was on a crusade, and if she wasn't prepared to support me, then she was getting in the way.

A couple more months of niggling remarks, and full blown drunken arguments, were enough to cause the end of our five year relationship. The final straw was another blazing row after a drunken night out.

She had stated, once again, that she wasn't sure she could live with me unless I relaxed and started to enjoy life again. This time I rose to it. I rounded on her, and informed her that she might not be sure she could live with me, but I was definitely sure I couldn't live with her. I had had enough of her constant nagging and moaning. She should leave. It was over.

There was a long pause. I'm not sure how long, but it seemed like a very long time. I looked into Laura's eyes and they were heavy with tears. Her eyes were pleading with me to take back what I had just said. I had taken this argument to a new level. This was now a breaking up argument. I could see in her eyes that she wanted me to apologise, and to bring this back to a normal argument. Not a relationship ending argument. But I didn't. I just stood there in silence.

Somewhere in my heart her tear-filled eyes were hurting me, but I kept it hidden. She scanned my face for a sign of emotion, but I gave her none.

I knew the severity of what I had just said, but I didn't care. My home life had been nothing but a distraction since my dad died. Laura had been sweet for a few weeks after my father passed away, but now my life felt like it was getting away from me, and she was a major part of that problem.

Laura ran upstairs, and I sat on the sofa staring blankly at the TV.

Normally I would give in and go upstairs to talk through the problem. This time I was going to ride it out, end this crap once and for all.

I remained downstairs for over an hour. I knew Laura was in turmoil upstairs. I could sense it. She was expecting me to make the peace. Through the ceiling I could faintly hear the noises of her sobbing. Normally this would tug on my heart strings, but it felt like something inside me had died. I no longer felt any desire to comfort her.

Eventually I made my way upstairs. I slowly went through my usual bedtime routine without saying a word to Laura, who was lying motionless in bed with her back to me. By now I was completely sober.

That night we lay in bed together, and I knew she was going to leave. Thinking about it made me feel down, but at the same time I couldn't find any motivation to sort things out. I just lay next to her in bed. I knew she was awake, and she knew I was awake. There was a weird atmosphere, neither of us said anything. Both of us had a knowing feeling that this was it.

It seemed like morning was going to take forever to arrive. Neither of us sleeping, just lying there, knowing this was going to be the last time we lay together. After five years of spending every night together. I wanted to just get through the night, and get on with the painful process of actually breaking up. Emotionally we had broken up that evening. Now she had to physically move out, and if she didn't want to move out, then I could ride out the weirdness until she left.

Gradually the sun began to rise, and the room became lighter and lighter. I could tell that Laura had been quietly crying most of the night. Trying her hardest to keep it quiet from me, but I knew anyway. Every now and then her shoulders would shake slightly, giving away the fact that she was crying. I just felt numb. I didn't know what I felt, whether it was relief, despair, I don't know. I was just numb.

My heart was telling me to sort it out, but my head was telling me it was a waste of time, and would be prolonging the inevitable.

All we were doing was arguing most of the time, and I now had something more important to do with myself. My relationship with Laura had started to become an unwelcome distraction.

I knew what was going through Laura's mind. She couldn't work out why I had started to behave like this. She thought it was probably the shock of my dad's death. Laura thought I should be able to get through that with her. She was wondering why I had changed. She had wasted five years of her life with me. She would never get those five years back.

I could also sense that she wanted me to say something, anything, in order to break the silence and attempt to sort everything out. She didn't know what to say. She didn't know what had changed. I didn't have the motivation to say anything.

As morning broke we both waited for the other to make the first move. Eventually I got frustrated with the waiting, pulled the duvet cover back, rolled out of bed and walked into the bathroom. As I left the room I heard Laura begin to sob again, a little louder this time, as the finality of the situation hit home.

In the bathroom I stared into the mirror. I wasn't thinking anything, I just stared at myself. I recognised the person staring back at me, but when I looked into my eyes they seemed empty.

Had I really changed that much? It didn't seem that long ago that we were on cloud nine, talking about kids, getting emotional when we attended friends weddings. Talking about the bits of weddings we liked, and what we could learn for our wedding. Where had that all gone wrong. I knew that Laura hadn't changed, so maybe that only left me.

I ran the tap and splashed my face with freezing cold water. That person was gone.

The person staring back at me in the mirror didn't care. That person was too involved in retribution and justice for all the fuckers in this world who were getting away with all kinds of shit. There was no god. You couldn't rely on the government to sort anything out. There was scum everywhere, and the only way that would ever change was if the good people in the world showed some balls and decided not to take this shit from anyone. Gradually the good would conquer the bad. The meek will inherit the earth? Will they fuck.

Laura moved in with her sister, and gradually moved her stuff out of the house. She didn't want to see me, so got on with moving during the days when I was at work. Each day I returned home to a slightly different, slightly emptier, house. It felt like Laura was moving the feelings out of our house. It left me numb and alone.

They say bad news comes in threes, and whoever 'they' are, I found it to be rubbish. Mine came in fours. After losing my dad, my grandparents and my relationship with Laura breaking down, the one real companion I had left, Steve my Staffordshire bull terrier, was about to leave me too.

During the day, when I was at work, I would leave Steve to enjoy himself in the garden. I would leave him with a load of bones from the local butchers, and he would spend the days playing happily with his bone, until he eventually got bored, and then paranoid that someone would steal his bone, and decided to bury it somewhere.

At lunchtime I would return home to take him for a quick walk and give him some company.

I genuinely believe that I loved Steve. He was a loyal and happy dog, and how many people do you know who are loyal and happy?

I 'lost' him on a Wednesday. I left for work that morning after popping outside to say goodbye to Steve, who was in his kennel gnawing on a bone. When I returned that lunch time he was nowhere to be seen. My back garden is fully enclosed, so there was no way he could have escaped of his own accord. I knocked at a few houses around my estate to see if anyone had seen Steve running around, but no joy. I was starting to feel a little frantic, but I had to get back to work. I calmed myself with the thought that he must have escaped, gone on an adventure, and would probably be waiting for me when I returned from work.

When I returned from work that evening there was still no sign of Steve. Another circuit of the estate proved fruitless, and I decided to put up some missing posters. I was anxious to get some news, being alone without Steve was causing me added stress.

A few days later a neighbour, who had seen the poster, called round to explain dognapping to me. Apparently it is one of the fastest growing crimes in the UK, and Steve was the most sort after type of dog. I was gutted. It meant I would never see Steve again. Outraged, I turned to the internet to learn more about this most heinous of crimes.

According to the MPB (Missing Pets Bureau) there has been a 141% increase in dognapping in the last 12 months. Sometimes they are ransomed straight back, other times they are stolen to order. I wanted so badly to find the subhuman scum that had stolen Steve, but I was impotent. Unless I could somehow try to buy him back on the black market.......

The internet produced a number of potential contacts in the area, but the emails I sent requesting a dog failed to get a response. I couldn't infiltrate the dognapping circle of trust. I felt impotent. Each passing day meant the likelihood of ever seeing Steve again decreased. I was at my wits end. I gave up trying and had to report it to the police, and leave it in their 'capable' hands. I never saw Steve again.

I knew I would never see Steve again. I felt a lump forming in my throat. I hated that feeling. I hated the people who had stolen my dog. I hated everything.

Laura was gone. Steve was gone. My grandparents were gone, and my dad was gone. I was alone.

A WORLDWIDE WEB OF DESERVING VICTIMS

"The thief is sorry he is to be hanged, not that he is a thief"
(Proverb)

A link someone sent me at work provided me with the inspiration I needed for my next targets. He had inadvertently opened my eyes to the perfect source of idiots, the internet.

The link was for a news item on the BBC news website, and was about a man who was called 'Britain's worst ever driver'. This man had two hundred previous convictions, including hitting a cyclist whilst driving a getaway car, stealing cars to order, and being a heroin addict. His lawyer described him as a 'likeable idiot', and believed that he "just doesn't understand the words 'don't drive'." His name was Michael Masterson and he lived in Bristol. He had been given yet another suspended sentence and told to behave himself. Thanks to this article I knew his name and the district of Bristol he lived in.

The internet is a wonderful thing. I turned to the website I always used, b4usearch.com.

With the information from the article on the BBC website I was easily able to find out where he lived. Now that I was single, and bored, I had plenty of time on my hands, so decided that if the legal system was unable to stop this idiot from driving, then I would see if there was anything I could do to help.

That is how I found myself cruising around one of the seedier areas of Bristol at 3am on a Wednesday morning. My main concern was being pulled over for kerb crawling. It would be difficult to explain why I was here at this time.

Even pikeys have to sleep, especially during the week, so 3am seemed like a good time to pay him a visit and set fire to his car. He had destroyed other people's cars, now I was about to destroy his.

I cruised around the area a few times, familiarising myself with the roads, and enjoying some of the delightful sights and sounds to be found in inner city Britain. I had the pleasure of watching a man spewing on the pavement outside someone's house. When I parked up I was able to hear the sounds of domestic violence from a couple of houses.

I parked up round the corner from his house and sat in my car observing everything around me. My senses were on high alert. My heart was beating fast. The rhythmic beating of my heart helped me focus on what I had to do. Once I was comfortable with my surroundings, and exit route, I was ready to set fire to Michael Masterson's latest car (I don't know why he had even been allowed another car). I took a deep breath and got out of my car. This was taking things to the next level. The work projects had been fun, and potentially damaging to my career, but this was taking things fully into the realms of criminality.

Earlier I had filled a petrol can at a nearby garage. Careful to leave my car behind so the CCTV couldn't pick up the registration number. I took the full petrol can from the boot of my car, and strolled confidently round the corner and towards his house.

The streets were quiet and empty. There were a few lights on in houses with their curtains drawn. I knew I looked suspicious carrying a petrol can round the streets of Bristol at 3am. My heart was beating even faster now. I was thinking twice about doing this. I wanted to turn round and go back to my car. Back to the safety of my car. I don't know what kept me going. Something inside of me kept me walking. Probably the devil may care, fuck it attitude that now drove my life. My head was telling me to turn back, but I continued walking.

Michael Masterson lived in a 1960s semi-detached house in an old, run down part of Bristol. The front garden, if you could call it that, consisted of a fine collection of bricks, a charming weather worn sofa, and lots of full rubbish bags. This was a look that a lot of houses on the street were in various stages of achieving. Parked on the drive was a 1989 Vauxhall Astra. It wasn't in very good condition, and in his hands represented a danger to the public.

The street was quiet. There were no people walking along, and no cars driving by.

I didn't waste any time emptying the petrol on and around his car. I lit a match and threw it onto the ground. Nothing happened. Panic set in. Just run. I kept telling myself to run. This was a stupid idea. I started hearing cars when there were none, and seeing shadows of people who weren't there.

I took a deep breath to compose myself. I felt like I was having a small panic attack.

I lit another match and threw it closer to the car. Again nothing happened. The panic was growing.

I heard a car. This time it was a car. It pulled into the street, the lights illuminated everything. I panicked, and dived behind the wall at the front of Michael Masterson's house. From my position on the ground behind the wall I looked up at his house. I was sure that the curtain in the bedroom window had twitched. I stared hard at the window. It felt like someone's eyes were peering at me, but I couldn't be sure, I couldn't really see anything. In my panic I could have been hallucinating.

There was no one there. Paranoia. It had to be paranoia.

I peered over the wall and watched as the car turned the corner at the end of the street. It was safe for me to return to my job.

This time the match ignited the petrol first time. Thank god. It was surprising how slowly the petrol ignited. In films there is always a massive explosion. In reality the petrol burnt on the ground and slowly snaked its way up to the car. I stood, mesmerised, and watched it snake across the floor. Once I was sure the car would burn I ran to the end of the street, turned the corner and walked slowly back to my car.

As I got to my car I heard a huge explosion as the Astra's petrol tank blew. The night sky was momentarily illuminated. I knew that I had succeeded.

I casually got into my car, switched on the lights, turned on the engine and pulled away. Only the smell of petrol gave me away. I hoped I wouldn't be stopped. I would never be stopped. This was going to be easy and satisfying.

Periodically I would return to monitor Michael Masterson, and it appeared he couldn't be without a car. Over the next few months he purchased, or stole, a couple more cars. Each time he got a new vehicle I returned and blew it up. In those few months I destroyed his next three cars. I then got bored of annoying him, and needed a new challenge.

I had lost all the nerves I felt the first time. I was now immune to the nerves, and feeling ready to take on anything.

I began spending hours pouring over news websites for information on people committing crimes. I wanted to find people who were getting away with little or no sentences.

I was amazed at how many there were. Too many for me to cope with. Every day people all over the country were committing crimes, being caught, tried, and getting away with just a caution, or a fine.

So much for Labour's "Tough on crime, tough on the causes of crime". I don't think so.

My next victim came to me whilst I was watching the local news. His name was Dave Dickson.

Dave Dickson had committed over three hundred burglaries in the Bristol area. These burglaries had been used to fund his drug habit. He had pleaded guilty to all his indiscretions, and was now being released because he had pleaded guilty.

Even though he had only (only probably isn't the best word to use) been charged with twenty burglaries, he had asked for a further three hundred burglaries to be taken into consideration. This 'honesty' was the main reason for his release. Apparently it showed that he wanted to change. The judge felt that because of his honest approach he was showing that he was truly remorseful, and therefore willing to change his ways. So the judge, in his infinite wisdom, decided that Mr Dickson should be allowed to walk free. He was to continue his rehabilitation in an environment that was more conducive for his rehabilitation, i.e. he should go home, carry on doing drugs and keep his head down for a bit.

Mr Dickson, a burly looking man in his twenties, was pictured triumphantly leaving court with his partner. Giving reporters the middle finger as he walked down the courtroom steps.

He was chav-tastic in his burberry cap, copious amounts of fake golden jewellery, and a lovely shiny shellsuit. He and his partner made a lovely couple. She was also massively overweight, and was wearing lots of gold jewellery and a lovely shellsuit, although her shell suit was made from pink velour. She had added the extra nice touch of allowing most of her pot belly stomach to protrude from underneath her small tracksuit top. It was a lovely image of modern Britain.

Dave Dickson left court looking so smug that you immediately wanted to smack him in the face. He was an ugly, fat specimen of a man. No wonder he kept getting caught. His getaways must have been some of the slowest on record. He had a face only a mother could love. As soon as I saw the smug look on his face I knew that this man had to be my next target.

The local news stations were outraged and appalled that the legal system had been so lenient, but no one was ever going to do anything. His case would be forgotten by the next day. Tomorrow's chip paper as they say.

It didn't take me long to plan a rough outline of what I wanted to do. Like all of my challenges, it involved giving him some of his own medicine. I wanted to provide him with an insight into the way that his behaviour affected other people. These people had no conscience, I was his conscience.

I knew that it would have to involve stealing something of his, it was just a matter of what, and how. I also needed it to be something that would go some way to redress the three hundred burglaries that he had committed, so it had to be something big.

Then it struck me. I wouldn't just rob him. I would rob him of everything he owned. Brilliant. That was the best possible way of getting back at him. It would take some serious planning. I laughed out loud when I thought of it, and the more I thought about it the more I liked it. I relished this challenge. I wanted something to occupy my time, and my mind. Since Laura had left I had become very lonely at home.

His address was easy enough to find on b4usearch.com. Now I would need to carry out some surveillance to find out a little bit more about his habits, lifestyle, etc.

The first opportunity I got was on a dreary, rainy, Wednesday evening. I ate as soon as I got in from work, then drove twenty minutes to the council estate where Mr Dickson lived. I parked about a hundred metres down from his 1930 (council owned) terraced house. I was parked on the edge of a cul de sac adjacent to his street, and settled into my waiting role with a stack of CDs, a bottle of coke and some crisps, and waited for some action.

After about thirty minutes the unmistakable frame of Dave Dickson lumbered out of his house. He was wearing another nice tracksuit and the same Burberry cap. This time there was a little less jewellery. Obviously the court appearance had been a special occasion, one which deserved a greater level of bling. He was on his own, there was no sign of his girlfriend, and believe me you wouldn't miss her if she was anywhere nearby. Maybe she was punishment enough for him. He jumped into his yellow Ford Capri, pulled out and headed in the same direction I was facing. I pulled out and followed him.

I followed from a safe distance. He drove for about five minutes to another house on the estate, parked up and went inside. Less than five minutes later he reappeared looking very pleased with himself, hopped (as well as an obese person can hop) back into the Capri, and drove home. It didn't take Sherlock Holmes to realise that he had gone to score some drugs.

He spent the next few hours inside. I assume he was getting high. I got bored and went home again. Maybe this was going to be a little more time consuming and difficult than I thought. If all he did was score drugs, and sit in his house doing drugs, I wasn't going to get much chance to steal any of his stuff.

The following week I again staked him out, and he again made the same visit to the same house. Then, just like the previous week, he spent the rest of the evening in the house. He only emerged to throw a full rubbish bag onto his front lawn, in what seemed like a council estate competition of

'Who can get the most rubbish bags on the lawn before the council sorts it out'. He was lacking the piece d'resistance, the sofa on the lawn. Only the slightly more upper class chavs could afford to have a sofa on the lawn.

I decided that midweek visits were pointless. All I was doing was watching him score drugs, and sit in his house doing those drugs.

If it carried on like this then I would have to rethink my revenge. All the hours sat watching his house had provided me with some ideas. There was the possibility of grassing him up to the police for carrying on with the drugs. He was definitely breaching the conditions of his parole. I doubted the police cared that much, they probably knew he had carried on, and hoped it was getting to high to burgle anyone. I very much doubted that someone who gets off three hundred burglaries, would get anything but an "oh, you naughty boy" for doing drugs. It didn't seem like a fitting punishment.

I opted for some weekend visits.

I had been in a very good mood recently. Having these projects was doing me the world of good. I didn't really think about Laura that much. I didn't miss seeing my friends. I wasn't doing anything apart from working during the day, and working on my projects in the evening. I had found myself a great form of escapism.

The first weekend visit proved enlightening. It was a delightful insight into a chav weekend. I got to the Dickson residence at 11am. I was worried that I might have missed them. I needn't have worried. The Ford Capri was parked outside, and there were no signs of life in their house. The first signs of life were a twitching of the curtains at 1pm. Mr Dickson's partner whipped the curtains open and revealed a truly glorious sight. A sight to behold. A massively hungover, virtually naked (except for a thong and vest) female chav. Again I was treated to the 'belly hanging out' look. No wonder Mr Dickson had turned to crime and drugs. I shook my head in disbelief.

Clearly they had some kind of engagement, as they were dressed, and outside in the Capri within ten minutes. Who knows what time they could have remained in their pit had they not had this prior engagement.

I followed discreetly as they headed across the Parkhurst estate to the local estate pub, the imaginatively titled 'The Parkhurst'. Estate pubs are brilliant for all the wrong reasons (fights, strange people, strange drinks), so I can't say that I was particularly looking forward to following Mr Dickson into the pub, but it was a necessary sacrifice.

I parked up a few hundred yards down from 'The Parkhurst' and wandered along the road, avoiding the children's bikes, carrier bags and bricks that had been carefully left on the pavement.

'The Parkhurst' was one of those old school flat-roofed pubs you don't see that much any more. Similar in design to a school mobile building, beige in colour with dark brown window edging. The pub itself was above ground level, and you entered up a small flight of stairs. The windows were well above eye level. Even if you were quite tall you would be unable to see through the windows from the outside. Probably a deliberate ploy to avoid potential punters being scared away before they got through the door. It definitely wasn't the kind of place you wanted to enter alone.

I walked in cautiously, and tried to have a quick look round without catching eye contact with anyone. This was tricky, as every person in the entire pub seemed to be looking at me.

The dimmed lighting made me seem even more suspicious as I stood in the doorway illuminated by the unwelcome sunlight from outside. I was having serious trouble adjusting to the new lighting conditions. I felt like I was sticking out like a sore thumb.

I lowered my head, in a similar way to subordinate animals in the wild, trying to physically show that I wasn't a threat, and walked up to the bar.

The barman seemed to have been waiting for me, and immediately asked me what I wanted, I didn't even have the chance to peruse the bar and see what was on offer. I could tell that he was deliberately trying to make me feel unwelcome. It worked.

I stuttered an order for a pint of Fosters, thinking that everywhere would have this generic beer. I was wrong. This was the sort of pub that had 'Tanglefoot', 'Sawtooth' and 'Two Druids Gruit' on draft. I went for a pint of 'Tanglefoot', and, upon my first sip, immediately regretted it. The reddish cloudy beer tasted like shit, and now I had to drink it all or stand out even further. I was socially out of place.

The one redeeming feature of the pub was a large selection of newspapers. I had something to occupy my time and help me blend into the surroundings. I was sure that the next newcomer would receive similar treatment and I would be forgotten.

Sitting in the corner pretending to read the paper meant I was no longer worth anyone's attention. This gave me my first opportunity to have a look at what was going on. It wasn't a pretty sight.

There were a family at a table across from me, all of whom were sporting lovely tracksuits and ear rings. They were looking chavtastic. The mother and father were relatively old when considered in chav terms, probably in their late twenties. They had three children, who I would guess ranged in age from the oldest boy, who looked about sixteen, to the youngest, a girl who looked about ten or eleven. The boy had ear rings in both ears, which looked very effeminate, but contrasted with his mean looking face. His hair was cut short all over, and he had a couple of lines shaved into the sides of his head. He was ridiculously skinny, and chain smoked the whole time I was in the pub. The girls were both dressed in velour tracksuits, and were clearly trying to imitate their WAG role models.

I was delighted to see that they all had alcoholic drinks, pints for the men, alcopops for the ladies, and they were all smoking. They certainly mature early on these estates. If mature is the right word.

Other sights to behold included young children, who were too young and short to use the fruit machines, being given bar stools so they could reach to put the money in. Starting them on the road to gambling early, which I suppose is in the interests of the landlord.

Other punters included a couple of skinhead youths showing each other their knives. A group of young men playing a game of 'try to hit your mates with a dart'.

In the middle of all this Dave Dickson and his partner were enjoying a nice romantic lunch. Gazing into each other's eyes, eating with their mouths open, and dropping food down their tracksuits. I realised why they were in such a hurry, food was only served until 2pm.

After an hour of watching this hideous scene, I couldn't take anymore and decided it was time to leave. I would try again the following weekend, this time on the Sunday, to see if there was any Sunday routine that would provide me with a window of opportunity.

The following Sunday proved to be a godsend. I was there at 11am the same as before, and waited for about half an hour before Dickson and partner left their abode. This time they were carrying suitcases. I watched from a distance, and was beginning to feel quite excited. This was looking like a holiday expedition, in which case the window of opportunity was potentially huge. Obviously it depended on what they were doing and where they were going, but the sight of the suitcases filled my heart with happiness.

I followed them to Bristol airport. The yellow Capri turned off to the long stay car park, and I carried on to the short stay. I parked up and went into the terminal to await their arrival. I hoped they didn't recognise me from the pub the previous weekend, but it was a risk I was willing to take. After all, I had already blown up three cars, so this was a walk in the park compared to that.

Bristol airport isn't very big. I looked on the TV screens and there were only half a dozen or so flights departing in the next few hours, most of them to European destinations. I doubted Venice or Prague was their destination. Another flight was to New York, but the one that stuck out as a classic chavacation destination was Palma, the airport which served Magaluf. My suspicions were confirmed when Dave and partner joined the Palma queue for check in. I was so happy.

I immediately left the terminal, safe in the knowledge that I probably had at least a week to enact my plan. I was sure it would never take that long, and I almost ran to my car to get the project started.

I already knew what I was going to do. I was going to subject Mr Dickson to a holiday house clearance.

First I had to find a way to get access to his house. I had read somewhere that the majority of people still keep a spare key hidden close to the front door, and was hoping, probably relying on this being the case. I would have happily smashed a window and then fixed it after I was inside, but this would draw unneeded attention.

The following evening at about 11 o'clock when everywhere was quiet I went back to the Parkhurst estate parked in my usual spot, and walked quickly down to his house. As is the case with a lot of 1930s terraced houses the front door was actually at the back, and you walked down an alleyway between two houses to get to their front door entrance. The front door area was also secluded by the kitchen or bathroom which extends out a few metres into the garden. This meant I could have a good search round without being spotted.

I tried all the usual places, under the doormat and under plant pots. I checked to see if a key had been tapped under a window ledge. No luck. I sat on the doorstep to consider what I could do to gain entry without the spare key. I didn't want to have to smash a window, that was far too noisy.

By now my eyes were fully adjusted to the lowlight evening conditions, and I noticed that one of the rocks at the side of the path looked a little bit out of place. It looked too perfect, too smooth, to be a normal rock. I stood up, went over to the rock, and gave it a tap with my foot. It slid along the path as though it was as light as a feather. I reached down and picked it up. It was very light, and underneath was a small catch. I slipped the catch to one side, a panel fell open and the front door key dropped into my hand. They even had a chav method of hiding their door key. Brilliant.

I opened the front door and crept inside. It is a strange feeling to be inside someone's house when you shouldn't be. I felt awkward, and wondered how a burglar did it, especially with the added concern that someone could return and catch them at any minute. I knew that the occupants were away for a while, but I was still nervous. I could never be a proper criminal.

I closed the door gently behind me and stood in the small kitchen getting used to my surroundings. To my left was the tiny kitchen, to my right the lounge. There was a pile of dirty washing up on the side, with food slowly cementing itself to the plate, waiting for their return. It smelled odd, and unpleasant.

The lounge was a reasonable size, the furniture was old and floral, but looked quite comfortable. I walked through the lounge past a collection of pizza boxes scattered on the floor, on past the stairs on my right, and into the dining room. The dining room wasn't a traditional dining room. It was full of cardboard boxes, I rummaged through a couple and they were full of odd junk, possibly from previous burglaries. I left the dining room and climbed the stairs.

Turning left at the top of the stairs I entered a personal nightmare. The boudoir. The bed was in the corner of the room with the sheets pulled back. Even in the darkness I could see that the bed sheet was covered in stains. At the foot of the bed, hanging from the ceiling was a 'love swing'. I knew what it was because I had seen one being used by some dirty Germans on 'Eurotrash'. This device was a strip of leather attached to the ceiling with two pieces of rope, like a traditional swing. I grimaced at the thought of it being used, but it was too late, the image was ingrained in my mind, and would probably haunt me for the rest of my life.

For those of you unfamiliar with the 'love swing' it is literally that, a swing made out of a strip of leather attached to the ceiling by two pieces of rope. The woman lies on the swing which makes it easier for the man to swing her to and from him, as the weight of her body supported by the swing. This swing is used to provide extra mobility during sex, especially if the woman is a larger lady

I can see why two incredibly overweight people would benefit from the device. Unfortunately, having seen the two of them, I was also able to vividly picture it in action.

Just as my shock and disgust at the 'love swing' was beginning to subside, I started noticing other horrifying sexual artefacts.

There was a large used vibrator gathering dust and pubic hair on the carpet. A strap on dildo was hanging on a hook near to the double bed. A set of shelves to the left of the bed contained a vast array of pornographic DVDs. Curiosity got the better of me and I examined the shelves to see what genres floated their boats. I wish I had never looked.

They seemed to enjoy a large variety of material, but they clearly had a favourite, cocrophilia. I imagine most normal people would not be familiar with this particular field of pornography, but let's just say it involves bodily emissions being shared with/on one another, but not the emissions you would expect. These emissions are better suited to a toilet than another human being.

I felt incredibly uneasy. I was starting to wonder what kind of house of horrors I had let myself into. Fred and Rosemary West popped into my mind, and I glanced around to check for any evidence of recent building work. There was none.

Just when I thought the boudoir of horrors could horrify me no further, I spotted a collage of sexual photos displayed proudly on the wall next to the wardrobe. I felt drawn towards it, and edged my way over knowing I was about to be disgusted, but unable to stop myself.

The collage contained about a hundred photos, all carefully cut out and framed, and which showed a variety of activities. These two were clearly very advanced swingers and doggers. The photos contained lots of different people, doing lots of different things to, and having lots of things done to them, by Dave Dickson and his partner. I won't go into details, but picture a battle scene from 'Braveheart', then make everyone fat, sweaty and naked. That is the best way to describe the collage. They were obviously first degree perverts.

I left the room appalled at what I had just seen, and very concerned about having to complete my plan if there was more of that in store. I paused for a moment and took a deep breath to compose myself before continuing. The bedroom had left me emotionally drained.

The council house had two bedrooms and a bathroom upstairs. I decided I would check the bathroom next, and save the other bedroom as a final treat. I wasn't ready for another den of iniquity.

The bathroom was small and dirty, as I had expected. At least it wasn't an extension of the sexually perverted theme from the bedroom. I could handle the fact that it wasn't hygienic. There was a sink immediately on my left, the bath was also to my left, and a toilet straight ahead. Even in the half light I could see stains on most surfaces. If cleanliness is next to godliness, then god was a long way away from these two reprobates.

I left the bathroom and reluctantly moved on to the second bedroom. I took another deep breath and tentatively pushed the door open with my finger. To my pleasant surprise it was actually quite a normal bedroom. Smaller than the first bedroom, it contained a bed, wardrobe and chest of drawers. That was all. No vibrators, no dildos, no porn. It must have been the guest bedroom. Although the guests in the collage seemed to spend most of their time in the master bedroom.

Now I was familiar with the house I had a better idea of the task at hand. There were no pets, so there was no reason for friends or family to come over and check the house. I should be free to get on with things in relative peace.

I was going to arrange for a house clearance at Mr Dickson's residence, so that upon his return he would find an empty house. All his worldly possessions, everything in his life would be removed. Maybe then he would begin to understand how three hundred people must have felt when they returned home to find that he had been in their house, and had stolen their things.

It may sound like this is an ambitious idea, but I had thought it through, and was very hopeful that I could get away with it. Even if I didn't get away with it, I would remain anonymous, so it wasn't as risky as some of the previous schemes.

First I would collect all the sentimental items from the house myself. It would look suspicious to a house clearance firm if personal things like family photos were left in the house. I had a holdall with me so I could at least start the ball rolling. The holdall enabled me to collect a lot of the sentimental items, photo albums, etc. on that first evening.

I felt happy when I left their house that evening. Even if the rest of the plan collapsed I had stolen things that would cause him distress, and that made me feel good inside.

The next day, Tuesday, I phoned in sick for work and made my way over to the Parkhurst estate. This time I parked up outside their residence, took out a pile of flat pack boxes, and calmly went round the back of the house and let myself in. There was no one around. All the neighbours must have been asleep or busy watching Jeremy Kyle.

Once inside I shut all the curtains that weren't already shut, and went about the task at hand.

I assembled the half dozen flat pack boxes in the lounge and took one upstairs. Once upstairs I went to work in the second bedroom (the master bedoom would have to wait). I wasn't mentally ready. After less than an hour I had fully packed all the clothes and various other objects (alarm clock, pictures, shoes) into boxes. So now the room consisted of empty furniture and boxes of belongings. I had been pumped full of adrenaline and worked quickly and efficiently. This was going to be easy, and I would be finished well before the end of the day.

Now that I had given myself a better idea of how long it would take, I was confident that I could phone and book the house clearance firm.

I had already spoken to a couple of firms to check on costs and the process. I was pleasantly surprised to find out that it would only cost me fifty pounds to book a firm. Obviously they made enough money from the tat they collected. They would clear the house in a few hours, asked very few questions, and were more than happy to accept cash as payment.

I made sure my mobile number was withheld, and phoned to make the booking for tomorrow in the name of Mr Dickson. The secretary at the firm wrote down my instructions. I informed her of the address, told her that I would leave the key and payment in a fake plastic rock outside the front door, and asked that they return the key to the same place when they were finished.

I told her that I was unable to get off work, so would not be able to be there in person, but if she needed to contact me she should email me at the same fake email address that I had used to inform the journalists of Cockburn-Emery's indiscretion. I knew that it was a means of connecting me to the two 'crimes', but I doubted anyone would ever make that connection. I doubted I would ever hear anything from Mr Dickson ever again.

And that was that, now I just needed to finish packing everything up, and I was free to go home feeling smug.

I went through to the kitchen to find some marigolds. These were essential for the main bedroom. I slowly made my way up to the boudoir, dreading the horrors in there. I threw the vibrator, duvet, sheets, collage and porn into the box. In the wardrobe I found even more porn, the largest dildo I had ever seen and some outfits that defied belief. Gimp outfits and a large plastic fist. I especially enjoyed the unclean crotch-less skin tight male cycling shorts. I was glad of the marigolds as I bundled it all into the box. The sex room required two boxes to complete the job, and took over an hour, proving to be the most difficult room to clear.

These boxes would provide a huge amount of amusement to the house clearance team. I was pleased that the dirty little pervert was going to be subjected to this further humiliation.

The bathroom took ten minutes. I moved downstairs and within an hour the lounge and kitchen had been completed. For a burglar he had remarkably few possessions. Pawned for drugs no doubt I turned my attention to the dining room.

I had briefly explored a couple of boxes the previous evening, and they appeared to be full of junk. I had left this room until last as it required very little work, everything was boxed up already. The contents of the rest of the boxes had left me intrigued. Now, in the daylight I decided to explore a few of the boxes.

I went through the boxes and, as I had first suspected they were full of items from various burglaries. There must have been about fifteen boxes in total and most contained similar items, mp3 players, jewellery, playstations, watches. I was shocked that he was arrested for burglary, but was still able keep all this at his home. What were the police doing, they certainly weren't bothering to check him particularly closely.

I had a sudden pang of social conscience and decided that I would try to return these items to their correct owners. I had bought a black marker pen with me and wrote 'Please leave' on all of the boxes in the dining room. I then left the premises, got in my car and drove home. I had started the operation at 9am, it was now only 2pm, and I was heading home, feeling pretty. Job done.

The house clearance team were due to come at 9am the following day, and I had been told that the entire job would only take a couple of hours.

I returned to work the next day. On my lunch break I drove into the city centre and used one of the public phone boxes to anonymously inform the police that there was a large quantity of stolen goods at an address on the Parkhurst estate. I gave the specific address, which I am sure they knew was Dave Dickson's. Despite continued requests for my name, I hung up and went back to my car.

The plan was completed. I wanted nothing more than to see his face when he returned home from Magaluf to find all his possessions had been stolen, and on top of that the police now wanted to question him about all the stolen goods he had been storing at his house. There might even be a chance he would go to jail, but I had my suspicions that it be another slap on the wrist from the police. I hoped I would be able to read something about the consequences so I could satisfy my curiosity, and would 'Google' his name from time to time, but overall I was happy with a job well done.

DRINKING SESSION

"You can't be depressed when you're pissed, it's not possible"
Jez – ('Peep Show')

I decided to take a break from my projects. Life was getting a bit weird, and I felt like I needed some normality back again. For a bit.

In the absence of any relationship to keep me at home I did what any man would do, I went out drinking with my mates.

There is an unwritten rule amongst men that you never talk about broken relationships. The only circumstances in which you would discuss a man's failed relationship with him is if he brings it up. But if he does bring it up it is considered soft, and poor form, so it should never really be discussed. No man wants to get into the details of why his relationship didn't work because it is seen as a failure. No man wants to discuss in any of it with his friends. Football, women and taking the piss out of each other are the main topics of discussion for men looking to forget relationships. I am not entirely sure that approach works too well. The fact that men don't have a proper support network, means that everything gets kept inside, which leads to further frustration. Men's drinking networks only seem like the best way to cope, but in reality they probably lead to even greater problems.

Thinking this didn't stop me getting heavily involved in my drinking networks. I was getting increasingly lonely and needed any kind of company. For a few weeks it was brilliant. Drinking when you are in the right mood is good. I had the chance to catch up with friends I had only seen sporadically for the last few years, which I thought was great. Laura had acted as a blocker to a lot of my friends. This fact helped me with the construction of evil Laura that I was working on in my mind to help me cope. If I had really thought about it, I would have realised there was a reason why I hadn't remained close to these friends, and there was also a reason why these friends were mostly single. They were selfish and shallow.

After the two week honeymoon period it was beginning to dawn on me that getting drunk and being an idiot wasn't the best use of my time. I hadn't even thought about seeking retribution for all the idiots, and was actually becoming one of the obnoxious idiots I had hated so much. I still carried on drinking, but in the back of my mind I knew that I had lost a really good relationship in pursuit of annoying the people who had annoyed me. All this time spent drinking in pubs and clubs was making me lose the motivation that I had enjoyed so much. The drinking was a huge negative influence hanging over me, but ironically it would also be the catalyst for the most shocking of all my acts.

It was after one such drinking session that I got back on track with delivering retribution to the scum in our society. It was completely by accident, but was the most serious of all the incidents to date. If I was caught I was probably going to prison for a very long time.

It had been raining most of the week, and it was predicted to rain for the entire weekend. So the difficult decision was made to spend another Saturday afternoon in the pubs in town. The day started as usual, watching football, playing quiz machines, talking rubbish, ogling women, and getting a bit bored with each other's company. Then blaming the boredom on our surroundings and moving on to another drinking establishment, until we got bored again. Eventually we would all be drunk enough to not be bored, and then talk about what a great night we were having.

As the afternoon turned into early evening a few of my friends went home to get changed and do their hair ready for going to a club that evening. Not being one of those men who has to spend more time on their appearance than a woman, I managed to persuade a couple of friends to stay in town and drink through.

Our poser mates went home to puff up their David Beckham sharks fin hairstyles, put on their ripped jeans and favourite underpants (as their pants would be on display over the top of their jeans), their sweatbands and jewellery, and trim their perfectly trimmed facial hair. Making a little line of beard along their chins to make it look like they have a defined jaw line, but instead looking like a small child growing bum fluff on their face to make them look older.

Strangely, once the posers had gone the atmosphere actually became a lot better. Everyone seemed more relaxed and it was great taking the piss out of the posers who had left. The drinks also flowed a lot more freely. My poser mates spend so much money on their appearance that they get really tight when it comes to getting a round in. There is often a round "stand off", where you start to notice some of your mates making the last inch of beer in their glass last forever, in an attempt to avoid being the next one to the bar.

You can tell they want to drink it, but the fear of getting a round in is too much. That round could mean that they can't afford ten pounds for the latest must-have hairstyling product. The revolutionary gel that can get their hair so high and bouffant that Newton would question his theory of gravity.

One of my friends who had remained behind to continue the drinking, was Mike Tiltman. I liked Mike, he was funny, he referred to a woman's bits as her 'Fonz', I don't know why, and he didn't either. He just liked the way it sounded. Another of his sayings that I liked was 'kissing baboons in the jungle' which meant he had gone down on a woman, i.e. I was kissing baboons in the jungle last night. He also had a fondness for fat women. I don't know whether he genuinely liked the larger lady, or whether he had resigned himself to that particular niche in life, and it meant that he never had to deal with the embarrassment or humiliation of being turned down, but he was a funny guy, and good company.

He was telling me about his latest 'get rich quick' scheme. He was always trying to make himself rich, and had earned himself the nickname 'Delboy' for his attempts at avoiding a proper job, and making himself a millionaire. His latest scheme involved the 'Free for collection' section of 'Trade It' magazine. He would collect the items and then sell them at 'Cash Converters' or on 'eBay'. His only overheads would be the cost of hiring a van, which he would buy once the venture was up and running, and the petrol costs. It was a cheap business. In the latest 'Free for collection' section there were washing machines, furniture, TVs, video machines. In fact, I was reasonably surprised at the sheer amount of stuff that people wanted taken off their hands for free. Our consumer society meant that people had so much stuff they were literally giving it away. I believed that his latest scheme could possibly work.

Having said that, he had me sold on a couple of previous schemes, all of which had gone tits up, so this was probably destined for the same result.

I have to admit I admired him. I would never tell him, but I wish I had the balls to try to make it by myself. Instead I stayed in a secure job, earning a steady wage, paying the bills, but bored out of my brain. I knew that the longer I stayed doing the same thing, the more deeply I would be entrenched in my life. Responsibilities, mortgage, marriage, children, would start to pile up, and all of a sudden I would be fifty years old and counting down the years until retirement and death. It's not something I liked to think about. Drinking helped me to not think about it.

The all day session was taking its toll, and I was feeling pretty drunk by the time the posers returned looking ridiculous. My drunken attempts at ruffling their hairstyles were not met with much appreciation. They were actually getting really annoyed. Where did it all go wrong for men, when did we start having to care so much about our appearance. I have a certain level of awareness, but that only goes as far as knowing what looks stupid. I would never wear a pair of speedos at the beach, I would never wear cycling shorts to play sport, but beyond that you cant go wrong with a pair of jeans and a t-shirt. I think that the men who spend the most time and effort on themselves are actually the ones who look the most stupid.

The drinking session continued, and at 10pm it was time to move on to a club. Clubs were great for my mates. So loud that the women can't hear what you are saying, which means making conversation isn't a problem, and so dark they can't see what you actually look like.

There is also the dancefloor for some strategic shuffling and grinding to alert your prey to your desired intentions. Although, based on the moves I see my mates pulling off, I can't see how anyone would be attracted to them. After a few drinks, some of the shapes they throw make them look like Michael Jackson trying to dance in a bouncy castle on acid. They are a danger to themselves and others.

Luckily the clubs are so dark that both the men and the ladies look a lot better than they would in properly lit surroundings. It's a winning scenario for all involved, until you wake up the next day feeling awful, and find yourself in bed with someone who looks disgusting and talks shit. Trust me, in my younger days, I experienced the 'walk of shame' on more than one occasion. Stumbling through town dressed in last night's clothes, looking like crap, standing out badly, and being stared at by the older generation who are already up and enjoying the day at 6am.

I tend to spend my time in clubs sitting at the side shouting into someone's ear, and them shouting into mine. When I get bored of that I laugh at the posers shuffling away on the dancefloor. Watching as they get blown out and keep going back for more punishment. It's like an ancient ritual where the male dancer dances his prey into submission. Sometimes watching a dancefloor reminds me of African tribes dancing around a fire, dancing themselves into a frenzy.

By the end of the night everyone is wild and all kinds of strange things happen (in England, not Africa). Men spill into the streets and start fighting each other, women stumble around crying and puking, and also fighting, which is a lovely recent addition to the drunken Englishwoman's repertoire. It's a beautiful image of modern England.

There was a point in the night when I actually chatted with my best mate about mine and Laura's relationship not working out.

I had been friends with Rob Wilson for years, we met at school, instantly hit it off, and had remained close friends ever since. Rob was the kind of bloke who, when he saw an attractive woman, would say things like, "I would put balls to that", or another one of his favourites was to shout, "Marks out of two?", and then answer himself with, "I'd give her one". A charmer. He was a real lad's lad, and the ladies seemed to love him. He was one of our group of friends I would class as a poser. He had the shark's fin hairstyle which he continually picked, tweaked and preened in front of the mirror. He spent ridiculous amounts of money on clothes which were 'in'. When he wasn't being a poser he was a good lad. Recently he was becoming more and more of a poser and our friendship was drifting apart a little bit.

Maybe it was the ease with which he picked up women that had made him into the man he was. He didn't seem to have much respect for them, but they still kept coming back for more. He was quite a good looking chap, he looked after himself, and after a few drinks he knew how to entertain a lady. Sober was a different story. When he was sober he found women boring, and they found him boring. He much preferred going to the gym to spending time with a girl. He just wanted the sex, nothing else. I suppose he lacked a bit of maturity, and because he could quite easily go from one girl to the next he never developed any relationship skills.

We had been mates for ages, and of all my mates, he was the one who could make me laugh the most. For a man, the most important quality to look for in a friend is the ability to make you laugh. Life is too short to waste it with boring, serious people. Women like friends who are supportive and open, men like idiots who can make them laugh.

Rob had noticed that I wasn't my normal self, and asked how I was coping since Laura moved out. I was a little surprised by his openness, and struggled to find my brave face. I said it was obviously painful after being together for so long, but these things happen, it wasn't meant to be, etc, etc, etc. I basically avoided saying anything meaningful. Rob took this as me not wanting to talk about it, which I sensed he was quite relieved about, I got the impression he only asked because he felt that it was what a mate should do. He wasn't too bothered about my response, as long it wasn't teary and long winded, he lived firmly by the motto that there 'were plenty more fish in the sea'. So, being single, and with his shark's fin hairstyle, he went off 'fishing' on the dance floor.

The best part of the evening, and its going to sound cruel, but it was funny, involved my mate Steve make a complete tit of himself. He had been shaking his funky stuff on the dancefloor, looking like a deranged gibbon, and frightening women away. I had been admiring him from a distance, and was disappointed when he started to make his way off the dancefloor. My amusement was over, or so I thought.

As he came to the edge of the dancefloor he spotted a girl who he thought was making some moves on him. She was moving strangely at the edge of the dancefloor, but still looked a lot more coordinated than Steve. He spotted her, and slightly amended his route off the dancefloor so he could sneak in a couple of thrusts in her direction, and see if she took the bait.

He approached her seductively, well not really, but I could see in his eyes that he thought it was a seductive approach. She shimmied one way, and then the other. To a casual observer, like me, it was obvious she was trying to simply get out of his way. To a drunken, sweaty, Steve, it looked like she was embracing his gyrations. What Steve didn't know is that the object of his desires was slightly disabled, and she wasn't actually dancing, she was trying to make her way past the dancefloor to the bar.

I had noticed her in the club earlier, and thought she was brave for coming to a place like this, and now she was being harassed by one of my friends as she tried to walk through the club. I went to her rescue and pulled Steve away. She probably thought he was taking the piss, but he was genuinely working his mojo. I apologised on his behalf.

To start with he hated me for ruining his chances, and thought that I was jealous that he was about to pull. That I couldn't stand the thought of anyone else with a woman now that I was single. He felt awful when I told him why I had 'ruined' his chances with her.

After a couple of hours of shouting in people's ears, and them shouting in mine, and with no desire to find a girlfriend amongst the peculiar gyrating people on the dance floor, I decided it was time to go home.

I didn't bother saying goodbye to anyone, I just left and wandered out of the club and onto the streets, which were remarkably empty. Normally you would expect to see someone getting sick, some girls screeching and men trying to break stuff, but tonight I couldn't believe how empty it was. At half one in the morning the town centre was normally a terrible place to be, but this lack of activity was actually very calming. I began my walk home and reflected to myself that this was a pleasant surprise. I might enjoy a forty five minute walk home instead of being a lazy arse and getting a taxi.

Walking through the virtually empty town centre at night, my route illuminated by the streetlights and shop windows, was a strange feeling. I think I felt safer when I could see the townsfolk being sick and fighting.

Occasionally someone would wander past, which was slightly unnerving. I had seen enough episodes of 'Booze Britain' to know that town centres in England were dangerous places at night. The calm feeling was beginning to be replaced by a slight nervousness that would probably have been more exaggerated if I hadn't been drinking most of the day. I was fully aware that if I showed any signs of drunkenness I was more likely to encounter trouble from the cowards who are looking for trouble with their gang of friends. I straightened up my walk and increased the pace a little bit to show I was fully aware of myself and my surroundings.

Towards the edge of the main town centre there is a large multi-storey car park which I often took a shortcut through on my walk home. However, it was rare that I ever walked home after a night out, especially as Laura was normally with me and wearing high heels. I had never used this particular detour at night. It looked ominous as I approached it. There were plenty of places where someone could hide away. I convinced myself I was being paranoid. After a few seconds of internal deliberation as I approached the car park I stupidly decided that the few minutes it would save were worth the risk.

The only light in the car park was spilling in from the street lights on the adjacent road, but this wasn't providing much in the way of light. There were a couple of cars in the car park, left there over night.

Within a minute I was regretting my decision to take this shortcut. The lack of people and poor lighting were very disconcerting, and it was about to get a whole lot worse.

I couldn't be one hundred percent sure, but I thought I heard some muffled crying. The acoustics of the car park made it hard to be sure, so I paused for a second to stop my own noisiness, and to see if I could hear anything more.

Waiting there in the dark, motionless, was awful. I could hear my heart beating, and my senses were on full alert. Adrenaline had kicked in and I was now stone cold sober. After thirty seconds, the longest thirty seconds of my life, I was beginning to calm down, and had convinced myself I was being paranoid. I had been walking pretty fast so maybe the noise of my walking had disturbed an animal or bird. In most situations like this, that was probably the truth. But in the back of my mind there was something telling me that this was a bit more serious. The paranoia returned and I began to wonder if there was a serial killer, or some dirty pervert hanging out in this car park. They all shared one common goal, getting me and abusing me. You hear about it all the time. Doggers in car parks, flashers, perverts. This car park was a perverts web, and I had wondered in. I was too far in now. It was just as bad to return as it was to go on.

I tentatively started walking again, a little slower and a little softer this time, just to make sure.

There it was again, the same noise. This time I was sure I had heard something. In fact, there was no doubt, I had definitely heard something. It was the same muffled cry as last time, but now I was a lot closer to the source of the cries. I stopped again. This time was worse than the last time. There was no doubt that something weird was happening. All my senses were telling me to get out of the car park, but something else stopped me in my tracks. My fight or flight instinct was going crazy and had frozen me to the spot. I couldn't make a decision. I was awaiting more information before deciding if this required fight or flight.

My sympathetic nervous system was processing all the external stimuli and trying to come up with the correct response.

Millions of years of evolution has endowed everyone with a set of automatic weapons that take over in the event of an emergency. At the sight of a sabre toothed tiger, your hypothalamus sends a message to your adrenal glands and within seconds, you can run faster, hit harder, see better, hear more acutely, think faster, and jump higher than you could only seconds earlier.

Your heart is pumping at two to three times the normal speed, sending nutrient rich blood to the major muscles in your arms and legs. The tiny blood vessels under the surface of your skin close down (which consequently sends your blood pressure soaring) so you can sustain a surface wound and not bleed to death. Even your eyes dilate so you can see better.

All functions of your body not needed for the struggle about to commence are shut down. Digestion stops, sexual function stops, your immune system is temporarily turned off. If necessary, excess waste is eliminated to make you light on your feet. Your suddenly supercharged body is designed to help level the odds between you and your attacker. Consequently, you narrowly escape death by leaping higher and running faster than you ever could before.

I was now a caveman. Danger had been sensed, but I couldn't work out exactly what that danger was.

"Wha cho starin' at?", the Afro-Carribbean voice was deep, and unmistakably a yardie's. It sounded ominous as it broke through the silence and echoed softly through the empty car park.

After the initial shock, I was able to register where the voice had come from. To my left there was a shadowy area by one of the car park fire exits. As my eyes adjusted to the light it became clear what I had heard and what exactly was going on.

The afro-carribbean chap was pretty big, much bigger than me. He was my saber toothed tiger. He was wearing a huge puffer jacket to emphasise his size, in fact all his clothes were huge, and far too big for him. He looked like a big black caricature of Brian Harvey. His dreds were tied up behind his head. He was staring straight at me, and he was as black as night.

By now I was also able to see who had been making the muffled cries. In one of his hands he was holding what looked like a small girl by her hair. She was still crying softly, and received a sharp blow to the head from the Yardie who told her to "shut the fuck up".

I was still frozen to the spot, undecided on the fight or flight option. Waiting for something to provide me with the impetus to make that decision.

"I said, what the fuck you lookin' at?", he had actually said 'starin' at' last time, but I didn't really want to split hairs with him about what he had and hadn't said.

I knew something bad was happening here, but I still didn't know what to do, or say. Somewhere inside me the Good Samaritan took over and I found myself asking the young girl if she was ok. The words didn't come out too easily, but I was able to sound relatively assured of myself.

Before the girl had a chance to answer, the yardie had punched her in the face, this time the punch was a lot harder than before. I was shocked. The punch would have been very painful to me, let alone this young girl. This was bad.

I looked back at the yardie, who was on his mobile phone informing someone that he had some 'white guy' messing in his business. I don't know why it mattered that I was white.

I used this opportunity to check if the girl wanted to come with me, she was now too scared to say anything, and just stared back at me terrified. I looked into her eyes and couldn't tell whether she wanted help or whether she wanted me to go.

I couldn't go. How could I leave this situation. After all the self righteousness I had felt recently. All my disappointment in everyone else. If I left now what kind of person was I? I was the kind of person I hated. I had been given this opportunity to make a real difference..…

"I'm phoning the police", I couldn't believe I had just said that. It sounded like someone else's voice. Someone had taken over my mouth and was trying to get me killed. What was I doing. She was probably a prostitute, and he was clearly no social worker.

Despite my inner doubts, I reached into my trouser pocket to get my phone. The yardie stepped towards me, releasing the girl at the same time.

I used this opportunity to ask again if she wanted to come with me, whilst also taking a few steps back to keep a 'safe' distance between myself and the approaching yardie. She shook her head and remained silent. I could tell she was still terrified. I wasn't exactly sure that my presence was making things any better.

The yardie was approaching fast. Why wasn't this a flight situation. My whole body was on high alert, and I immediately noticed when he had reached into his coat pocket and produced a knife. It wasn't a huge knife, the blade was only four or five inches, maximum, but it was still a knife. The situation was turning into something even more dangerous.

Fight or flight. Looking back, flight was the best option. I think it was a combination of the alcohol, my nihilistic approach to life since Laura had left, and the feeling that this was an opportunity to do something about the scum in society that casued me to act in the way I did.

The yardie was clearly expecting me to be frigtened off by him approaching with a knife. So when I lunged forward towards him he was visibly shocked and disoriented.

Using all my strength I grabbed his wrist with both hands and forced the knife upwards towards his throat. The element of surprise and the adrenaline rushing through me made it a lot easier than I had expected, and in a split second I had forced the knife into the side of his neck.

He staggered back, with a look of complete disbelief etched across his face. Even in the half light I could see the dark red blood trickling down his neck. I looked deep into his eyes, more out of curiosity than anything else, and found myself fascinated by watching him. The adrenaline flowing through me made everything move in slow motion. Just like the car crash. At no point did I feel any remorse, or any worry, about what I had just done.

His legs gave way and he fell awkwardly to the floor. He was still staring back at me in disbelief and holding his neck. Holding on to life for as long as he could.

The moment seemed to be lasting forever. In reality it lasted less than a minute, but time stood still for me.

Finally his eyes closed, and everything had a sudden calmness. The car park fell silent. Time started to return to normal speed. I wasn't sure, I had never seen anyone die, but I suspected that his life was over. As 'normality' returned the seriousness of the situation hit me. I should phone the police. They would understand what had happened. That would have been the logical conclusion to this situation, but I wasn't thinking clearly and decided to leave the scene of the crime. Once I had made that decision I could never admit to this crime. It was a poor decision, and one I would live to regret, but I was under a little of bit of pressure when I made it.

It had been a surreal few minutes, something I would need to think about in more detail at a later time. Right now someone had just witnessed me stab, and possibly kill, another man.

It was dark in the car park, but not so dark that she wouldn't recognise me if she saw me again. She hadn't wanted to leave the yardie, so I was guessing that she wouldn't be overly happy that he was now dead.

"Have you got a phone?" I asked, aware that I needed to leave the scene as soon as possible.

She nodded.

"Give it to me".

Having just seen what I was capable of, she was in no mood to argue. I took her mobile phone, searched the yardie's coat and took his phone as well. I switched both mobiles off and pocketed them.

I didn't have a criminal record so there was no need to worry about finger prints.

When I was nine I was caught playing knock and run. I had been put in a police car and driven home. I doubted the police would be able to link the two crimes.

Some of the knock and run skills were required now. Having acquired her means of communicating with the police, or anyone else for that matter (he probably had some 'friends' who might also be interested in finding me). I now needed to get as far away from the scene as possible, as quickly as possible, without using any form of transport that could be linked back to me. I also needed to avoid main roads.

The adrenaline was still pumping through me making it easy to concentrate. I mentally mapped out the best route in my mind, and started running. It seemed too easy.

Avoiding CCTV and main roads were my main concerns, but that was going to be difficult for the early part of the journey home. I was in the middle of town. Luckily I had lived here for long enough to know a lot of shortcuts. I hadn't previously been very observant of CCTV locations so I scanned streetlights and the edges of buildings for cameras, and tried to stay in the shadows.

I was out of the multi-storey car park. The first few minutes of my journey were along the edges of department stores and through the parks in the town centre. A relatively well concealed route, and not many people along the way who would take any notice of me. Just the occasional drunken idiot.

I got through the town centre without encountering anyone, keeping my head down to avoid any CCTV shots of my face.

Then came the riskiest part of the journey. I needed to get across one of the main roads to gain access to the canal towpath. Once on the canal towpath I would be fine. The canal would take me out into the suburbs and from there I knew lots of back streets and footpaths that would keep me from prying eyes. The main problem was that there was no route to the towpath that didn't involve me being exposed. The road I needed to cross was full of taxis and police cars throughout the night. There were also traffic lights which meant people sat in their cars studying everything. Add to that the curry houses and kebab shops, and this street was probably as busy during the night as normal streets are during the day.

I crouched at the edge of one of the buildings, behind a cluster of bushes, and watched the street. It seemed even busier than normal, but that was probably just my anxiety. The only way I wouldn't be anxious was if I was at home. I knew I couldn't stay crouched here for long, but the road seemed too busy to cross.

As I was waiting it occurred to me that I hadn't once thought about what I had just done. Maybe it was the heat of the moment, which meant I didn't have time to dwell on my actions. I really wasn't that bothered. The only thing that bothered me was being caught.

Two minutes had passed by as I waited for my opportunity. It had felt like a lifetime, and the road was still just as busy, if not even more so.

In the end I decided to bite the bullet. I was looking more suspicious hiding behind a bush than I was if I casually wandered out onto the road, and tried to blend in with the rest of the people who were drunkenly milling around.

I crossed to the least busy side of the street, which was tree lined and away from the bright lights of the kebab shops and curry houses. I avoided eye contact with anyone, just looking at the floor or straight ahead, hoping not to be noticed.

It was a nerve wracking few minutes, but I reached the stairs down to the canal, and quickly descended down to the dark, quiet, and relative safety of the towpath.

I felt my entire body begin to relax as the adrenaline flowed out of my system. I had to remind myself that the towpath was actually a dangerous place. I would never normally go this route home at night on my own. I picked up my pace. I knew I would be home within an hour. I could assess the night when I got home.

The towpath was quiet. There was the occasional noise and flash of lights as cars went by on the road a few metres above the embankment, but no people. Normal people avoided the dark towpath at night. I wasn't a normal person that night.

I skirted round the edge of my housing estate, avoiding main roads, and sticking to the pathways that zigzagged across the estate. I was home. I hadn't seen a single person since I descended onto the towpath. It was 2am.

Once inside my house I felt safe, but was strangely affected by the complete silence. This was the first time my mind had anything to think about other than getting home. I stood in the lounge in the darkness and tried to decide what to do next.

There was no way I could sleep. I didn't know whether I should be worried by the nosey neighbours. I had stumbled home late at night plenty of times before. This was different though. I didn't even want them knowing I had been out that night.

I left the lights off and stood in the darkness waiting for my eyes to become accustomed to the dark.

After a few minutes I went through to the kitchen. Even in the half light I could see blood stains on the hand I had used to stab the yardie. I washed the small amount of blood from my hands, took a beer from the fridge and went back to the lounge. I needed some stimulus to help me think. I put the TV on, muted it, and lay on the sofa watching the images on the TV. The images flashed up, but I wasn't taking anything in. My mind was elsewhere.

My mind raced over the events of the evening, and there was one major thing that affected me. Would I be caught? I didn't even care that I had just stabbed someone. He was subhuman scum.

I didn't sleep that night. The flickering light from the TV kept me company as I mulled over what had happened, and what I would do now.

There was nothing to connect me to the crime. I had a clean criminal record. No one knew I was in the vicinity at the time of the crime, and no one would ever think that I could be responsible for such a heinous crime.

The only real concern I had were witnesses and the possibility of good CCTV evidence. There was nothing I could do about that except wait. I wasn't going to get all wound up worrying about that. What's done is done. It is what it is.

There was also the slight chance of being recognised by the prostitute who had been so ready to stay with that scumbag. I didn't mix in the same circles as her, so she was never going to come across me again. Even so, it was a risk I didn't want to take.

I had a set of clippers, and decided to shave my head. The only time I might come across the prostitute would be a random meeting in town. With a different hairstyle she would never recognise me. People look completely different with shaved heads, and I had shaved my head before so no one would find it suspicious.

I went upstairs to get my clippers, and sat in the dark slowly running the clippers over my head. The feeling of the clippers and the soft hair falling down my back made me feel relaxed. It was 5am by the time I had finished, and for the first time that night I felt like I might be able to sleep.

I needed to shower first to get rid of the hair. There was no way I would be sleeping if I was constantly irritated by loose hair in the bed. The loose hair was more likely to keep me awake than the incident that evening. I hadn't changed the sheets since Laura had moved out, and sleeping in the bed after cutting my hair would mean I needed to change the sheets. I couldn't be arsed with that.

The sun was beginning to rise, and I showered in the half light of the morning. By the time I had finished showering I felt completely refreshed, and had given up on the idea of getting any sleep that night.

It was Sunday, and the key thing now was for life to get back to normal. I tried to remember what happened on a normal Sunday so I could get on with a normal life. Sometimes that meant visiting my parents for Sunday lunch, that was the last thing I needed after murdering someone and staying up all night. Sometimes I met up with friends for a few drinks. I wasn't in the mood for that. In the end I decided to keep a low profile and avoid anyone else. I couldn't face having company, and needed to make sure I was fully rested before I returned to work on Monday. Monday at work had to be like every other Monday.

The phone rang a couple of times during the day, making my heart jump. I didn't bother answering it. I had a couple of texts from friends giving me details of their conquests the previous night, and what an awesome night it had been. I thought it had been a boring night, but then I don't enjoy crappy dancing and shouting in people's ears all night.

I needed to keep my mind occupied. Every time I had a spare moment with nothing to concentrate on I found myself worrying about being caught. I needed stimulus. I was still impressed at my lack of remorse.

I watched films, played games on the internet, looked for reports of the incident, and drank lots of tea, but this wasn't enough to stop me thinking about being caught.

Only time would lessen the worries. I would have to ride this one out.

NORMALITY

"Normality is just a consensus of opinion"

Getting up for work on Monday morning was done on autopilot as normal. On this occasion I was actually looking forward to work. Looking forward to doing something that would keep me occupied. I was nervous about stepping back into normality, and worried about the fall out from Saturday night. I was also intrigued and excited about the reaction. A mysterious yardie stabbing wasn't something that happened every day where I lived. It was going to cause a bit of a stir. The social anthropologist in me was interested in people's reactions.

In the end it wasn't as big a deal as I had expected. There was nothing reported on the internet, and nothing on the local news. Maybe the police were looking into things and didn't want to release details to the press just yet. Or, more likely, it wasn't considered that important a crime. The press aren't interested in that sublevel of society, and the people who read their papers aren't interested either, they would rather pretend that part of society doesn't exist.

Despite the lack of coverage, when I pulled into the car park at work and parked up, I half expected someone to collar me as soon as I stepped out of my car. I sat in my car and looked around for the police sting operation. I don't know exactly what I was expecting. Maybe a SWAT team assembled on the roof ready to snipe me down. No one did, and I walked into work as usual. Flashed my pass at the security guard who was too busy looking at porn on the internet (he thought he was safe with the screen facing the other way, but I could see the images reflected in his glasses). He didn't even notice me walk past, and I wandered up the stairs to my office. The whole routine was the same. Get a coffee from the machine, some idle chatter about nothing to colleagues at the machine, and sit at my desk. Even my inability to concentrate on work was the same, although for very different reasons.

Some of my colleagues noticed I was a little quieter than usual, and suspected I had overstretched myself at the weekend. They knew I had recently split with Laura, and that my reaction had been to go out drinking. In reality, on this day I was busy scoping out all the local news websites to see if anything had been reported.

At 10:42am it happened. Top story on the local news website, replacing the 'Pet Cat Shot in Head' story, was the headline 'Local Gangland Stabbing'. At first I thought it wasn't the story. I had assumed it was a killing, not a stabbing, but as I read on it became clear that this was the crime that I had committed. I was relieved that it wasn't murder. Despite my initial indifference, in the aftermath of Saturday night I had been quite concerned that I had killed another man, even if he was a very bad man.

'Gangland Stabbing'? I couldn't understand how the police could have got it so wrong. It was never a gangland attack. I was confused. Were the police just being idiots? Maybe it was deliberate misinformation from the police, or more likely, they would be under less pressure to solve a crime classified as a gangland attack. The report was interesting;

"A gangland stabbing in the St Paul's area of Bristol on Saturday night has been linked to rival yardie gangs. The stabbing happened at approximately 01:00hrs on Sunday morning in the Viceroy multi-storey car park. The victim has been named as Delroy Green, but he is known by many other aliases.

A police spokesman has stated that attacks of this nature are very difficult to solve. Criminal gangs seldom speak to police and prefer to sort out issues of this kind internally. CCTV footage in the area has proved inconclusive, and police are appealing for any witnesses to come forward."

The report went on to cover some background on yardie crime in the UK;

"Yardie gangs are very small, and there is no structure to their criminal activities, which means that they often fall out and gangland assassinations are common. Revenge attacks are common in yardie society, even small disagreements can lead to excessively violent consequences. The police are expecting further violence in the coming weeks and have advised people to be extra vigilant in the St Paul's area of Bristol.

Yardie is the slang name given to occupants of the government yards in Trenchtown, Jamaica. Trenchtown was originally built as a housing project following devastation caused by Hurricane Charlie. Yardies began arriving in the UK during the 1950s, when the UK was experiencing a post-war economic boom and the British government encouraged immigration to fill job vacancies. Yardie was originally an affectionate term, but due to the recent violence, is now associated with criminal activity.

Yardie criminal activity grew in line with the increased use of crack cocaine, but in recent years they have branched out heavily into prostitution and other drugs. The cycle of violence means that the average life expectancy of a yardie is only thirty five."

I still didn't understand how it could be construed as a gangland killing, but I was happy with that theory. In the cold light of day I had realised that I should have phoned the police, but now it was too late, and it seemed I would get away with it. The prostitute must have either given the police false information, which would be bizarre. She would have known it would lead to gang warfare. Or, more likely, she had left the scene, the police were not even aware she had been there and were putting two and two together and making five.

Over the next few days the nervousness I had been feeling quickly subsided. Everything I read about the crime confirmed the same story. It was also starting to become a self-fulfilling prophecy.

The following weekend there were two yardie murders in the St Paul's area. Each one added more evidence for the initial police theory. Especially as they were both knife attacks.

I wasn't feeling particularly guilty about my actions. If anything I had acted in self defence (kind of). If he hadn't pulled the knife on me the situation would never have arisen.

Within two weeks of the crime I was completely over the nervousness I had first experienced. I now had to cope with the boredom of being home alone with nothing to do.

After living with Laura for so many years I was enjoying having my own space, but finding it strange not having continuous company. Time seems to pass a lot slower on your own. Activities that we previously enjoyed together, watching films, eating, were now boring to me. I couldn't enjoy anything as much when I did it on my own.

I was finding television gradually more and more annoying. Every time I watched the news I was appalled and embarrassed by the state of the country and the people in it.

Each morning I got up early, sat in traffic for an hour on the way to work, to do a job which offered no satisfaction and no degree of self worth. After spending the majority of my waking hours sat at a desk staring at a computer screen, I then get back in my car to sit in traffic for another hour. I then get home, eat dinner, watch TV for an hour or so, feel tired, go to bed, and so begins the daily cycle all over again. The cycle of life was grinding me down.

I know a lot of people view their work as their raison d' etre, unfortunately I am not one of those people. There are jobs which must be thrilling every day, but not many. I needed something else to stimulate me.

I was feeling like a robot, lumbering through life, on autopilot every day, with no purpose. No reason for me to be here. Who cared about a life insurance leaflet, or a pension's poster? Not me. The only thing that kept me going was the hatred I was feeling for all the idiots in the world. At work, and at home, I was waiting for the next person to do something annoying, anticipating how I would be able to make sure these wankers got what they deserved.

It was that or nothing, and if I had nothing what was the point in living.

THE DATE

"Dating should be less about matching outward circumstances than meeting your inner necessity."

It was at this point that Rob decided it would be a good idea for me to go on a date. He saw shallow encounters with women as the solution to any problem. His latest conquest, which had lasted an impressive two weeks so far, had a friend who was single and interested in meeting up with me for a date. She had recently split from her boyfriend after he had been unfaithful. It wasn't a good idea, she would have all kinds of man issues after being cheated on, and I wasn't bothered enough to make any effort.

I wasn't really in the mood for a date. I had a lot of things on my mind, and knew that I wouldn't be brilliant company. I don't know why I decided to give it a go, probably boredom and loneliness like most people who go on blind dates.

I had planned to take Georgina (the date) to one of the bars in town on the Wednesday night. Wednesday night should be quiet so we could talk without being disturbed by the lairy weekend crowd. We had spoken on the phone and she seemed ok. A bit shy, but then so was I when it came to working my mojo with the ladies.

By the time Wednesday night came I was actually looking forward to the date. It was a welcome distraction from sitting at home doing nothing.

I made a bit of an effort. I showered, shaved, wore a shirt and splashed on enough after shave to knock out an elephant. I enjoyed making an effort. I hadn't made an effort with my appearance in a while. It felt good.

I decided that I was only going to have one drink, and was going to drive into town. I arranged to pick Georgina up on the way.

When I arrived to pick her up I was surprised to see an elderly man answer the door. I had assumed she lived with friends, or on her own, but she had moved back in with her parents after the split with her boyfriend.

He eyed me up and down, and I could tell he had taken an instant dislike to me. He was probably one of these people who instantly dislikes everyone. He had that look about him. I instantly disliked him right back, but was cordial with it.

I was invited in for a minute whilst Georgina finished getting ready upstairs. It was awkward. I sat on the sofa and entertained some small talk with her parents. They asked all the standard questions about what I do, where I live, etc. I answered with the standard answers, trying to make myself sound better and more interesting than I was. All the time I was looking to the stairs, hoping and pleading with the stairs to make Georgina appear.

I think she had heard me come in and hurried down after about a minute to save me. It had felt a lot longer than a minute. She looked nice when she came downstairs. I don't know what I was expecting, but the pessimist in me was expecting some slightly ugly and desperate girl, but she was actually quite attractive. She looked even nicer when she caught me staring and smiled. Things were looking up.

We said a quick hello, and then she hurried us out of the door. On the way to the car she apologised for making me wait with her parents. I lied and said it wasn't a problem, but we both knew it had been awkward and weird, and that her dad could be a bit of a twat.

In the car on the way to the bar she chatted away, asking a few questions about me and trying to work out why I was single. I think she was suspicious that anyone who is single must have some kind of problem. I was remarkably relaxed and answered well. I didn't explain that my last relationship had ended because I was obsessed with seeking retribution against strangers, and went with the 'grew apart' version of events. She didn't dwell on the subject for too long, which was good, and went straight into talking about her work and how boring it was and how some of her workmates were complete idiots. We had something in common already.

We were still talking and laughing about the idiots we worked with when we parked up and went into the bar. This was good.

I got her a drink and we settled down in a quieter part of the bar. This was an exciting but strange part of dating. I hadn't done this in years and had forgotten that it could be quite good.

After the good start things went rapidly downhill.

As we sat and drank the first drink I became acutely aware that I didn't really have many topics of conversation, and she was doing most of the talking. This is fairly commonplace, women love talking, but I started to feel awkward.

I resorted to the friend (and enemy) of many men in this situation and decided to leave my car in town and drink instead. It would help me relax….. Georgina seemed a little surprised that I had changed my mind. I could see that she was confused about my change of heart, and was thinking that it was because of her.

My response to that wasn't text book. "Don't worry. It's not because of you. I just fancy drinking". What an idiot. I might as well have said it was because of her. As soon as the words were out of my mouth I knew I had made a gaff. I felt myself going red and wanting to escape. The fight or flight mechanism was definitely in flight mode. Flight took me to the bar again. Georgina hadn't even finished her drink. I had nervously finished mine ages ago.

Four more rounds later and I was starting to feel a bit tipsy, and a lot more confident. I felt like things were going brilliantly. I was now talking more than her. In fact she wasn't talking that much at all. Georgina had ducked out on the last couple of rounds, but that was rationalised in my steadily inebriated brain, as women not drinking as much as men.

As it turned out I was ruining the night, whilst thinking it was actually going brilliantly. I was starting to get a bit lairy. I could see her looking round the bar. I didn't wonder why, but she was hoping that no one she knew could see her with this drunken idiot. I was being massively inappropriate, telling stories about sexual encounters, and even tried to turn the conversation around to what she liked in the bedroom. I felt like we had no boundaries, but in reality I was getting hammered.

Georgina suggested that we should leave. I didn't realise she meant leave and go home, and thought it would be a great idea to go dancing. I hate dancing. I can't dance. I look like a right twat, but in my drunken state I thought that having a dance together could be a bonding exercise. I would rub up against her, it would be irresistible. I hadn't been this drunk in a long time.

I reluctantly dragged her to a club a few minutes away. I was still doing all the talking, or to be precise I was doing all the slurring. We got to the club and I paid for us both to get in. In my drunken state this was still a great idea.

Once inside Georgina was horrified to see some of her work colleagues. She anxiously waved over to them, hoping that I wouldn't notice. I was delighted to see them, and staggered over to their table to introduce myself. I spilt my pint on the shoulder of one of them, and then apologised profusely. I then spilt my pint on the lap of another of Georgina's colleagues. It was at that point she dragged me away. I took the dragging as her cue for us to get on the dance floor.

I took the lead and pulled her onto the empty dance floor. We were still in view of her workmates, who were watching my ridiculous gyrations and laughing their asses off. Georgina wasn't laughing, she was hugely embarrassed and barely moving, just staring at me like I was subhuman scum. I was too drunk to notice.

It was at this point I broke my thumb. I tried a three hundred and sixty degree spin, lost my footing and fell heavily on the hand I was using to try and break the fall. Even though my alcohol induced anaesthetic was strong, it still hurt. Georgina looked at my thumb, could see there was something seriously wrong, and used it as an excuse to leave. I didn't want to leave. My thumb would be ok. We were having too much fun dancing. She insisted we leave. I was adamant that my thumb was fine and we should "stay out dancing". We left.

Once outside she wanted to phone an ambulance. I was having none of it, and suggested the alternative of getting a taxi back to my house. She didn't seem too impressed with this option. She preferred the taxi back to mine, dropping her off at home on the way. Reluctantly I agreed. Even in my drunken haze I saw that we didn't need to rush things. Although I planned to try again once we were in the taxi.

I still thought we had got off to a really good start. We didn't need to take things to the next level already. This could progress a lot more slowly, a lot more naturally. Let things take their natural course. Georgina's natural course was to never see me again, but I couldn't tell that at the time.

Then came the next bitter blow. There were no taxis available for the next hour. I saw this as the ideal opportunity to get back in the club for some dancing. She saw it as the ideal opportunity to get her dad to pick her up. It was at this point I began to notice that things maybe weren't going as well as I thought. The only reason she would phone her dad is because she is really desperate to get away from me. The penny dropped. I didn't take this rejection too well, and got a bit arsey.

After an uncomfortable few minutes on the street I gave up on trying to rectify the situation and we stood in silence until her dad arrived to pick her up.

Surprisingly she was actually still concerned about me, and my thumb in particular. My thumb was hurting like hell, but not as much as my pride. I stubbornly insisted that I was going to walk home, but by now her dad was out of the car. He had sensed there was a 'situation' and suggested that I needed to get to hospital. I didn't take his interfering too well, and got a bit abusive.

In the end he insisted that I get a lift to A & E. My thumb was causing me a lot of pain, and I reluctantly agreed. Georgina got into the back seat of the car, but when I tried to follow, her dad insisted I sit in the passenger seat. As he pulled away a surge of drunkenness and pain overtook me. Before I knew what I was doing, I was sick into the foot well and all over my own feet. This seemed to end all charitable thoughts from

Georgina's dad. He ordered me out of his car. I was now so embarrassed that I gladly got out. I think we all hoped that we would never ever see each other again.

I somehow stumbled home. I don't remember how. The beer radar must have kicked in.

I woke up the next day stupidly hung over, hugely embarrassed, and in all kinds of pain. It had been a school night, so now I had to phone in sick and go to A & E where I spent a few hours waiting and thinking about what a twat I was. Helped by flashbacks, and texts from Rob, to remind me. He thought it was awesome.

My thumb was reset and put in a little plastic cast. I would never be able to bend my thumb again. A constant reminder of that night, which ranks as the most embarrassing night of my life.

The episode with Georgina, and her dad, left a sour taste in my mouth. I was never going to try that again. Even people who seemed normal were turning out to be idiots. I needed a break from people, they just pissed me off. My life had taken a dark turn.

A FACIAL

"Justice denied anywhere diminishes justice everywhere."
(Martin Luther King)

The Georgina incident, combined with the yardie incident, seemed to have broken a boundary. I was now prepared to take myself to another level. Past practical jokes. I was now starting to think about taking my actions into the vigilante arena. If I could stab someone then I could do anything. The police were inept, they would never find me. It was time to take on some even bigger idiots.

I was scanning news sites on the internet and constantly tuned to Sky News. I needed to find some injustice, something that I could change.

I found something on a regional news network. A man who had thrown acid in his wife's face had recently been released from prison, just three years after he was sentenced to eight years inside. Good behaviour meant that he was now coming out five years early. His behaviour must have been extremely good, saintly in fact, to make up for throwing acid in his wife's face. All she had done was ask for a divorce. The attack was premeditated; he knew that he could get away with a few years in prison, whereas her entire life would be ruined.

Understandably his ex-wife was furious. She had been left disfigured for life, and was still going through numerous facial operations at the time of his release. She was questioning how he could now get back to a normal life, when she could never do that. She was still not allowed out into direct sunlight during the summer months. Plastic surgeons were trying their best to make her look normal, but she knew she was always going to be stared at by strangers, and her face even frightened her own children.

I shook my head as I contemplated what she must be going through. Three years of your life, versus a lifetime. She must be furious with him, with the justice system. I didn't know the guy, but I hated him. I could feel my hatred for him building inside me. The more I thought about him, the worse it got. I could feel it eating me up inside. I was going to find him, and he was going to experience what he had done.

I didn't know much about sulphuric acid, but that was easily changed by a quick search on the internet. I discovered that I could buy ninety eight percent sulphuric acid online. It was a slightly surprising discovery, given that this was such a dangerous substance. Is the internet a good thing or a bad thing?

I didn't want to buy it online that was far too traceable. The internet again came to my rescue. Sulphuric acid is apparently commonly found in car batteries. Buying a car battery was a lot less suspicious. Hundreds, maybe thousands, of car batteries must be sold every day. The following day I went to Halfords and purchased a cheap car battery, using cash of course.

Now I had the house to myself it was easy to get on with my business without any suspicions being aroused.

I slowly dismantled the battery. I was wearing industrial rubber gloves that I had picked up from the local garden centre. I eventually got to the battery cells that contained the acid, pierced a hole and let the contents drip into an empty beetroot jar.

Once the job was done I looked at the acid in the jar, and at the mess I had created by dismantling the car battery. The act of taking the battery apart had taken my mind off the hatred I held for this man. I looked around at the mess that surrounded me and wondered what I was doing. This didn't feel like the right thing any more.

I needed to snap out of it. I *was* doing the right thing. I went back to the internet and re-read the articles about the attack and his release from prison. I read the interview with his wife, and looked again at the photos of her face. This was enough to convince me that I was doing something that needed to be done.

The offenders name was Jermaine Jeffries. Like all these types of people he returned to his old hang outs when he left prison. He lived in the St Pauls area of Bristol. There were only a few parts where people gathered socially, so I staked out the main street that contained all the bars and pubs. I had seen his picture on the internet. His face was burnt into my memory. I would recognise him immediately.

I spent four consecutive nights parked up on that street, waiting, with only my anger to keep me company. The jar was at home, awaiting its moment.

On the fourth night I saw him emerge from one of the bars. It was last orders and he had been kicked out. He was with another woman. I wondered if she knew anything about his background. She was all over him, and vice versa, so I guessed she probably didn't know he could potentially one day throw acid in her face.

They were both clearly drunk. I got out of my car and started to follow them from a safe distance. He was a lot taller than I had thought. Maybe six foot five inches. She was short, especially in comparison. He had long hair and reminded me of Bono. His face was slightly evil looking, with beady little eyes.

They stumbled along slowly with their arms around each others waists. I became aware that I was having to walk suspiciously slowly to stay behind them. I couldn't overtake them. I used some stalling tactics to fit in. I stopped and pretended to tie my laces. I got out my mobile and stopped to make a pretend call. They didn't look round once. They were too engrossed in each other.

Luckily they only had to travel a few streets to get to their destination. A standard terraced house, possibly a bed sit. I watched them go inside and returned to my car. Seeing him had made me hate him even more. I hated that he was enjoying his life, whilst his wife sat at home thinking about the rest of her life with nothing but sadness.

It was late, I went home. I didn't sleep well that night. I wanted to get back there and get him.

I worked the next day and all I could think about was that evening. My feelings fluctuated from extreme hatred, to questioning whether I was doing the right thing. One minute the time couldn't go quick enough, and I was itching to get it done. The next, I wasn't even sure that I was doing the right thing. I needed to banish those thoughts if I was going to carry it out.

That evening I sat in my car about fifty metres down from his house. I watched and waited. The jar was on the floor by my feet, waiting for the moment. I didn't see him that evening. I waited for over four hours, and went home.

The following evening I did the same thing. After two hours of waiting he emerged. This was the moment. I reached for the door handle, but paused. I wasn't thinking anything. I don't know what made me pause. I saw him walking towards me. I snapped back to reality and pulled the handle. The door clicked open, but again I paused. I couldn't bring myself to push the door open. I was frozen. I watched him walk passed. He cast me a glance as he went past my car, but didn't really notice me.

The anger I had towards him, was now replaced with anger at myself. What the hell was I doing? I released the door handle and slumped back into the seat. I geed myself up with thoughts of the next time. There would be another opportunity tomorrow night.

I went home disconsolate. I was all talk, and no trousers.

I decided I needed a back up plan. If I was too much of a coward to carry it out, I was at least going to scare him.

I wanted him to live in fear. If I couldn't physically harm him, then I would psychologically harm him. If I was unprepared to carry out the physical act then something else was required. I made a back up plan to leave the acid on his doorstep with a note to make him think. It read;

"THIS ACID IS FOR YOU.

ONE DAY, WHEN YOU LEAST EXPECT IT, YOU WILL GET THIS IN YOUR FACE.

EVERY TIME YOU ANSWER THE DOOR. BE AFRAID.

EVERY TIME YOU WALK DOWN THE STREET. BE AFRAID.

WATCH YOUR BACK, JERMAINE"

That was ominous enough. I wanted him to spend the rest of his life waiting, worrying. That was possibly a better punishment.

That night I sat in my car waiting, knowing that the situation would be resolved, one way or another.

I would be glad when this was over. I had experienced some emotional turmoil over the last week of planning.

I sat and waited. An hour went past. No signs. Another hour. Maybe this wasn't going to be resolved tonight. This emotional rollercoaster was going to drag on for another night.

Jermaine had a visitor. I was puzzled, no one had visited him on any of the previous evenings. This wasn't good. He had to be alone when I got him. Another evening was going to be wasted. I put my car keys in the ignition and prepared to start the car.

It was at that moment that Jermaine's visitor, who was walking up his path and almost at his front door, pulled on a balaclava. I froze, holding the keys in the ignition, but not starting the engine.

Jermaine's front door opened, and the mystery man threw a liquid in his face. I knew exactly what was happening. He screamed and put his hands to his face.

Someone had done it for me. Shit. I couldn't believe it. I was so surprised I almost laughed. The man in the balaclava turned and ran. He ran straight past my car. I looked in my rear view mirror to watch him as he disappeared down the street. As he turned the corner I caught of glimpse of him as he removed his balaclava. I had no idea who he was.

I was in shock. I needed to get away. If I was found sitting in a car, outside his house, with a jar of acid, I was in all kinds of bother. I started the car and was gone.

A WEIRD PLACE

"Alcohol may be man's worst enemy, but the bible says love your enemy."
(Frank Sinatra)

I was in a weird place. I didn't feel like I belonged in normal society anymore. I was being less sociable at work, and noticeably less sociable with my friends and family. I didn't have the energy or desire to bother with people anymore. They were all just an embarrassment to themselves.

My mum was worrying as usual. Every week I would have answer phone messages from her, wondering why I wasn't answering her calls. I would eventually phone her, but I felt like I had nothing to say. The conversation was forced and unnatural, and was making me feel even worse than not phoning at all.

I was no longer leading a normal life, doing normal things. I had nothing normal to talk about with anyone.

Nothing really interested me. If I had been able to look down on myself I would have seen someone who was very depressed. It wasn't healthy, but I couldn't see it. I was living it, and from the inside it didn't seem so bad. Classic boiling frog syndrome.

I was claiming lots of time off work through fake illnesses, and using the same excuse to avoid social situations. One week it was the flu, then migraines, anything that didn't require a doctor's note. The only thing that motivated me and occupied me, was the thought of the next person I was going to get.

I watched the news constantly. When that wasn't enough, I read the news on the internet for inspiration. Every evening was spent with the computer and TV for company, looking for the next victim.

I had become unconcerned about my appearance. My hair was longer than it had ever been. I was unshaven a lot of the time. I was constantly being reminded I needed to shave by my manager at work. I didn't wash my clothes as often as I should. Personal hygiene was no longer a major concern, and my manager could go fuck himself. The power crazed little twerp.

I was ambling through life. To begin with time seemed to stand still, but then, and I cant pinpoint when it happened, I lost all concept of time. A month went by without me even really noticing. It had seemed like only a few days. The lack of any routine meant life was rolling by and nothing was happening. I was given a disciplinary at work. I didn't care. It's all bullshit.

The days go on and on... they don't end. All my life needed was a sense of someplace to go.

I was getting so used to my own company that I could feel myself moving from being unsociable, to getting paranoid by the thought of having to be in any kind of social situation. My lack of faith in anyone was making me retire into myself. I was the only person I could trust. I was the only person who seemed to have a decent perspective on life. I was the only person who adhered to any morale code.

Work had gone from being boring but bearable, then a distraction, and was now something that was beginning to become a source of anxiety. I dreaded talking to people. I had nothing to talk about. There was no way I could talk about my sideline activity, but there was nothing else I wanted to talk about. I found myself being increasingly rude, and simply ignoring people in my office. They would say good morning, and all they would get in return was a look of indignation. They were mostly fucking idiots anyway. It amused me to be rude to these imbeciles.

I felt I was stripping myself of my social skills. I was becoming like the lonely child in the playground who has no idea how to act with the other children. I was standing at the side of the adult playground, worried, confused and frustrated, and hating everyone.

The increasing isolation was taking me further into a weird place.

I was finding it impossible to track down any targets for retribution. There wasn't anyone who appealed to my sense of injustice. There was a severe lack of opportunities. My confidence had been shaken by my inability to carry out my last opportunity. When I needed them most, when it had become the main focus of my life, it seemed that fate was stopping me from fulfilling my potential.

I phoned Laura.

I don't know what made me do it. Maybe subconsciously I knew I was sinking into trouble, and she was my only way out. I wasn't sure what else to do, who else to talk to. I suspected, deep down, that it was a bad idea and the wrong thing to do, but I did it anyway. I was feeling so lost, and she was the only person who had ever seen my vulnerable side. She was the only one who I could let see me in this state. Despite what had happened between us I still felt she was my best hope for finding a way out of this. And I knew was that I had to find a way out.

Laura's mobile rang for what seemed like ages. In my mind I could see what was happening at the other end of the line. She had picked up her mobile, and seen that it was me who was calling. She knew she shouldn't answer, but something inside her made her want to. It was the same thing that had made me call. Even though I knew it was a bad idea, I couldn't stop myself. I guess that once you have had that connection with someone you can never properly let it go. A part of you will always be attached, and no matter how many weeks, months or years go by, you will always feel that connection, and you will always be there for that person. Even if sometimes it is only curiosity that keeps the connection alive.

Laura finally answered and said hello.

"Hi Laura, it's been a while." I tried to sound confident, but even I could tell from my voice that something was wrong, and Laura would surely pick up on it.

She tried to sound distant, but the fact she had answered meant we both knew she still cared.

"It certainly has, five months I think." It was a blunt response from Laura, but what I had expected. She wasn't exactly impressed with my attitude prior to the break up, and rightly thought that I was the reason that our relationship had deteriorated.

I hated talking on the phone. I wanted to get to the point, and I wanted to talk to her face to face. Face to face meant that the awkward silences wouldn't be anywhere near as bad as telephone silences.

I spoke again. It had been good to hear her voice, and this time I was able to sound a bit more confident. "I was just wondering how you were doing, and whether you wanted to meet up for a chat."

The line fell silent for what seemed like ages, then a confused Laura asked why I wanted to meet up and why I thought she would want anything to do with me. She was making sure I knew that she was still angry with me, but also making sure that she was leaving the door open for us to meet, as long as I had a good enough reason.

"I just feel a bit weird at the moment, and don't have anyone to talk to." I was clutching at emotional straws. I felt I could trust her, and that if we met up I could be more open with her about my feelings than I could with anyone else.

There was an even longer pause this time. She was making me work for this. She asked me what I thought that it would achieve.

At this point I heard a man's voice in the background, which startled me slightly. The envious devil inside me took me over, and I immediately demanded to know whose voice I could hear. I knew it was none of my business, and was a little surprised at the way I had reacted. Maybe there were still some feelings there. Even though Laura said that the voice was 'no one', I was troubled, and knew there was something up. I had recognised the voice from somewhere, I couldn't place where, but I knew that it was not a good thing.

I persisted with my enquiries about who she was with, and I got slightly aggressive. Laura snapped back that it was Rob Wilson. I was horrified. He was supposed to be one of my friends. I hadn't seen him recently due to my residence in the weird place. But he had been a mate for years, and there was only one reason why he would be with Laura right now. I knew how men, and Rob especially, worked. He was there because he was trying it on with Laura. My stomach turned, I felt a cold wave rush over me. Laura was gabbling something. I wasn't listening. My mind was turning over the worst case scenario. I was imagining them sleeping together, laughing together. Him touching her, him kissing her, him sleeping with her. This was too much.

Laura's feeble attempts to explain things fell on deaf ears and I hung up. That plan had backfired. I was now in an even weirder place.

Feelings of disappointment and jealousy washed over me. One second I was in a rage with them, the next I was feeling so low I felt like I couldn't go on.

I went to the kitchen and got a bottle of tequila.

I wasn't normally a spirits drinker, but I had numerous bottles of spirits which were gifts from relatives returning from holidays. Now they were going to come in useful. Now they would support me through this shit.

I could hear my mobile phone ringing and ringing in the lounge. Obviously Laura realised that she had ruined me. Now she wanted to talk and try and ease her conscience. Well, she could kiss my ass.

I went out into my small back garden, sat down at the garden table and took a huge swig from the bottle of tequila. It was quite late. The tequila burnt my throat. I enjoyed the burn. It was dark and quiet in my garden. I lit a Marlboro Light. I relaxed in the darkness of my garden, drank tequila and tried to forget.

Eventually the sound of my mobile ringing stopped. The back garden was silent. It was ten o'clock and the neighbours were indoors, probably watching some crap on TV, pretending to enjoy their blissful, routine, suburban lives.

I drank some more tequila. I was starting to find the numbness it brought quite comforting. I drank some more. After about half an hour the bottle of tequila was two thirds empty. I was starting to feel quite hammered, and a little hostile towards the world. Luckily it wasn't long until I passed out.

I woke at 2am. I was still in the garden. I was feeling cold, ridiculously hungover, tired and most of all, worried by the fact that I had to get up for work in five hours. This was definitely a weird place, but it was better than the place I was in after hearing Laura with Rob. Alcohol had been my friend that evening. Alcohol is a loyal friend.

I felt awful at work. All day long I clock watched. Until one of the worst working days of my life was finally over.

I had been looking forward to having something to take the edge off the hangover all day. As soon as I got in I loaded up a shot of tequila and banged it down. That did the trick.

Something had changed in me since last night. I think that if I had met up with Laura and we had chatted, she would have been able to help me. Maybe we would even have sorted things out and gone back to the way things were, back to normality. In my mind I had made the discussion with Laura the final avenue for escape, now it was closed, not only closed, but well and truly slammed in my face. I was going to have to get to grips with what was happening to me. I was changing.

I lay on my sofa with the tequila and a shot glass on the table in front of me. The TV was on channel 501, Sky News, as per normal. I was absentmindedly reading the news that was scrolling across the ticker at the bottom of the screen and wondering what I was going to do with myself.

I was slightly amused by the story of a priest up North somewhere who believed that Christmas might be a slightly offensive term to some other religious groups, and was suggesting that his parish refer to Christmas as the 'Winterfest'. Little things like this kept my mind off Laura and Rob, but there was nothing sustained in my life, except the alcohol, that kept me preoccupied.

I couldn't stop thinking about Laura and Rob. I wondered what they were doing together right now. I wondered how serious they were about each other. How long they had been together, and what all my other so called friends thought about their relationship. I pictured them together. I could see her love making 'face', and his sweaty body writhing about on top of her. I was putting myself through hell, and I couldn't even see it was because I still loved her.

I was driving myself mad, and now the bottle of tequila was empty. Luckily, or unluckily, there was a bottle of Ouzo from two years ago, which was now my new friend. It tasted just as bad, if not worse, than the tequila, but in a weird way the more disgusting the drink, the better it felt. Almost, like I was trying to punish myself.

I continued to 'punish' myself for the rest of the week, and the punishment continued into the weekend. The Ouzo was finished on Thursday, quickly followed by the Jamaican Rum, and by Saturday morning my new best friend was Jack Daniels. The JD was the last of the spirits. I would need to leave the house at some point to get some more. I think in a short space of time I had achieved borderline alcoholism. Impressive stuff.

To begin with I had felt rough at work the day after drinking, but gradually it was getting easier and easier to drink more and more, and I would feel fine the next morning.

Suspecting I was descending into alcoholism (but not really caring) I went on the internet to read a little bit more about alcoholism. The first page I visited talked about the CAGE theory, which was essentially four questions, which you probably shouldn't answer whilst drunk;

1. Have you ever felt like you have needed to Cut down on your drinking?

That was definitely a 'No'.

2. Have people Annoyed you by criticising your drinking?

I don't ever speak to anyone, so that's a 'No' as well.

3. Have you ever felt Guilty about drinking?

Drinking is my friend, why would I feel guilty about having a friend. That's a 'No' too.

4. Have you ever felt like you needed a drink first thing in the morning (Eye-opener) to steady your nerves or get rid of a hangover?

YES. I did this morning.

One out of three suggests I am definitely not an alcoholic. Self rationalising is brilliant.

I had also only been drinking heavily for a week, surely that couldn't constitute alcoholism. I decided to confirm that I wasn't an alcoholic by attempting AUDIT (Alcohol Use Disorders Identification Test) on the internet. This test involves 10 questions about your frequency and volume of consumption, whether you drink first thing in the morning, whether you have failed to do something expected of you because of drink, ever felt guilty about your drinking and forgotten what you did the night before. They all sounded like things that happen most of the time when you get drunk. Did that make me an alcoholic? I don't think so.

I had phoned to say I was too hungover to play football, and I quite often forget what I did the night before, everyone does. I was able to rationalise this as normal drinking behaviour.

That evening I finished off the rest of the Jack Daniels. I was disappointed to say goodbye to Jack, he had been my favourite friend, but also my last friend. I now needed to leave the house. The numbing effects of the alcohol were kicking in, and I was feeling pretty good. I grabbed my coat and left the house for the short walk up to the local off licence.

After purchasing two bottles of vodka, at £5.99 they were the cheapest spirits available, the rest of the day was spent alone at home with only the internet and the TV for company. Although over the last few months I had become used to the internet and the TV as my everyday companions.

The next month followed much the same pattern. Work during the week, drinking on my own in the evenings and all day at the weekends. I had given up speaking to anyone.

Phone calls and people at the door were ignored. Answer phone messages were listened to, text messages and emails were read, and then ignored. Laura had phoned a couple of times, and texted to say that we needed to talk, but eventually she gave up. I didn't need to talk to her, I knew exactly what was going on.

My curtains were permanently closed, and the occasional visitors who knocked at my door were ignored. I wasn't even curious as to who they were.

It was at this point that I experienced a mini breakdown at work. Like Michael Douglas in 'Falling Down', but on a smaller scale.

I had a week where I simply did not care about anything, or anybody, at work. I could sympathise with how the 'Old School Daft Racist' must feel every day. I decided that I wasn't going to take any crap from anyone. I was in a seriously bad mood, and I didn't care. I didn't care about my job, and I certainly didn't care about the idiots at my work.

It started on the Monday afternoon. Mondays are bad, even at the best of times.

I had been drinking heavily over the weekend, and this Monday I was really feeling the effects of withdrawal. I had stumbled through the morning session at work, not doing a lot, keeping my head down, drinking obscene amounts of coffee. I could feel my mood sinking further and further as the day went on. By lunchtime all I wanted to do was go home. The afternoon loomed ahead of me, and I wasn't sure I could take it.

I grabbed a sandwich from the work shop, and spent that lunchtime alone in my car, eating and listening to the radio. Avoiding human interaction was the best course of action.

When I returned to the office I was in a slightly better mood. Keeping my own company, and not having to be around the idiots in my office, had calmed me down, but that was soon to change.

It was about 3pm. I went to the toilet. I finished my business and was washing my hands when the Head of Marketing, Crispin Matthews, came into the toilet. As he urinated he started talking to me. Firstly, I didn't really appreciate the fact that he felt I should stand and watch him urinate whilst he talked to me. Secondly, he was giving me grief about something that was entirely his fault. And thirdly, he was talking shit just like he always does. He expects people to just take his boring chit chat about his stupid posh life. Well, today he could take his boring chit chat, and his boring life, and fuck off. He was going to listen to the sound of someone else's voice for once.

He wanted to know why I hadn't been to see him for the new posters we were going to put in branches. He was making it out to be a poor effort from me. He wanted to know why it was taking me so long to run them by him for sign off. He had a very confrontational attitude, which was the last thing I needed.

The reality of this situation was that I had booked in a meeting with him, which he had cancelled, and subsequently gone to the gym instead. The next attempt I made was booked in for 10am, and he hadn't even got into work that day until 10:45am. So that was cancelled too. It was a similar story with a 4pm meeting, which was cancelled so he could leave early as he had been given the opportunity to test drive a Porsche.

He had also abused his position on a number of occasions prior to that. In my first few weeks in the office he had tried to assert his authority by telling everyone that my work was poor, and that a man in his position deserved, in fact, demanded, better from me. I was new to the job and he just wanted to make sure I was aware of his importance.

With these incidents fresh in my mind, and combined with his attitude and infidelity, I snapped.

I could feel my blood pressure rising, but he had his back turned and had no idea how annoyed I was becoming.

There was no one else in the toilets, so I sensed this was a good opportunity to give him a piece of my mind. I opened the toilet door, reached round and flipped the door signage over to 'Closed for cleaning'. I didn't want to be disturbed.

"Well, Crispin, 'F.Y.I.', there is something you need to understand" I paused to stop the anger boiling over into a rant. I wanted this to be a calculated attack.

"In terms of these posters, you need to shut the fuck up and listen to me for a bit". He had finished his business, and turned to face me. He was about to say something. I could see his outrage. It made me pleased. I stared at him, fixed him with a threatening look, and repeated that he needed to shut the fuck up.

He was a small man, physically much smaller than me, so I took the opportunity to walk closer to him, invade his personal space and look down on him. He may have been the most powerful man in the department, but right now he felt impotent, and I could tell he hated it.

"The meetings have all been cancelled by you. Therefore it is your fault that you haven't seen the fucking stupid posters. You are too busy going to the gym (although that obviously isn't working out too well for you), arriving late to work, and leaving early. If you actually did a proper days work then this would have all been finished a long time ago. Instead you sit in your office getting people to stick their tongues in your ass all day, because you just love how good that feels. Being a weedy little loser, you just love this fake work power. You aren't better than me. You are just a short, slightly balding, little twat. I imagine that you probably got bullied at school. I bet you weren't very popular, and now you just love the way things have turned out."

"Have you any idea…" he tried to start a defence, but I cut him off.

"I'm not interested, Crispin, vis-à-vis your thoughts, you can stick them up your poncy little ass. I really don't care about you, or your opinions, or your life, or what you think you are going to do to me. I just don't care. I hate you more than anything. I look at you, and you make me want to puke."

Now he was silent. Obviously shocked that someone could hate him so much. I had maybe overdone it a little bit. He had caught me at the wrong time.

"Crispin, my good man. Everyone hates you. They all pretend to like you because you have an influence on their career, but in reality they all curse you behind your back. You are probably the most hated man in the department. There are probably people in there who hate you even more than I do. I expect your own family hate you as well, especially if I told your wife about you and Faye at the Christmas party last year."

"You wouldn't", he wasn't convinced with his own words. He could see how much I hated him. He cast a hopeful look towards the door. He was desperate for someone to come in and rescue him.

"Oh I would Crispin. I think you know that I would enjoy it too." I was warming to this.

"Do you know what the beauty of this little tete et te is? There are no witnesses. If you wanted to report me for this, I would simply lie, and say it never happened. I have some of the obnoxious emails you sent insulting my work. So I can prove you don't like me. Your word against mine, it would get messy, but as you can probably tell, I don't care. I could also tell your wife about Faye, so you assess the risks and let me know how it goes.

Thanks for taking some time out for a little chat-ette", I was being facetious now, using the kind of idiot business speak that Crispin loved so much.

I ended the conversation by giving him a pinch and a gentle slap of his chubby little cheeks, and with a big smirk across my face, I left the toilets.

He was a loathsome character, but somehow he was in the first class cabin of the work gravy train, he deserved taking down a peg or two.

That got me through the rest of the day. I saw him a couple more times that day, both times I flashed him a grin, and he looked away. I felt like our roles had been reversed. I now had a strange hold on him. He no longer felt so powerful around me.

I knew he would do everything within his power to harm my career, but I didn't care, so it was an irrelevance.

Later that day I attended a long brainstorming meeting to generate ideas for re-improving and re-energising the personal loan application form. The head of loans, Robert Creamer, attended. As did Faye, who was still reeling from her wedding day fiasco.

As a warm up to get the creative juices flowing, everyone was asked to say who, from the team, they would like to be stranded on a desert island with, and why. I said another guy on my team so we could play football with coconuts, or whatever. I wasn't interested. Next person please.

Robert Creamer, an oily man in his fifties with slicked back hair and a permanent tan, said he would like to be stranded with Faye for 'obvious reasons'. Everyone laughed, including Faye, who gave him a cheeky little smile. He had influence over everyone's careers so they had to laugh. They all laughed loudly. I thought the laughing would never stop.

The laughing did stop, and everyone paused to prepare themselves for the next contributor. I used this natural break to provide my take on Robert's comments. Fresh from my encounter with Crispin I was full of confidence and didn't give a shit.

"So Robert, does that mean you want to fuck Faye?" I enquired with what sounded like a genuine question.

"Er, no" he paused, struggling for an excuse, "it just means I like her company." He wasn't convincing. Everyone knew he had been insinuating that he wanted to sleep with her. He knew everyone knew that. It had seemed funny at the time, and a little risqué. Now I had forced him to face the consequences of being a smarmy prick.

The brainstorming session died shortly after my question, and we all awkwardly agreed to reconvene at another time. I wouldn't be welcome. I didn't care. I had done myself a favour getting out of these pointless brainstorms.

My career was screwed. I didn't care. I enjoyed upsetting these idiots. These massive corporate idiots.

I carried on the drinking at home for a while, but the toilet incident with Crispin seemed to have changed my outlook on life. I felt stronger, and I was starting to feel like drinking wasn't the answer.

I think it was probably about a month later that I finally snapped out of my drunken reverie. I had finished another rubbish week at work, and been home on the Friday evening drinking heavily and had passed out. I was awoken the next day by an awful smell. I was fully clothed and lying on my sofa covered in my own puke. I also had a serious case of the shakes. I could easily have choked on my own vomit and died that night.

I tried to convince myself the shakes were just part of a bad hangover, but I knew they weren't. I knew another shot of vodka would get rid of the feeling.

The awful smell was emanating from my bin, which hadn't been changed in over a week. I had fish and chips last Monday, and the remains of the fish were rotting at the bottom of the bin bag. I pulled the bag from the bin, and was revolted by the sight of hundreds of maggots crawling all over the outside of the bag. I gagged and went for the front door as quickly as I could. I threw the bag outside onto the lawn, and went back inside to pour boiling water into the bin to kill the remaining maggots.

I looked into the bin and watched the dead maggots floating on the surface of the scummy water. I was mesmerised, my mind was off somewhere doing something on its own, I just stared at the dead maggots floating in my bin.

Eventually, I don't know after how long, I snapped out of it. Something in my brain had changed. I felt energised. I went upstairs, showered quickly, got dressed and frantically went about cleaning the house.

I was still shaking and sweating, but the act of cleaning kept my mind off the shakes. I started with the front garden. There were bin bags in the front garden, the symbol I associated with the people I hated was now there in my own front garden. I cleaned for hours, until it was starting to get dark. I was still shaking, but the house was spotless. I had washed clothes for the first time in a month. The recycling of underwear was over.

I sat on the sofa and looked around me at my spotlessly clean house. This was the cleanest it had been since Laura moved out. The cleanliness made me feel normal again. There was vodka in the kitchen cupboard. I went to the cupboard and took the vodka out. I could feel my body yearning for alcohol. I was physically withdrawn from the alcohol, but I wasn't mentally addicted. I emptied the remainder of the bottle down the sink and went back upstairs to shower again. Showering helped me feel like I was washing away the last few months of my life. It was a baptism, I was starting anew.

I often find the shower is the best place to think. The sound and feeling of the water raining down brings me a degree of serenity. It feels like I am the only person in the world, and I am able to think about problems and people clearly. Whilst in the shower I accepted that I was moving towards a severe problem with alcohol, and that I already had a severe social inclusion problem.

I hated work, I hated socialising, and I hated life. Before I had embarked on all of this I had only hated work, and even hate was too strong a word to describe my attitude towards my job. Apathetic was probably a better description.

I had loved life, loved people and been a generally happy person. Somewhere along the way I had become eaten up by my hatred of things I could never really change.

I would never describe myself as someone who had goals in life, but this was certainly not the way I had envisaged things turning out. Somewhere in the last six to twelve months I had changed, my life had changed. Everything had changed for the worse.

I stood there in the shower, and for the first time since my father's death I began to cry. Not a wailing, sobbing cry. I had my eyes closed, and the shower washing over me, but I could feel the tears fall a few centimetres down my cheek before they were washed away. It felt like the water was washing away this strange part of my life. When I got out I felt better. I felt like I was starting to change for the better and I was ready to start again.

I was determined to put this part of my life behind me. I had not achieved anything. All the time, all the effort, the relationships and friends I had lost along the way, and I had not really achieved anything. Some of the schemes had been amusing, some had bought short term satisfaction, but had come at the cost of everything and everyone around me.

I didn't know what I was going to do, how I was going to start the process of getting my life back on track. I finally knew that drinking wasn't the answer. The last month had been the worst month of my life. I was still physically needing a drink and that feeling would be with me for a while yet, but psychologically I was strong enough to ignore the cravings.

Lying on my bed in complete silence seemed to ease the physical cravings. It also gave me a chance to replay the events of the last twelve months, and really think about the effects my actions were having on me and the people around me.

Let's not beat around the bush, I had nearly murdered someone. I could rationalise this as self defence, that was certainly what I considered the best coping mechanism. At the time I was coping with the death of my father and the breakdown of my relationship with Laura. I was using alcohol as the crutch to support me, and an unfortunate series of events had led to that incident in the car park.

It felt like self therapy. In my mind I was discussing and rationalising that incident, and starting the process of understanding and moving away from the person I had become. I would never forget what happened, but I believe that in the right (or wrong, whichever way you look at it) circumstances almost every person is capable of what I had done.

Soldiers kill people in wars, police officers who live in middle class suburbs with their families and lead very ordinary lives, will kill people in the call of duty. On Sunday they could be having friends and neighbours over for a barbecue, on Monday they could be shooting and killing an armed robber. Look at the Charles De Menezes case, an innocent man was shot seven times in the head from close range, the circumstances made the police act that way, and later that evening they will have all gone home to their families. They have to rationalise their actions, and now I had to do the same. I knew that only time would properly help. I had to accept that in the short term it would be difficult. There was no one I could ever turn to for help. This was a secret I had to keep.

None of my other schemes had been anywhere near as serious. A few made me laugh, especially the work projects. I had enjoyed them, and the victims really deserved what had happened. I wondered whether I would do something similar again if the opportunity arose, but decided I couldn't. That could be a dangerous and slippery path. I had to let go.

I lay on my bed for hours thinking everything through. I was trying to come up with a plan to get things back to normal. Firstly, I needed to think about what I now considered normal so I could work out how to achieve it. I wasn't sure if normal included trying to get Laura back, or returning to a job I hated. My job had directly contributed to me seeking a form of escapism. I wondered whether I had unresolved issues with the death of my father. His death seemed like the trigger which sent me to another level of frustration.

People around me had always considered me a closed book. Past girlfriends, my parents, they all thought I was a difficult person to get close to. I lost count of the 'chats' I had had with girlfriends about 'opening up' and 'discussing my feelings'. I didn't consider this something that men needed to do, and I still felt that way. Even now, when I was at my lowest, I wanted to get through it on my own, and I knew that I could.

It was Saturday evening. In my previous life, Saturday night had been the best night of the week. Whether I was staying in with Laura watching a film, having a meal or out socialising, I was always doing something I enjoyed on a Saturday night. Not on this Saturday night. I was lying on my bed alone, in complete silence, trying to sort my head out, wondering where my life was going, and what I was going to do. At least it was taking my mind off the alcohol cravings.

Always find some way of justifying your actions. Inadequate coping mechanisms will cause mental instability. You have to learn a selection of coping mechanisms, you aren't born with the ability to cope, you develop it.

I had been lazy and used alcohol as my coping mechanism. Now I needed willpower and focus to get me through this, and out the other side. My coping mechanism would be to rationalise what I had done, focus on the future and getting back to a normal life. I needed to understand the steps I needed to go through to get my life back.

I was already on the first stage, accepting there was a problem. Giving up alcohol was a good first step. The next stage was to get my old routine back. The routine of going to work, meeting up with friends. Doing things. Socialising. This sounded like an easy plan, but it had been a long time since I had anything that resembled my old life. I was scared.

Work would be the same. I had been a bit rough round the edges, unshaven some days, shirts not ironed, not properly hygienic, but I had been able to maintain a level of work that meant no one really thought I was losing my grip. Or so I hoped.

The real problem lay in finding the courage to return to the social group I had previously inhabited. For a start, it appeared that my best friend was now with my ex-girlfriend. I didn't know how serious it was, but paranoia told me that I was probably forgotten. They were now ingratiated into the group as a couple. Fully integrated in my old social network as a couple. That would be awkward for me, and them. If you add to that my strange behaviour, which wouldn't have gone unnoticed, trying to re-establish those links was going to be tricky, and potentially very embarrassing and degrading. That step in the process could wait. I would get back into work life first, get that part of the routine sorted out, and see how it felt. Maybe I needed a new circle of friends, but how the hell do you do that. The internet? That sounded awful. I could cross that bridge another time.

Shortly afterwards I fell asleep. I had been thinking about my life for seven hours and it was 4am.

CUPS OF TEA & THE INTERNET

"It's important for us to explain to our nation that life is important. It's not only life of babies, but it's the life of children living in, you know, the dark dungeons of the Internet."
(George W. Bush)

I awoke on Sunday morning feeling refreshed. I had sweated a lot in the night, but I felt better for it. I had sweated out the toxins. My body was cleansing itself after the weeks of abuse. I also awoke to a clean house for the first time in months, which instantly put me in a good mood.

I went downstairs and made a cup of tea. I felt happy, and life felt good. I couldn't remember the last time that I had felt happy. It was definitely a long time ago.

The sun was shining through the kitchen window, the radio was on, and the sound of another human's voice was comforting. I sat on the kitchen work surface, sipped my tea and looked out of the window.

After finishing my cup of tea I hopped off the work surface and went through to the lounge. Sunlight filled the lounge. I could see some disturbed dust particles flitting through the sunbeams, and thought to myself that it had been a long time since I had even noticed something like that.

Tomorrow I would have to go back to work, and, for the first time in a long time I found myself looking forward to something. I was actually looking forward to having something to do. I had positive energy again.

I pottered round the house, went to the shops, and then relaxed for the rest of the day. It was a pleasant Sunday. The kind of Sunday I used to enjoy, before Sunday became a day of sitting in the house all day scouring the news and internet for someone to abuse. I read the Sunday papers without wanting to find a story about someone who needed to be taught a lesson. I just read them out of interest, like a normal person.

Sunday went by slowly, but that was a good thing. Before, when I was obsessed and drinking, the weekend would be over before it had started. I would wake up for work on a Monday morning feeling rough and disoriented, and the week at work would seem to last forever.

That following week I found work a lot more interesting than usual. I took on additional work to keep me occupied. I didn't let the idiots annoy me. They were still idiots, I could see that quite clearly as they went about their day without actually doing any work. The managers were still talking 'in terms of' everything. Saying utter crap like, in terms of delivery, in terms of Peter, in terms of blah, blah, blah.

I kept my head down and worked. I didn't get annoyed when the recycling bin got filled up with teabags by the inconsiderate idiots at my work. I didn't even wonder what happened when I saw John Simmonds in the canteen. I was disgusted when I saw the bogeys some people wipe on the walls whilst they urinate, but I didn't feel the urge to wipe bogeys in their faces like I would have before. It really did feel like that part of my life was behind me and I was starting a new chapter.

The working week went quickly. I hadn't touched any alcohol in the evenings, although Monday and Tuesday had been bad days. I had sweated profusely all of Monday evening, been irritable, felt nauseas, and found it impossible to concentrate on anything. Tuesday had also been pretty bad, but much better than Monday, and Wednesday was better again. It wouldn't be long until I was physically back to normal.

I had only used the internet for normal things, emails, a little bit of poker to ease the boredom. I also played a few games of pool against some Americans, which basically turned into a slagging match between me and a seventeen year old boy. He had seen my profile, noticed I was twenty eight, and was giving me abuse for being old. I felt compelled to tell him it was past his bed time and that his mummy should come and tuck him in. He then beat me 5-4 and had the last laugh, but it had taken my mind off having a drink, and was more of a normal activity than going out to burn criminal's cars, or burgle their houses.

I had enjoyed arguing anonymously with someone across the other the side of the world. I found it therapeutic; even if it was a seventeen year old kid giving me abuse. I had become too used to keeping my own company in the evenings, this was a good way to ease myself back into socialising again.

The following evening I played more pool, and this time chatted amicably with a thirty year old Canadian about what he did, how he was, etc. I also chatted to some more Americans.

Before I knew it Friday at work was over, and the weekend stretched out ahead of me. I had no plans, but felt like I needed plans. As much as I had enjoyed the internet in the evenings, I didn't fancy a whole weekend of pool and poker on the internet. I know it sounds like most men's dream weekend, but those are the men who have a woman. The grass is always greener. Trust me, I needed some company, and teenage Americans were not the kind of company I needed.

I didn't want to drink any alcohol, so there was no point in contacting my old drinking network. They would be spending the weekend in pubs and clubs chasing women, getting blown out by women, and gradually lowering their expectations until they end up going home with someone that they really shouldn't. That wasn't the kind of company I was after. I didn't really know what kind of company I was after. I just knew I needed some company.

It was then that I decided internet chat rooms were the safest option in the short term. I wanted to speak to Laura, but didn't have the courage. At that point I didn't know myself what I wanted from Laura. I wasn't sure if I was just curious about her and Rob's relationship. After hearing his voice in the background, in my own mind I had blown the relationship up into something huge. I was convinced that they were probably engaged and that marriage was imminent. That wasn't what I wanted to hear right now. That could set me back. I wasn't strong enough for that.

I also didn't know if I wanted her back. A lot had happened since we broke up, and a lot had happened to cause us to break up. I didn't know if we could get over that, even if both of us wanted to get back together. Some people say you should never go back, maybe they were right. I wasn't sure I believed that, but it comforted me, and was better than admitting I loved her and was too much of a coward to sort things out.

What if I did want to get back together, and all the old feelings came flooding back, but she didn't, and she blew me out. I couldn't take that right now.

What if she did want to get back together, but I didn't. I had already put her through enough, and there was no way she deserved to be hurt by me again.

I couldn't contact Laura, not now. Maybe in time I would sort it out in my own mind. It could be that I just wanted to apologise for my part in the break up, and let her get on with her life. Whilst I was unsure myself, it was unfair to make contact with her.

That left me with the very limited choices for social interaction. I could go to a supermarket and try to make conversation with people, but that would just freak people out. Or I could go and prop up the bar in the local pub, which was equally as sad, especially as I would be drinking coke. That didn't leave me a lot of options. I could hire an escort (expensive) or the internet (cheap).

That evening, after watching a film and drinking tea all afternoon, I decided that I was bored enough to try out a chat room as the answer to my loneliness. There are chat rooms for everything you can ever think of on the World Wide Web. I knew the internet was a vast expanse of information and people, but I had no idea just how many tastes and subjects it covered. Then I remembered the story of the German guy who had eaten someone he met on the internet, with their consent. They had met in a chat room for people who fantasised about eating people and being eaten themselves. Now if there were chat rooms for that, then I could surely find something I wanted to talk about.

I sat at my PC and thought about the things I used to talk about with my friends. I missed our conversations about fantasy football, films. Actually, I just missed chatting, full stop. A quick google search later and I had found a forum for discussing football. There were about a hundred different conversations going on, and I could join in on any conversation, or just listen in on the conversations other people were having. I could even join in multiple conversations at the same time.

This was amazing and exactly what I was looking for. There were so many additional benefits to conversing this way. When I went to make myself a cup of tea I didn't have to make a massive round of tea, and I didn't miss out on anything. All the responses were typed up and waiting for me on my return. After an hour or so of eavesdropping on other people's conversations I felt I had enough experience of the process to be ready to join in.

Someone had posted (added a comment on the forum to start a new conversation) their belief that Alan Shearer was the greatest footballer of all time, and, in my opinion, he was wrong. I typed my thoughts, and posted my response.

'Chaser247', who had posted the comment, thanked me for my comments, agreed with some of what I said, and added what he thought of my comments. He, I assumed it was he, also joked about some of the players I had suggested were better, and inserted a smiley face. I smiled at his comments, and thought to myself that he seemed alright. Maybe I was making a friend.....

My visions of dirty perverts, sat in darkened rooms, preying on children on the internet was quickly evaporating. I realised I had been taken in by the media hype.

Another hour or so and the evening was almost done. I said my goodbyes to the other people on the forum and turned off my pc. Tomorrow I would visit a movies chat room speak to other people who thought 'Scarface' was the greatest film of all time.

I made another cup of tea. I was clearly substituting the alcohol with tea, but that was ok in the short term, apart from some unfortunate side effects. I was visiting the toilet an extraordinary amount, and was abnormally devastated when I ran out of milk, but I could live with that.

It was now nearly eleven o'clock. I watched some TV and thought about the evening spent discussing football on the internet. I had really enjoyed it. This is why Tim Berners-Lee invented the internet. He had wanted to facilitate the sharing of information amongst researchers, and now he had facilitated the sharing of information amongst everyone in the world, and I was very thankful for that. I was turning into an internet geek, but I was enjoying it, and there was nothing else I could do for company.

I wondered how specific these chat rooms could get. Maybe there were people out there going through similar experiences to me. People who wanted to speak about their experiences and advise others on how to cope. They were bound to be people talking about alcohol problems, but I didn't really see my problems as alcohol related. I was thinking about people with relationship problems. I logged on.

It didn't take long to find a website which hosted chat rooms about relationship problems. They had every kind of problem you could ever imagine, and some you could never have imagined that were very specific problems.

There was a room for couples with a bisexual male about to 'come out' to his partner, poor women. A room for straight females who want anal sex from their partners, and who need to discuss their options. 'Involuntary celibacy', for people in marriages where their partner is ill or reluctant. Revenge forums (probably best that I avoided that one). 'Save your relationship', offering impartial advice to help people sort out their differences. 'Broken hearts that still ache', which is fairly self explanatory. 'Lost and Alone'. One of the scariest rooms I found was called, 'My mum said I'm a mistake', I didn't want to go in there. It sounded like there was a lot of pain in that room. 'The depressed and idiotic' sounded intriguing. There were so many different rooms, or communities as they are better known, on the internet. This was insane.

I registered to use the site which consisted of a couple of personal details, a password and a username. I chose the username of 'loser123', I was feeling like a bit of loser for doing this, and went back to the chat rooms to decide on which one to join. In the end I went into the 'Save your relationship' room. There were five hundred people in there, and about forty different conversations.

I scanned the titles of the conversations to see if there was anything that might resemble my problem. The problem of not knowing whether my ex is seeing my best friend, and whether or not I want them back. I wasn't expecting anything that specific, so was pleasantly surprised when I found a conversation (or thread to use internet parlance) titled 'My ex is with my best friend'. I entered the room, and was greeted pleasantly by the incumbents of the room.

They all typed 'hello' and someone asked me why I was called 'loser123'. I told them it was all I could think of when I registered, and that they shouldn't read too much into it. 'Cowgirl187' asked me to tell my story. I felt like I was being bombarded with questions and asked to take a back seat for a while and just listen in on the conversation. The other people in the room returned to their previous discussion.

They had all been debating whether you should/could take your ex back if they had left you for your best friend, and then subsequently wanted you back.

The people in the room were able to discuss the problem from a variety of angles. There were people in there who wanted to be taken back, those who were considering taking someone back, those who had taken someone back and it hadn't work, and some who had taken someone back and, up to that point, it was working out ok. It was interesting to hear the different perspectives. Those with negative experiences, not surprisingly, thought that you could never get over the thought of your ex and best friend together. It was too hard not to think about them being intimate. Apparently it would often arise during intimate moments, during every day life it was not a problem. These people shared experiences of becoming intimate with their partner, and suddenly their mind would start to imagine their friend in the same situation, doing the same thing. That sounded horrible.

At times I would struggle to work out what they were saying. The online community has a lot of strange abbreviations to make it quicker to type. Some of the more common examples are;

LOL – lots of love, or laughing out loud.
MOF? – male or female.
BBL – be back later.
IMHO – in my humble opinion.
OMG – oh my god.
ASL? – age, sex, location?

And some more obscure internet language;

IANAL – I am not a lawyer.
BTDT – been there, done that.
TIC – tongue in cheek.

And my personal favourite;

YABA – yet another bloody acronym.

After about half an hour of listening to these people discussing their individual problems I started to realise that that's exactly what they were, individual problems. It was good to know other people were going through a similar things to me, but ultimately it was something that only I could sort out, and the only way I could do that, was by confronting the problem.

I thanked everyone in chat room and said my goodbyes. I logged off knowing that I would have to speak to Laura. I would sleep on it and make sure I felt the same in the morning.

THE CONFRONTATION

"A woman drove me to drink and I didn't even have the decency to thank her."
(W.C. Fields)

Sunday morning was good. I awoke refreshed, and without the fuzzy headed feeling you get from drinking the night before. I dozed in bed, enjoying the feeling of a warm bed and no need to get up.

As I lay there, eyes open, staring at the ceiling, I wondered whether I should revisit things with Laura, or whether it was better to move on. I remember people telling me that once you leave someone, you should never go back. I wasn't sure I agreed with that philosophy. I believe in second chances for everything, but I suppose there must have been something wrong in the first place to cause the relationship to break down, and maybe that problem would always be there. Or maybe it was me being a prick, and now I was no longer a prick.

This time, deep down, I knew that I was the reason the relationship had broken down. I believed that I had changed for the worse, which caused the break down, and now I was feeling normal again. The last time I felt this good I had been with Laura, and we had been happy together. This gave me the confidence that contacting Laura was the right thing to do. I knew that I had sorted myself out. It just depended on what Laura had been through since we split up.

I got out of bed, showered and got ready for the day ahead. I would wait until the afternoon to phone Laura. That would give me the chance to compose myself and maybe do something with my day so that I had something to talk about if idle gossiping broke out on the phone. I didn't want to tell her I had been alone all weekend using the internet to try and sort out my emotional problems. That sounded awful.

I mowed the lawn, pulled up some weeds and trimmed the edges of the garden with my strimmer. Now I could tell her I had been gardening, which sounded like a lot better use of my time.

I managed to prolong the phone call until four o'clock. I reasoned that most people are free to chat at that time on a Sunday. I didn't want her to have any excuse to fob me off. It was taking enough time and courage to make the call, I couldn't have it postponed.

As it turns out, I was too apprehensive to phone. I sat in my lounge in silence looking at her number on my phone, one click of a button away from making contact, and I couldn't do it. I had switched the tv off to help me maintain my focus, but now I was just sat in silence, feeling unsure of what I was about to do. Continuously getting Laura's number up on the screen, then getting rid of it. Getting it back up again, pressing 'dial', then immediately hanging up.

I couldn't shake the feeling that I was about to make a mistake. That I didn't really know what to say. I didn't want to look foolish, and ruin everything, and, like most men, I wasn't very good at talking on the phone. I went through the awkward 'phoning' stage when I first courted Laura, it's a necessary evil. But, as soon as we got together, phone calls became short and sweet. They were simply for making arrangements, not for discussing her day at work, her workmates' new kittens, her friends relationships or anything. Phones were for sorting out times and places to meet. More often than not a text would do instead.

Every time my phone screen faded to save battery I would tap the button to get the number up again, but it was no use. I just couldn't do it. She had probably moved on. Maybe, probably, definitely with Rob. I was prolonging the inevitable pain and finality of finding out the details. I didn't want to find out over the phone. I didn't want to find out at all.

I took the cowardly option and sent her a text. I kept it short and sweet. I didn't want to appear needy, or play the emotional blackmail card. I wanted her to want to meet up. I wanted to arrange to meet her, and see if she wanted to do the same. If she did then there was hope.

I had read somewhere that women always need 'closure' when a relationship finishes. I didn't think we had 'closure' on our relationship. It had ended abruptly, and Laura had very little idea what was going on in my head. At the very least she would be curious to see me again. Or so I hoped.

I sent her a short text and waited anxiously for a reply. A minute passed. Surely she should have replied by now. We were together for five years, I expected an immediate response. Five more minutes passed. Now I was worrying. Was she showing everyone the message, had she simply deleted it, was she discussing what she should do with Rob. Were they laughing at me.

I needed something to take my mind off it. I needed vodka, but, as had been the case recently, I settled for a cup of tea instead. The act of making the tea calmed me down, and the warmth of the cup in my hands was comforting. I sat on the sofa and turned the tv on to try and distract myself, it didn't really work, but the noise from the tv was better than silence.

Another hour passed and still no response. I had now moved into the 'accepting depression' stage. I was starting to mourn the loss of our relationship. Maybe I was being premature, but if she wanted to see me, and if she cared about our relationship, she would have responded by now. I had obviously hurt her too much, and now she didn't want anything to do with me. Or, even worse, she was happy with Rob, and didn't see the point in raking over old ground with me.

Whichever way I looked at it, it was now over in my mind, and I had to properly start the process of moving on.

Then my phone beeped. It was Laura. She did want to see me. It wasn't a text laced with emotion, and simply said, "Hi. Let me know where and when, and I will meet you".

Why had it taken her over an hour to get back to me? I had agonized over my life so much in that space of time. I texted back immediately, saying that I would like to meet the following evening at 7pm in the local pub, Ye Olde Butchers Arms. Laura responded with an "Ok", which didn't leave her open to much interpretation.

I wanted to get more information on how she was feeling before entering the lion's den, but knew I had to leave it there for the night, and hope for the best the following evening.

My feelings were weird. What was going to happen? At least our meeting would answer that once and for all. Whether it was me, a mutual decision, or Laura's choice. Whichever way, I would know and I could move on.

I didn't sleep too well that night. Morning eventually arrived, and the need to go to work was a welcome distraction.

I couldn't concentrate at work, Laura, and the uncertainty of the evening ahead preoccupied me. The day dragged along. Finally, it was time to go home.

I ate a small dinner, I didn't have much of an appetite. I showered and got ready. I didn't know what to wear for a night of deep discussion. I knew that looks didn't really matter between us anymore, we were past that stage, but I decided to make an effort anyway.

I looked sharp in my tailored jeans and black shirt, simple, but effective. I always believed that if you looked good, you felt good, and if you felt good, you were good. It's all about self perception. I left the house for the short walk to Ye Olde Butchers Arms. As soon as I shut the door behind me the enormity of what I was about to do hit me. Getting ready had distracted me from the task at hand, but now I was walking into the situation I was nervous. It had been a while since I had even seen Laura, and we had ended badly. My mind was filled with thoughts of her and Rob. I was tempted to turn back. What if Rob was there with her? How would I react? I was running through the worst case scenario in my head, trying to convince myself that it could actually be that awful, so I wouldn't be a coward if I turned back. My recently found resolve kicked in, I knew I was scaremongering myself, so I ploughed on. On to Moscow……

I got there at almost dead on 7pm, and there was no sign of Laura. It is a woman's prerogative to be late, but it's still annoying. I got a pint and settled down in a quiet corner of the pub. There was no way I wanted all the locals listening in as I aired my dirty laundry. This was my first alcoholic drink for a few weeks, it tasted good, and helped me feel less nervous. I was sure I wasn't an alcoholic, so it wasn't a problem for me to have a couple of sociable drinks.

Laura eventually showed up twenty minutes late, and I was already half way through my second pint. I had been drinking nervously, and convincing myself that she wasn't going to show up. I was delighted when I saw her, something inside me leapt as she came through the door.

Like a true gentleman, I stood when she entered the pub, and asked what she would like to drink. The whole time I was scanning her (not in a weird, perverted way), for clues about her state of mind.

She looked good. I hadn't seen her for so long that I had forgotten how attractive she actually was. On top of that, she had clearly made an effort for our rendezvous. She must have been thinking the same thing as me when she prepared for the evening. Her dark hair was cut to just above her shoulders, and much shorter than last time I had seen her. I liked that she looked a little different. She was wearing a black skirt, cut just above her knees, and she had great legs. Her white blouse was open enough to show some chest, but not a huge amount. I was beginning to realise that I was having the same feelings as the first time I had ever seen her.

With this realisation in my mind we settled down at the table. The first few moments we just looked at each other, until I broke the ice and asked how she was.

"I am ok, thanks" she replied, not giving anything away, and leaving the conversation very much in my hands.

"Cool. I don't want to start the evening on a sour note, but why could I hear Rob's voice in the background when I phoned you recently? Are you guys together now?" I blurted it out straight away. I had been planning to discuss this issue much later in the conversation, but curiosity (and the fact that I didn't want to open up and embarrass myself if she was with Rob, and there was no point in me trying to sort things out) got the better of me.

Laura paused. I didn't like that pause. I had wanted her to answer immediately that her and Rob were not an item, and that there was a perfectly innocent explanation for him being there. This wasn't good.

She looked straight at me. I knew exactly what that look meant. She wanted to lie to me, but she couldn't. There had been something between her and Rob. That look said it all. She had done something with my best friend.

I felt numb, but proceeded to explore this painful area. "So are you two together?" I asked again.

Laura looked down at the table and nodded.

I felt even more numb. Last night in bed I had run through a number of scenarios for the way the evening would pan out, and this was one of the worst.

"Oh", was all I could say. My mouth was dry and I couldn't concentrate on talking. How could Laura do this? How could Rob do this?

I looked up at Laura, she raised her head and looked at me. I could see tears in her eyes. I didn't know what the tears were for, she had made her choice. I should be the one who was upset. Seeing her tonight had made me want her back, for the briefest moment. And for the first time in months, I had some clarity on what I was feeling and what I wanted. Now that was gone.

I looked down again and fiddled with my pint glass. I couldn't look her in the eye. I couldn't talk. I needed to compose myself and decide what the next step should be.

The way I saw it there were three options. I could just leave, go home, forget Laura and move on with my life. Or, I could stay and find out what had happened, get some 'closure', and go home knowing why things had turned out that way. Then forget Laura and get on with my life. The final option was to stay, talk to Laura, see if she wanted anything further from me, try to get back together and take the huge risk of trying to make the relationship work again.

Option one won. I thanked Laura for coming and got up to leave.

Life is about choices and decisions. I had made my choice to give up on the relationship all those months ago, and she had made her choice to start seeing my best friend. Two particularly bad choices that now left us in an emotionally messy situation, but choices that were ours to make, and now ours to face the consequences.

I could tell that Laura still had feelings for me, and I could also tell she was wishing that she had never made the decision to get together with Rob. I could see it in her eyes. As I said earlier, he was a nice enough guy, and good looking, but I know them both really well, and I know they would never make a good couple. The only reason they would stay together is to justify the heartache their involvement had caused in the first place. They would feel socially obliged to stay together, because if it didn't work out then everyone would think they had behaved disgracefully by going behind my back. People will forgive true love anything, but lust, without a thought for anyone else, is a different matter.

I walked away from the table towards the door and turned to look at her one last time. She was looking at me. I could tell that she wanted me to come back, and if she had asked me to, I would have. She said nothing, and I left the pub.

I walked through the dark car park. I was annoyed, which was better than being upset. I couldn't understand why Laura would go with my best friend. The only reason I could think of was to upset me, but I thought I knew her better than that. I thought she was a better person than that.

Just as I reached the other side of the car park my mobile started to ring. I knew it would be Laura, and for a moment I thought about ignoring it. I paused, reached in my pocket and checked that it was her. I knew the best course of action was to ignore it. To keep walking. To get on with my life.

I answered the phone.

She quietly asked if I would come back inside. I thought that we could talk forever, and maybe even get back together, but that ultimately it would never work between us again. I had decided that in the last few moments. There was no amount of talking that would paper over the cracks. There was nothing that could hide the insecurities that would always be there.

Somewhere inside me something was telling me there might be some detail, some significant detail with our situation. Something that would mean we could make it work. There was something Laura could tell me that would shed new light on the situation. Something that would make it easy for us to get back together, and make it work. I had no idea what this piece of information might be, but I was willing to speak to her and find out if it existed.

I answered Laura and told her I would be there in a second.

I had given in. I had left the door ajar. I had shown willing.

It is decisions like these that change your life forever. We make decisions all day, every day, that will have a slight impact on your life, but it was definitely decisions like these that shape the rest of your life. I sometimes try to think about how life would have been if I had done something differently. If I had stayed with my first girlfriend from school, where would I be now, would I be living in the same small town, married, with children. Ultimately this kind of daydreaming is a pointless, but enjoyable, exercise. You should try it, you can while away many hours by mapping out alternative lives, and you can always make them worse than your own to make you feel good. Never make them better. As I walked back into the pub that night, I was already wondering what the implications of this choice would be.

Laura was watching the door, and smiled as I walked back in. We could both tell that all the old feelings were there, just her smile made me feel alive, but now there was a whole load of weirdness that was tangled up with those feelings. It would take some serious untangling. There would be a few knots that would be difficult to undo, and we might want to give up or cut the knots. Ok, that's the end of the analogy.

I got another drink, and asked Laura if she wanted one too. She declined. I think she wanted to be thinking clearly when she explained the situation.

I sat down and Laura gave me a really big smile, immediately I was suspicious. I wasn't sure, but I knew her well and suspected that she was about to lie to me, or at least massage the truth a little bit. This wasn't a good start, and was not a good foundation upon which we could rebuild our relationship.

She tried to explain that her and Rob weren't serious, and that they had only had a couple of drunken nights, and a couple of dates. She tried to justify it with the fact that I had disappeared from the social scene, which had made getting together with Rob easier to do. I didn't like the fact that she was trying to apportion some of the blame to me. I didn't say anything, and let her get on with explaining her situation.

As she carried on I realised that all I was hearing were clichés.

If she had known there was any chance of us getting together it would never have happened, etc. That didn't wash with me. She should have had enough respect for what we had, even though it was over, not to do it. I know that it happens a lot, and that circumstances make the chances of your ex getting together with someone from the same social group more likely to happen, but I would have respected what we had. I would never have tried to get together with one of her friends. This wasn't going very well, but every time I looked into Laura's eyes I felt like I could forgive her anything.

She then went on to make things even worse by stating that all my so called friends believed it was ok. Everyone else didn't see a problem with it. Well, in my eyes, they were idiots. I would like them to imagine how they would feel in the same situation, and then tell me they thought it was ok.

I couldn't believe she was telling me this, but at the same time I was starting to realise that if I had any chance of getting my old life back, then the best way to achieve it was by getting back together with Laura. I saw no other entry point, and I really didn't fancy having to start my life again from scratch. It sounds awful, but I could see my life without Laura ending with loneliness and internet romance, and that thought frightened me. It sounds like a heartless thing to say, but if you had spent the last six months with no one for company, and had resorted to drinking yourself silly every night, then you might start rationalising your life and your feelings in the same way. Also, it would be a great way to get back at Rob for what he had done. He was a wanker.

In the back of my mind I also thought that maybe once we got back into the swing of things then there was every chance that time would sort things out. Time is a great healer, as they say.

I listened for a bit longer. Laura wasn't saying anything that was making me feel any better. But I knew I still had feelings for her, and she had feelings for me. I decided to just interrupt her and put something out there for her to consider. If she didn't like it, she could throw it right back.

"Laura, can I stop you for a second. It is obvious we both still have feelings for each other, so why don't we stop talking about all the crap that has happened in the last few months, and get on with just being together again?" Laura looked puzzled, so I tried to make it a bit clearer.

"We need to just try things out again. See how it goes. I don't want to discuss the weirdness that we have been through. I want to try and make it work. I want to forget what has happened. I want us to start dating again, like we did when we first met, and see where that takes us. Dwelling on the past will only make things worse. I want to see if the future can work. What do you think?"

She looked confused, but I could tell she knew what I was getting at. Her confusion was brought on by wondering whether or not it was a good plan. Women like to discuss things, a lot. I didn't think that would help. Fundamentally, my plan meant ignoring everything that had happened. We had both made mistakes, and I had made the biggest mistake, so why keep going over them. As women tend to want to talk things through, this course of action suited me more than Laura, but I could tell she saw the sense in moving on and drawing a line under the last six months.

"Ok", it was a tentative 'ok', and I had a feeling that there was more to come.

"There is one thing, though"

There was always one more thing, but I let her continue.

"What happened to you? Did something happen to you? Was there something specific that happened to make you change in those few months before we split up?"

I hadn't been expecting such a blunt question, and was slightly taken aback. I knew that there were certain events, my dad's death for example, which were contributory factors. But it was mainly my attitude towards life, and my intolerance of the people around me, that had caused the change. I didn't know whether I should tell Laura about that.

I thought for a moment, and then decided that I was going to tell her everything. Maybe then she would understand what had happened to me, and how that had changed me, and our relationship. Or maybe she wouldn't.

I felt a wave of optimism run right through me, and decided to plunge head first into the full story of the last few months. I went through everything, from Brian Cockburn-Emery, the woman at work with the fake breasts, Dave Dickson, the yardie, to the brief flirtation with alcoholism.

Some of the stories she found amusing, others I could tell she thought were crazy. It felt good letting it all come out. I hadn't mentioned anything to anyone throughout the entire time, and I now realised that was probably the main problem. I had no way of releasing my tension. My annoyance with the world had been eating me up inside. All I needed to do was speak to someone about my feelings.

I should have been able to laugh at the annoying and selfish people, instead of letting them get me down. There were always going to be annoying, selfish people in my life, and there was no way that was ever going to change. There was nothing I could do about that. Twats are a fact of life.

"Give me the courage to change the things I can, the grace to accept what you can't, and the wisdom to know the difference between the two". I had not had the grace to accept what I cannot change, and had definitely not had the wisdom to know the difference. I saw that now, and felt quite sad that I had wasted so much of my life, and affected so many of the people that I cared about in the process. This was becoming a rollercoaster of an evening. I needed another drink.

Talking so openly with Laura had, at first, been a cathartic experience, but now it was leaving me with a feeling of deep sadness and regret. Recounting the stories was, in the main, quite amusing. There were some details that I could tell were making Laura slightly uneasy. The yardie story was especially tricky, and required some acute story telling to convey the strange nature of the event.

Her main concern seemed to be the fact that I had kept it all hidden from her. I understood how it must have made her feel. It was like I was leading a double life. I could see that her mind was working through the possibility that I had done this once, so what was to stop me from doing it again.

The only thing she said throughout the time I was recounting my story was "I can't believe I didn't notice what was going on".

What that really meant was, "I can't believe you lied to me all that time". I couldn't work out whether this was something she could, or couldn't, forgive. I was trying to read her face, but she was being deliberately nondescript. I could sense that this wasn't going as well as I had hoped.

I finished narrating the last few months of my life, and sat back in my seat. I then began to feel slightly concerned. Laura wasn't saying anything. She was just staring intently back at me, trying to match the strange behaviour I had described, back to the person she was looking at. I think from that point onwards I had changed in her eyes. She no longer saw me as the same person, and actually thought I was a bit of a freak.

I sensed this, and tried to persuade her that I no longer needed to resist everything in my life that annoyed me. That I had got it out of my system. I no longer needed to act against people who infuriated me. I was a changed man. But I could see that it was falling on deaf ears. Her expression remained the same.

Laura got up to leave and stared back down at me. I was slumped in my seat, exasperated. She informed me that she needed time to think about what I had just said. She would be in touch.

Oh shit!!

I knew that this was probably quite a lot to take in, especially the business with the yardie, but I had acted in self defence. Surely she could understand that, and all the others things I had done. They were strange, but they were understandable. Other people must have thought about acting against things in life that frustrate and annoy them, but most people just grumble and complain and do nothing. She must be able to understand why I would spend so much time and effort getting back at these people. The people I targeted were idiots. All of them were idiots.

Laura left, and in my heart I knew that it was over. She would not be able to look at me in the same way ever again.

Now I knew I shouldn't have said anything.

Why had I suddenly felt the need to open my heart.

I ordered another pint and sat back down at the table to smoke, drink, and think.

THE WAIT

"How much of human life is lost in waiting."
(Ralph Waldo Emerson)

I awoke the next day feeling light headed. The pub session had turned into serious drowning of my sorrows, and now I could feel that I needed another drink to take the edge off the day ahead.

The last thing I could remember was boring the arse off the barmaid about my lack of understanding when it came to women, and my inability to keep my mouth shut. I felt a huge pang of embarrassment as I remembered her feigned interest, but clear boredom, at all the rubbish I was talking. I hated that feeling. I had experienced that feeling too many times in my life. Waking up and realising that you have been a complete tit the night before is an awful feeling. Especially when you add being physically unwell to the mental anguish. To make things even worse, I had to include the fact that it was a work day, and I now had the prospect of nine hours sat in front of a computer. It's a dangerous equation. A self-imposed, self inflicted day of shitness.

Throughout the working day I had flashbacks from the night before. Each one embarrassing, some quite worrying. The details of my conversation with Laura were gradually working their way back into my mind. Cold pangs of regret filled my body as each memory returned. I continuously checked my mobile phone, hoping she had tried to contact me. Hoping that she had decided I wasn't a complete freak. Hoping that we could have some kind of future together.

There were a couple of shocking recollections from the night before. Towards the end of the evening as I had stumbled across the pub, using my beer radar to locate the toilets, I had tripped (or maybe just drunkenly collapsed), and fallen at the feet of a couple who were trying to enjoy a quiet drink together. I remembered looking up at them from the floor, and laughing at them as they scowled down at me. I was scum. I hated people like me.

As I remembered the incident I realised I was actually shaking my head at my own actions. I was disappointed in myself. I was equally disappointed when I recalled throwing up on my next door neighbour's car bonnet. He would be so pleased when he found it.

All in all, it had been a tremendous evening.

As disappointed as I was with my behaviour, and as rough as I felt at work that day, my main concern was Laura.

The more I thought about it, the more I realised that it had been a heinous error to tell her anything about my time apart from her. I had promised myself from the outset that no one would ever know what I was up to. I knew that most people wouldn't understand, and I was right. Even my own ex-girlfriend, who knew me better than anyone, couldn't understand.

There was no contact from Laura during the day at work, and none that evening. My mind would not rest. The tiredness of work and drinking wouldn't provide me with the solace of sleep.

I toyed with the idea of initialising contact, but had no idea what to say. I wasn't sorry for what I had done. I was sorry that it had led to the breakdown of our relationship, but not sorry for the other people involved. They deserved everything that came to them. Every single one of them.

Sometimes women just need time. That's what I told myself. She probably wanted to discuss our problems amongst all her friends and get a balanced view.

I could just imagine what Laura was up to right now. Sat at home, surrounded by a group of her friends, drinking wine, gradually getting louder and louder as the wine kicks in and they compete against one another to crowbar their views into the conversation.

'Dirty Dancing' and 'Pretty Woman' DVDs on the coffee table. They won't be watched. Tonight is for talking, and they will talk, and talk, and talk. The main topics of conversation will be me, me and Laura, Laura, our relationship, our past and our future. Great. At the end of the evening they will all be drunk and emotional.

I hoped that Laura would have enough discretion to omit some of the details of my activities. My activities would spread across Bristol within a day if she mentioned it to her horde of friends.

I dropped Laura a quick, non committal text asking that she keep the details of our discussion private. She didn't respond, but I wasn't that bothered. She must know that this wasn't something that should be made public. I was sure that she wouldn't betray my trust. At the same time something at the back of my mind made me concerned that she might now hate me, and take great delight in ruining my life. She wasn't that kind of person, but then I never thought she would get with Rob, and she did.

I wondered how long it would take for the results of the debate to filter their way back to me, and what form those results would take. Despite the drunken, and often hysterical, nature of a ladies night, they always seem to stumble their way towards a plan of action.

As things turned out it didn't really matter what the outcome was.

ROADKILL

"Sleep, sleep, beauty bright,
Dreaming in the joys of night;
Sleep, sleep; in thy sleep
Little sorrows sit and weep.
(William Blake)

I waited a couple more days, but there was no word from Laura.

The feelings for Laura, the ones that I felt returning that night in the pub, were subsiding quickly and being replaced by annoyance. Annoyance that she could leave me in the dark for so long. Annoyance that she couldn't make her mind up, and annoyance that all this time was being wasted. My life was on hold and was being wasted whilst I waited for her to make a decision.

She could either live with what I had done, or she could decide to move on. I had made it clear that I was happy to move on together. I was willing to forget her time with Rob. I had extended the olive branch. I had opened myself up. The Rob episode was a painful one to forgive, so surely she could forgive me and move on.

A few more days passed and the feeling of annoyance was gradually edging towards a feeling of anger. I didn't even know if I wanted her back anymore. It had been nearly a week since I had spoken to Laura in 'Ye Olde Butcher's Arms' and I hadn't even had a text. I was being stubborn and had not contacted her, but the ball was in her court, the decision had been left with her. She was the one who 'needed time to think'. How much time did she need? What was there to think about? She either wanted to work things out, or she didn't. It was really starting to piss me off.

At the time, when she left the pub, I thought that it was probably over. In the first few days following our meeting I had become optimistic that something might be salvaged. That we could work on sorting things out. These feelings were now gone completely. I decided that the answer probably lay at the bottom of a bottle of vodka.

It had been a while since I had drunk on my own at home. It felt good, and remarkably comforting. The slight sting of the vodka as it hits your throat, followed by the warm feeling in your chest. The knowledge that your feelings and emotions are about to be numbed. That is a good feeling in my situation.

I didn't want to think about Laura anymore. I didn't want to worry about what she was thinking and feeling. I just wanted to get on with my life, and a night on the booze seemed a good way of starting that process. The vodka would help me flush Laura out of my system. I would feel rough in the morning, but a heavy drinking session might be the punishment I needed to get myself over Laura and back to reality again.

I drank hard. As soon as one vodka was down, another one was loaded up. The television was on loudly, but I wasn't really watching it. The radio was blaring in the kitchen, but I wasn't listening, and a CD was playing loudly in the lounge. To anyone who had looked in on my house that evening I would have looked insane, it was chaos, but I was enjoying myself. Partying on my own.

When Laura lived with me I was never allowed to have the TV and music at the same time. I decided that tonight I was going to enjoy all the things that I was never allowed when we had lived together. This was going to prove to me that I was better off without her. I would leave the toilet seat up. I wouldn't bother washing up my plate after dinner. I would laze on the sofa in just my underpants. I would watch testosterone fuelled TV. I would even download some porn and just leave it playing in the background.

I was wasted. I was Martin Sheen in 'Apocalypse Now'.

In my drunken state I was likening his physical journey to the metaphorical and emotional journey I was about to take to forget Laura. Purge her from my system, and get on with my life. In reality I was just a wasted idiot acting like a prat in my own house.

Then disaster struck. I ran out of vodka. I needed to think about a plan of action to get more alcohol. The stimulus from the TV, stereo and radio was now confusing me. I stood, confused, in the centre of my lounge, too drunk to think straight. The local Pakistani convenience shop was the answer.

First, there was the annoyance of having to get dressed. Common sense disappeared and I prepared for my journey to the shop. I say journey, but it's about a ten minute walk in normal circumstances. These weren't normal circumstances. I hadn't been this drunk in ages.

The act of dressing and undressing, when inebriated, becomes hugely complicated. Something that you have been doing with ease since you were just a few years old, is now nearly impossible. I went upstairs to begin the dressing experience.

The first obstacle, the trousers. Trouser legs are impossible to find, and I kept getting the wrong trouser leg. I couldn't understand why. Trousers were too confusing. I gave up on the idea of trousers and went for shorts instead. It wasn't that cold outside, and I reasoned that wearing shorts made it possible that I could jog there and back. In reality drunken jogging was never going to happen. I would make it about one hundred metres, feel as though I had run a mile and have to stop for breath. In the end it would have been quicker to walk the hundred metres.

I sat on the edge of my bed and wrestled a pair of socks on to my feet. I got knackered chasing my feet around with a pair of socks. It was like my feet and the socks were magnets and completely opposed to each other.

I went back downstairs and realised I had forgotten to get a top. I couldn't be bothered to go back upstairs so decided that a bare chest, covered by a coat, would be fine. The final part of the dressing process would prove to be the most difficult. Shoes.

Laces that should undo with the slightest tug, will instead form some of the most amazing knots in the world. Undiscovered knots, for which there is no known release. After struggling with tying my laces for what felt like an hour, I gave up. Flip flops were the answer. I sat on my sofa to remove the socks which had taken forever to put on. I lolled from side to side on the sofa as I tried to get some purchase on the socks. Now they did not want to come off. The little fuckers.

I hadn't tried it before, but who was to say that flip flops and socks were such a bad combination. In my enlightened inebriated state I was sure it could work. It did. The socks were pushed into the crack between my big toe, which wasn't very comfortable, but it worked, and I felt like a genius. A drunken stupid genius.

The final part of my interesting 'look' was the overcoat. I went for a parka jacket to finish off the look. Grabbed a pile of loose change from the side, and stumbled out into the street, looking like a hobo beach bum in an Arctic coat.

The walk to my local shop was mainly through the housing estate alleyways, with a quick trip over the main road and into the next estate. It would normally take about ten minutes, but I needed to add a few minutes for the 'vodka effect', i.e. the inability to walk in a straight line.

As I walked the fifteen minute journey to the local shop I realised that the vodka was having its desired effect. I hadn't thought about Laura, or the situation, since I had first started to feel drunk. As 'The Eagles' say, some people drink to remember, and some people drink to forget. I drink to forget. I wondered if you could really define all people into those two types of drinkers. I have certainly experienced both. Many of my friends become emotional and reminisce when they have a few drinks. But there are also a lot of my friends who get drunk and live for the moment as I was doing now. Then there are the teetotallers. So there are three categories of drinkers. Jesus, I was clever. Three categories. Amazing.

That was the last thing I remember thinking before the accident.

I found out later that whilst I was waiting to cross the main road someone had swerved to avoid a cat, mounted the pavement, and ploughed into me. My life ruined for a cat, it's strange how things work out.

I remember continuously waking up and then passing out again. Looking at the stars in the sky. Numb. No pain. Lying on the pavement, the man who had hit me standing over me. He looked worried. I passed out again. My eyes were closed, in the darkness I could hear him talking to someone. He was describing me as a tramp. Even in my state, slipping in and out of consciousness, I can remember being slightly offended. Then again, I was topless, wearing a parka jacket, shorts and flip flops with socks.

It seemed that because I was a tramp he was prepared to drive off and leave me. He had probably been drinking, why else would you leave the scene of the crime. Another example of the scum in our society acting without a thought for anyone but themselves. Bastards.

As I fell in and out of consciousness I became aware of him searching me, which obviously wasn't a good thing. I couldn't move, but I could feel his hands all over me. Hand raped by a stranger.

I wasn't aware of any pain. I passed out again. This time I passed out properly, I have no idea how long for, but the next time I was conscious I was in a hospital room. Everything was white, blindingly white. I couldn't bear to keep my eyes open, but for some reason my eyes were remaining open. I couldn't get them closed.

I lay there awake, with my eyes open, confused.

A wave of panic spread over me. I couldn't move at all, I couldn't even move my eyes. I could hear something, a machine probably, constantly beeping somewhere to my left. All I could see was the ceiling. I could hear, and I could see, but I couldn't move. I passed out again.

The next time I awoke my eyes remained shut. No amount of concentrated effort could force them open. I could hear people talking somewhere in the room. I recognised one of the voices as my mum's.

They were talking about me, and judging by the conversation, my mum was discussing my situation with a doctor. It must be a hospital.

The doctor was being reassuring. Telling my mum that most people recover from a vegetative state within a few weeks and make a full recovery. My mum was a mess. When she spoke I could hear that she was on the verge of tears. It hurt to know that it was because of me. Even though the accident hadn't been my fault, there was no way I would have been out there on the main road, as drunk as a lord, if I hadn't let myself go off the rails.

I had let my life get away from me and this was the consequence. In fact, all I had done was try and dish out a bit of karma, and now karma was biting me on the ass. That wasn't supposed to be how karma worked. Maybe karma didn't like me messing in its business.

I listened to the details of my accident and my current condition. I had been unconscious for a week, but had been showing some signs of brain activity in the last few days which was promising, apparently.

I definitely had brain activity. I felt like a fly on the wall. They were speaking as if I wasn't there, but I could hear everything. It was strange, but interesting, to hear people speaking so candidly about me in my presence.

The doctor believed that I, like most people, would come out of my coma within a few weeks. This was the most common scenario, but even then, people have remained in comas for months and still made a full recovery. As time progressed I was less likely to make a full recovery, but the doctor hoped and believed that we could have a quick resolution. In other words, he had no idea, but my mum seemed to take some comfort from his words, so that was good.

I heard my mum thank the doctor, and then I heard the door open and close. I listened intently and could make out some faint sounds. Someone was still in the room.

My mum had remained in the room. I could hear her settling down into the chair next to my bed and then fiddling around for something in her hand bag.

She began to softly cry. I hadn't heard my mum cry since my dad's death. I wanted to cry, I felt like I was crying inside.

"Are you crying too?" I heard my mum's voice again, as she leaned forward to wipe a tear from my eye. I could tell that her question was not one she expected me to answer.

Inside I was screaming that I was sorry, and that I wish I hadn't put her through this so soon after the death of my dad, but I couldn't do anything. I was trapped inside my body, able to think, able to hear, but unable to communicate or move.

"What were you doing? What has happened to you in the last few months?" again these weren't questions that my mum expected answering. They were just thoughts on her mind that she was saying out loud. The kinds of questions she wished she had asked before my accident. Questions that never get asked until it is too late. This was therapeutic for her. She could talk to me about anything she wanted. Tell me exactly what she was thinking, hope that I was listening, but just happy that she was saying them out loud to me.

My behaviour hadn't gone unnoticed by my mum. She knew that I was having some problems, but assumed that it was because of the death of my father, and that it was all part of my grieving process. She had wanted to talk to me, but I was always a closed book, and seemed to prefer to sort these things in my own time. She blamed herself for not talking to me, for being a coward and hoping that the situation would sort itself out.

It was horrible. I just wanted to reach out to her, give her a hug and tell her that it wasn't her fault. But all I could do was lie there and take it all in. Hoping that one day I would come out of this and tell my mum not to worry. That it wasn't her fault. That it was all my fault. I didn't even know if I would remember all the things that she had talked about. I hoped and prayed that I did, otherwise it would all have been wasted.

My mum was constantly crying and upset, and it was killing me.

I was having trouble sleeping, in fact that was an understatement, I wasn't sleeping at all, chronic wakefulness. All this information I was taking in was unsettling my mind. I couldn't sleep at all. Occasional dozing was all I managed.

People opening their hearts to me was something I was getting used to. Everyone who visited me wanted to open their hearts. To tell me things that they wished they had said before my accident. It was interesting, but also frustrating. I was permanently in one way conversations. I wanted to offer my opinion, or in some people's cases, just tell them to shut up.

Laura came and had a deep conversation with my mum right in front of me. She explained everything about the breakdown of our relationship. My obsession with getting back at the people who annoyed me. How it had consumed my life and made it impossible for our relationship to survive.

Thanks Laura, my secret was well and truly out now. I wondered how many other people knew.

She even went through our attempted reconciliation and how it had left her confused. She had been unable to speak to me because she wasn't sure who I was anymore. She had wanted to get in touch, but didn't know what to say.

At least I was now getting an explanation. Even if it had taken a near death experience to bring Laura to me. Laura being there was the only positive thing in all of this mess.

She was still unsure about whether it could ever work again, but the accident had made her realise how much she cared about me. And that maybe there were enough feelings there to give things another go.

This revelation pleased me. It gave me something to look forward to. Even the chronic wakefulness couldn't stop me from enjoying the possibility that all my mistakes could now be forgotten. There could be a new chapter in my life.

My mum clearly had no idea what was causing the changes in my attitude. She was grateful to Laura for providing her with some understanding behind my recent erratic behaviour. They both agreed that the root cause was the death of my father. I still believed that I was heading down the same road whether my dad had died or not, but I was starting to think that it could have been the catalyst for some of the more extreme things I had done. Everyone else couldn't be wrong.

I even had a visit from Rob. He was feeling bad about what had happened between him and Laura, and was keen to blame it all on drinking. I couldn't care less about him at the moment. He had burnt his bridges.

Another day passed, and my frustration increased. I was alive inside, but dead outside. It was embarrassing having tubes to take away my bodily fluids. It was embarrassing when the nurse had to clean me and check my bed sores.

The next day my mum came again and read some of the well wishers cards to me. It was weird. My mum was teary. All the messages were really emotional. It felt like everyone thought I was dying, but I felt so alive. I felt full of energy. Caged up inside my body. I was counting the seconds until I woke up again.

I was looking forward to waking up properly and letting people know that I had heard everything. I wanted to tell my side of the story, and get on with my life. If anything this had been a positive experience. I was seeing a side of people that was normally hidden from me. It was making me empathise more with other people. I was seeing positive characteristics again. I was slowly regaining my faith in people.

I was beginning to understand that the issues I had with other people's behaviour were actually my problem. There were always going to be people that I found irritating. Some people were always going to find me irritating. That was just a fact of life.

I had let it consume me, whereas normal people just got on with life and looked for the positives. I got myself into a vicious circle, where I looked for everything that was annoying and became annoyed, and determined to seek out more annoying people, which then annoyed me even further.

I had now been in this state for over three weeks. I knew, from the conversations that my mum was having with the doctor, that the longer I stayed in this state the less likely it was that I would make a full recovery. This panicked me from time to time, but I was feeling mentally ok. Just a little bit frustrated and claustrophobic.

It was about halfway through the fourth week that I started dreaming a lot. The chronic wakefulness had started to pass a week earlier, and I found myself able to gradually catch up on the missed sleep. It felt good, but by the end of the fourth week I was sleeping a lot.

It was rare for me to be awake. I was having the same continuous, vivid dream. I was spending less and less time in reality. The dream felt like my reality to me. Every time I woke it felt like I was still in the dream for a few minutes. It would take a while for my brain to register the reality.

The dream involved me as the central character. Everything was seen through my eyes, and felt through my feelings, but the dream itself seemed to have no bearing on my life, and became more and more random as the days went by.

The dream began in a forest, a very pleasant forest. The sun shone through the trees and everything was green and vibrant. I was in the body of a large black horse. Although I would take on the form of many different animals as the dream progressed.

In the dream I was happy. I drank from the streams that ran through the forest, ate the lush grass, and made my way through the day at a leisurely pace. To begin with I never encountered any other animals, or people for that matter, and I enjoyed the solitude. I was happy just to wander through the forest and plains, without a thought about the lack of life around me.

The dream always ended in the same way. I would curl up under a tree as the sun went down over the mountain range at the far side of the plain. I would wake from the dream, back in the hospital room feeling happy.

The days passed, and the dream progressed in pretty much the same way, with only the occasional detail changing. Sometimes I would spend all day in the forest doing nothing, but some days I would wonder what it was like on the other side of the plain. I would run across the plain towards the mountains. Strangely, I wouldn't ever appear to get closer to the mountains, no matter how fast, or how long I ran, the mountains were always the same distance away. In the beginning I didn't let this bother me, but as the dream progressed I became more bored of the forest, the plain and the solitude. I began to try harder and harder to reach the mountains in the distance.

Every time I ran until I could run no more and I needed a rest. Every time I rested I fell asleep, and when I awoke from the dream I was back in my hospital bed, feeling frustrated. When I fell asleep again, and returned to the dream, I was back in the forest and the mountains were far away across the plain.

The frustration was passing over into my waking thoughts. I no longer had much grasp of what was going on around me. I heard voices, but couldn't make out who they were or what they were saying. I had given up my interest in reality and couldn't wait to fall unconscious and return to the dream. I had to find out what was happening at the mountain range.

I lost track of time, I don't know if anyone was still visiting me. When I was awake I felt hazy, but mostly I was asleep, and my perception of time had gone.

I was no longer enjoying the repetitive nature of my dream, I was bored with the lack of company, and I was bored with the forest. Its lush green grass was just pissing me off. I spent my days at the edge of the forest staring at the mountain range, amazed that I couldn't get there. Then something happened.

I was lying down at the edge of the forest looking at the mountains, wondering what was on the other side, feeling frustrated at my inability to get there, when an armadillo strolled by. He was the first living thing I had seen in my dreams, and I felt excited at the prospect of having someone to talk to.

He completely ignored me, and casually continued his shuffle along the edge of the forest. Slightly offended, I got to my feet and trotted after him.

Even though I was making a lot of noise as I trotted through the forest the armadillo continued to ignore me. I pretended to loudly clear my throat, but he still ignored me. In the end my impatience caused me to shout out to the armadillo.

"Excuse me, why are you ignoring me?"

The more direct approach seemed to work, he stopped in his tracks, but remained facing away from me. He didn't seem scared at all, even though I could crush him with one hoof. The armadillo remained still, and seemed to be waiting for me to make the next move.

I spoke, "I have been in this forest for god knows how long. I haven't seen or heard anything or anyone. You are the first thing I have seen and I want some answers".

The armadillo remained perfectly still, but something about his demeanour gave away the fact that he was annoyed and irritated by me. After a long pause the armadillo spoke.

"You are an idiot". I thought this was a bit harsh.

There was something familiar about the voice, but I couldn't place it.

"You are such an idiot". He repeated.

Then it hit me. I hadn't been able to place the voice, but now I could. It was mine. It was like when you hear yourself on an answer phone, and you think it doesn't sound like you. But this was definitely me.

I demanded that the armadillo turn around, but the armadillo didn't move. My aggressive approach didn't seem to be working, but I was in no mood for a softly softly attitude. I was confused and worried.

I moved forward to try and get around to the other side of the armadillo, but as soon as I began to move, he shuffled on. I sped up. Even though I was a horse and infinitely faster than the armadillo, I couldn't overtake him. He always stayed a few feet ahead of me. I felt the same frustrations as the mountain range. Trying to reach something that should be attainable, but failing to do so. Trying and failing seemed to be a common theme in my dream.

I stopped running and, in the same instance, the armadillo stopped. I don't know how he timed it so well, but then you should never try to rationalise a dream in the middle of having it. I tried again to get some information from the armadillo. I decided to try a new approach.

"So, Mr Armadillo, what's your name?" I was going to lure him into a false sense of security.

"What do you think my name is, you idiot." It wasn't a question, and he was becoming more and more belligerent, the sarcastic little bastard.

Despite being angry, I decided that this was at least a kind of a question, which could lead to a conversation, which could sort out what the hell was going on in my brain.

"I think your name is Andy. Andy the Armadillo".

I could sense he thought I was the biggest twat he had ever met, and he verbalised that for me, "You are the biggest twat I have ever met".

"Thanks, but I think you will find that if you could meet yourself then you are the biggest twat you could ever meet", it was a lame put down, I was normally a lot sharper than that in real life, but at least it showed the cantankerous little chap, he was getting on my nerves, and I had had enough.

There was a pause. A stand off. I had a feeling that even though he was immensely annoyed with me, he was about to say something. He wanted this conversation over, and he knew that he could only do that by telling me something about what was going on.

Eventually he spoke up, "I am you, and you are me." He was still facing away from me.

"That's a bit cryptic. What is it supposed to mean?"

His response wasn't what I was expecting, "Oh for fuck's sake, just fuck off and leave me alone". With that he disappeared down a hole which I hadn't even noticed before.

I shouted after him, but this time there were no expletives in response. He was gone. I was confused, but at least he had given me something to think about, something to do.

I sat down at the foot of a tree, as I normally did, with a view across the plain to the mountains in the distance. My thoughts turned to armadillos. Why was I an armadillo and a horse?

What are the traits of an armadillo? Defensive. Lonely. Timid (well this one certainly wasn't). I didn't understand how that was relevant to me. Suddenly there was a bright flash of light, and I saw my mum's face looking down at me from the sky.

All armadillo thoughts were gone. My mum looked concerned, but then her son was a horse, so she probably had reason to be concerned. She looked like she was crying, but I couldn't be sure. Her face slid away, and was replaced by a bright light flashed directly into my eyes, it was unbearable. And then, as suddenly as it had started, it was over, and I was dreaming again. I didn't give it a second thought.

I was still in the same landscape, but I was no longer a horse. I had now morphed into a badger. This was getting ridiculous, I felt like I was in a rubbish Disney film.

I remembered the armadillo. Now I was a badger I could follow him down the hole. I looked around, but the hole was no longer there. I was frustrated, but now that I was a badger my attitude had changed. I had developed an inner resolve, the change in me was almost tangible, and nothing was going to annoy me or get me down. Being a badger seemed a lot more positive than a horse.

I was thinking about how I would get to the mountains, how I could find out what was on the other side. It was all I could think about, I was ready for the journey. Even though as a badger I was a lot less mobile than a horse, I had a strange confidence that I could make the journey now. I had the same confidence on my first attempt as a horse, which had ebbed away with each failed attempt.

I set off across the plain, scurrying at first, worried about being away from the safety of the forest and exposed to possible dangers. I had only seen an armadillo so far, and although he was obnoxious (and possibly me), he didn't pose much of a threat to a badger.

Eventually, when my energy levels dropped, and I became more comfortable with my surroundings, I slowed to a walking pace. The sun was shining, I was in a good mood, and, unlike previous attempts, the mountains were definitely getting closer and closer.

This cheered me up. I wondered what had changed to make this journey successful when previous attempts had failed. I was pondering this when once again the bright light appeared, beaming down on me from the sky as I looked upwards.

This time I couldn't see anything apart from the blinding light, but I could hear Laura. She sounded very distant, she was pleading for me not to go. I could hear her saying "please don't go", over and over again. I didn't understand what she meant, not to go where? Not to go to the mountains? The light subsided again and I was alone on the plain.

I paused and thought about what had just happened. Did she mean I shouldn't go to the mountains? Even if she did, there was no way I was going back to the forest. I had lost all perception of time, but I had been alone in that forest for what felt like a very long time, and I didn't want to go back. I didn't want to waste my time feeling lonely in the forest. I moved on, a bit more apprehensively this time.

The mountains were still getting closer, but I was moving a little bit slower than before. The weird visitation from Laura had left me feeling disturbed, and for the first time I wasn't sure that I was doing the right thing. Something was holding me back.

I don't know how long it took me to get across the plain. The concept of time in dreams is strange. You can't monitor it. I needed to dream up a badger watch. It must have been less than a day as it had remained light throughout my journey across the plain.

Now I was close to the foot of the mountains, and they weren't very daunting at all. It was still light, and I was pretty sure I could be over them before night drew in. I decided to rest for a bit, and lay down on a large rock at the foot of the mountains. The sun was out and the warmth of the sun and the rock combined to make me very drowsy. I nodded off to sleep.

Back in reality things weren't looking so good for me. Laura and my mum were by my beside, as they had been for the entire ordeal. It had been well over a month now, and for the last week or so I had barely been conscious. The doctors were saying that I had entered stage two, and that the outcome of the coma would soon be known. Stage two didn't last very long, and normally resulted in the patient slipping into a deep vegetative state from which they rarely return. The one positive note was that there was a slight chance I would wake. These were the two possible outcomes, but it was rated 90/10 against me waking.

There had been a couple of occasions when I had started to slip away, but the heart monitor had alerted Laura and my mum to the danger and I had been revived by a team of doctors. It was on one of these occasions that Laura had crossed over into my dreams, and I had heard her begging me not to go.

As Laura sat at my bedside and stroked my head, I awoke in my dream with the feeling of something nuzzling up against the top of my head. It felt nice. Through tired eyes I could see a friendly looking deer staring down at me. As I gradually pulled focus I began to notice that the deer looked familiar. There was something Laura-esque about her. I think it was the eyes. The eyes looked very familiar, they were welcoming and friendly, but at the same time hinted at an inner sorrow.

She continued to nuzzle me until I was fully awake. I sat upright on the rock and for the first time I noticed that she had a passenger. There was a horrible looking little weasel perched on her back staring at me intently. I could immediately tell that he didn't like me. It's never a nice feeling to be instantly disliked, so I made it obvious that the feeling was mutual. This negativity spoiled the serenity of my surroundings.

"Why must you go to the other side of the mountains?" The deer spoke and I knew that it was Laura. It was nice to have someone else in my dream, but it was even nicer to have Laura in my dream, even if I was a badger and she was a deer, and sex was physically impossible. I had enjoyed her nuzzling me, and was definitely going to be a lot happier if there was more of that in my dream. I was also enjoying the fact that she wanted to talk to me, unlike my only other companion, the armadillo, whose sole purpose seemed to be giving me abuse and being rude.

I decided to ignore the strange weasel and explain myself to Laura. "I have been in the forest you can see on the horizon across the plain. I have been there for ages, I'm not exactly sure how long, but it feels like a very long time. The only other living thing I have met is an armadillo. The armadillo was obnoxious, gave me abuse for about an hour, and then disappeared. As you can imagine, it has been pretty boring, so I decided to see what was on the other side of the mountains. I have tried to get across to the mountains before, when I was a horse, but I never made it. But now I am a badger it seems I am able to get here and I am ready to see what is on the other side."

"I see" said Laura, "but I would like you stay on this side with me".

"I would like that too, but how long are you going to stay for? And what are we going to do?"

"I think you should see what is on the other side of the mountains", the weasel piped up. "Maybe we can meet you on the other side". I could tell that the weasel had an ulterior motive. That he wasn't a nice character. He was trying to sound helpful, but I could tell he was being a wanker. Unlike the armadillo and the deer, the weasel did not sound like anyone I knew. Maybe he symbolised something, rather than being someone.

I couldn't believe that I had met three animals and two of them seemed to hate me for no reason. This was putting a sour note on my meeting with Laura. If I had thought about it then I would realise that dreams are always bizarre, but I shouldn't question it until I woke up. In reality, there was a strong possibility that I wasn't going to wake up.

"Don't be stupid, weasel", Laura's voice brought me back from my reverie. "You know that we can't meet anyone on the other side".

They seemed to know a lot about the other side of the mountains, so I asked what was on the other side. Neither of them knew, or at least they said that they didn't know. I suspected they knew.

Then things began to get very, very strange.

Firstly, a fox walked past, stopped, looked me straight in the eyes, and said in a broad cockney accent, "I like it here, I could stay here forever, don't bother me. Life was crap before anyway.", and then carried on walking along the path at the foot of the mountains and disappeared.

Then a large black bear lumbered out from behind a rock about a hundred yards from my rock, and began slowly walking towards us. Strangely none of us seemed threatened by the bear. When he eventually got close to us he looked at me in disgust and told me in a deep American accent that I was weak. Apparently I was weak for wanting to go over the mountains. He was going to find a way out of here even if it took forever, he would never give up, and he would eventually find another way out.

The weasel suddenly became animated. He was running along Laura's back whooping in delight. Then he loudly proclaimed that he was going with the bear as the bear was a winner. With that he jumped from Laura's back, scampered across the floor and climbed up onto the bear's back. The bear roared loudly, and arrogantly, gave me one last dirty look, and trundled off in the same direction as the fox.

The procession of strange animals continued when a jolly otter ran past, pausing briefly to inform me in a Scouse accent that the bear and fox were talking bollocks, and that he was going to see what was on the other side. He was sure it was something amazing. He was very optimistic. I had been doubting my plan to scale the mountain, but the otter made me feel that maybe I was doing the right thing. I smiled as I watched him scurry up the side of the mountain and then he disappeared over the ridge and was gone.

As I gazed up at the top of the mountain, thinking that going over the top was a good idea, something strange happened. Laura disappeared. It went a little darker and fell completely silent. It may have been completely silent before, but now I was alone I noticed it.

I felt different, and when I looked down it became apparent that I was no longer a badger. I ad changed back into my normal human form. I had hands again. I stared down at my hands.

I looked back across the plain to see if anything was happening, but in the half light I was unable to see to the other side. It was getting darker and colder. I was scared.

A wave of panic set in. I needed to know what was happening. For the first time in my dream I was scared. Everything felt ominous, something bad was about to happen.

Then I heard my father's voice It was coming from over the ridge of the mountain. All he said was "hello, son" as he appeared over the ridge of the mountain. Within moments he was stood just a few metres away from me, behind him in the distance I could see a light glowing powerfully over the ridge of the mountain.

He looked good. Much better than the last time I had seen him. I could tell he was happy. It made me happy to see him so happy. His appearance comforted me.

He extended his hand to me and said, "Come with me, son. It's amazing on the other side of the mountain. Everyone is there."

I paused for a second. I had so wanted to make it to the mountains and get to the other side. This wasn't how I imagined it. But it felt good. Actually, it felt better than good. It felt amazing.

I decided to trust my father. I took his extended hand and began to move slowly up the side of the mountain. I would say walk, but we weren't walking, it felt like we were floating to the summit.

I felt brilliant. The happiest I have ever felt. I felt like I had accepted my fate, that I was ready for whatever was on the other side. A new life beckoned, and it wasn't going to have any of the old frustrations. No thoughtlessness, selfishness, and none of the annoyances that had marred my other life. I knew that the resistance I had felt towards everything before was gone.

Just as I was fully accepting my new life, I heard Laura's voice again. I turned back towards to the plain to face the direction that the voice seemed to be coming from. I was almost at the ridge. The glowing light beckoned.

The same bright light pierced through the sky and I turned away to escape its harshness.

Behind me the light was getting brighter. It was illuminating my father's face. He smiled at me and let go of my hand. He looked happy, and used his eyes to signal for me to go to Laura.

I turned around again to face the light and work out what was going on. Laura's voice was getting louder and louder, and the light was getting brighter all the time.

I was confused. One moment I was happy, now I didn't know what was going on. I turned back to face my father and ask him what was happening, but he was no longer there.

I looked up to the summit and saw my dad approaching the edge. He turned to me, smiled and waved, and told me that he would see me again, soon. Then he disappeared, and I was alone again.

The light was now so bright that I couldn't see anything but the white light that now surrounded me. It was like I was floating in the light. There were noises racing into my head from all directions. Annoying voices. Voices and beeps. I could hear Laura's voice in the background, and several other voices. The voices were raised and sounded urgent. Panic set in.

THE AWAKENING

"Dreaming. -- Either one does not dream at all, or one dreams in an interesting manner. One must learn to be awake in the same fashion: -- either not at all, or in an interesting manner."
(Friedrich Nietzsche)

I was quickly becoming more aware of my surroundings. I could hear a steady, constant bleeping, and was now able to pinpoint where the noise was coming from. The bright white light was subsiding. Every time I opened my eyes it became easier to see without being blinded.

I started to make out shapes and shadows, and they gradually turned into people, a window, a machine, a poster.

I felt paralysed. I wanted to move, but something stopped me from even making the slightest movement. My eyes were now almost fully adjusted to being open again. It was still uncomfortably bright, but I could see people I recognised. Laura and my mum. They were both happy, but crying. It was a bizarre scene to wake up to. It was bizarre full stop.

Men in white coats were checking machines and monitors all around me.

I still couldn't move properly, although I was now becoming aware of my fingers. It felt like I was moving them, but I couldn't be sure.

"His fingers are moving. That's a good sign", said a male voice from somewhere to my right.

I was now able to keep my eyes continuously open, without squinting against the light. Everyone was in focus. I could see my mum on one side of my bed, and Laura on the other. I felt them both reach for one of my hands and squeeze it tightly.

The wave of panic I had experienced earlier, when I was first starting to wake up was now gone, replaced by an overwhelming feeling of happiness. Happiness mixed with disorientation, confusion and frustration.

Neither Laura, nor my mum, said anything. They were both still teary, I was mesmerised watching the tears roll down their faces. I wanted to talk, but I couldn't. My throat felt like it was full of sand. The muscles I needed to talk were so underused that I couldn't get even get them started.

My mum must have seen that I was trying to talk. She comforted me and told me to relax and get some rest.

I wanted to talk. I wanted to know what had happened to me. I wanted to discuss my dream with someone whilst it was still fresh in my mind. I knew that the dream memories would fade, and I wanted to know what the dream meant. The dream had to mean something. I had almost died. If I had made it to the other side of the mountain I was sure that I would have died. Something had bought me back. It wasn't my time yet. But it had almost been my time.

The frustration of not being able to express myself was building up inside me, and making the monitor beep a little faster. A doctor leaned over the bed and asked me to remain calm. I was over the worst and was on the road to recovery. He said that it would be a slow process, but that all the signs were good. He was now hopeful I would make a full recovery. All I needed to do was rest and recuperate. My mum and Laura concurred with the doctor, and I began to relax. The beeping on the machine went back to a steady and less alarming rate.

I was now fully aware of my surroundings, and could move my neck slightly to look around the hospital room. I had a lot of tubes going into me, my nose and arm especially, but there was also an uncomfortable feeling in my groinal and anal region. I was slightly repulsed at the thought.

The doctors left the room and my mum and Laura settled in to the two comfy armchairs to the right hand side of my bed.

As women do, they talked. They talked to me for a long, long time. Normally this kind of intense chatter would be too much, but today I felt comforted by the continuous talking. They filled me in on my accident, my condition, and even found time to fill me in on all the local gossip. I wasn't particularly interested in the local gossip, but I happily listened. I didn't want the talking to stop. It reminded me I was there.

My accident was a hit and run. In parts of the UK one in five accidents are now hit and runs. The proliferation of uninsured drivers means they know they cant be traced and it makes more sense for them to run away.

I had vague memories of the guy who hit me standing over me as I lay on the floor, but I would never recognise him. I had been found a few minutes later by a man walking his dog. It was lucky that he had arrived so quickly otherwise I would definitely have died. My mum began to cry as she told me how close it had been.

My mum started to question what I had been doing out there, at that time, dressed like that (she definitely believed that you should always wear clean underwear, just in case you get knocked down by a bus). She realised that it was a stupid and inappropriate question, and said that it didn't matter. I didn't mind, she was just being a mum.

From the analysis of the accident scene carried out by the police, they had been able to establish that the car had probably been speeding, as was usually the case with car accidents. The car had swerved for some reason, probably to avoid an animal. Having lost control, the car mounted the pavement and ran straight into me. My mum added that blood analysis had shown that I had been drinking heavily that evening. I know what my mum was insinuating, she obviously believed that, had I not been so drunk, I might have been more aware of the danger and been able to avoid being hit. I didn't blame her. She was just worried for me. She had suspected that I had been drinking heavily even before the accident.

The accident had happened six weeks ago. Despite all the media coverage and calls for witnesses to come forward, there had been nothing for the police to use. It was proving a fruitless investigation. Another great example of someone looking after themselves without a thought for my life. Human nature to self preserve.

At this moment in time I wasn't that bothered. I was just glad to be alive, but I knew that once I was fully recovered this could be exactly the sort of thing that would eat away at me. Especially considering how I had been before the accident.

Once the details of the accident were done, they turned to my condition.

They had almost lost me at one stage a few days ago, but it seems that had acted as the catalyst for me to start improving. Something I had experienced in my coma had jolted me back, and over the last few days all the signs were that I was recovering. I had woken a couple of time, and garbled something about a weasel and an otter, before lapsing back into unconsciousness. Then today I regained consciousness.

It had been amazing to witness as I had been virtually motionless for nearly a month after the accident. Previously I had been steadily getting worse. Then, all of a sudden, it was like I had decided I was bored of gradually deteriorating, and was going to give it one last try.

I moved my head slightly to look round the room. There were cards and flowers everywhere. It's a bit odd that men get flowers when they are ill, I would never want flowers in a normal situation, yet when you are in trouble it is somehow appropriate for you to be sent flowers.

The mention of the weasel and otter rang a bell somewhere in my head, but my dream had been all but forgotten already.

At that point Laura and my mum suggested it was time I had some rest. I was feeling very tired. By now I was able to speak ever so slightly, but it took a lot of effort to state my agreement with a strained 'ok'. I was frightened about being left alone, but I didn't want to admit that to Laura and my mum.

My mum kissed me on the forehead, and Laura placed a kiss on my lips. My heart leapt, and I knew then that I had all the same feelings for Laura, and I could sense she felt the same way. Later that night, in a state of paranoia, I would question whether I was getting sympathy affection from Laura, but there and then it felt genuine.

They walked to the door, opened it, turned back to say goodbye and left the room.

I was very tired, but I still felt a great loneliness when I was left alone. I had just spent over a month alone in a world of my own. I wanted company now.

I tried to sleep. It didn't go well. I was scared that if I fell asleep I wouldn't wake up. I became paranoid that I was still dreaming. That this wasn't happening. That I was still in a coma. But I couldn't risk going to sleep, just in case it was real. The paranoia and tiredness was making me feel awful. The doctors had given me a button to press if I required assistance. I could feel the plastic tube in my hand, and gripped it tightly. I wanted to press it, but I didn't want to seem weak, and I didn't want to waste everyone's time.

The memories of my life before the accident were coming back. Aided by the paranoia, I was remembering all the negative aspects. Splitting from Laura. Her time with Rob. The drinking and the loneliness. I questioned why she was here now, was she only here out of sympathy? Was she that kind of person? I didn't know what was going on, paranoia isn't very nice.

Eventually the tiredness got the better of me and I passed out.

I awoke early the next day with Laura and my mum already in the room waiting for me to wake up. Sunlight was coming in through the blinds, and I could smell coffee. This seemed like heaven compared to my night time paranoia. I smiled at them and tried to fully wake up as quickly as possible.

I had been moved out of intensive care a few days before. The doctors thought that I was on the verge of regaining consciousness, and felt I should be moved to a private room to ensure that I would come round in a comfortable environment.

My mum was glad to see me moved from intensive care. She had found it too depressing. She didn't like being surrounded by the other families who were watching their loved ones, hoping for the best. She had found it very distressing, especially when people had passed away.

Just two days ago a lad from Liverpool, who had been involved in a nasty accident on a building site, had passed away. He had been in intensive care for two weeks before passing away, and my mum had got to know his family quite well in that time. She felt their pain when he died.

There had been a number of families who had seen loved ones pass in the time that I had been in there. Each one got harder and harder for my mum to see. It was steadily getting her down, and making her question my chances of survival.

An American man on the same ward as me had been in a coma for over a year. The hospital believed that the best course of action was to turn off the life support machine, but his family were deeply religious and believed that he should maintain the right to life no matter what. They were all over from the States, and had been here since he was admitted to intensive care after he was injured in bizarre squash accident. He had collided with the wall chasing a shot, knocked himself out and landed awkwardly on his neck. It is amazing how these things happen.

My mum was about to continue with the details of other patients on the intensive care ward, when I blurted out that "They should keep his machine on".

I don't know where my comment came from. I shouted it out without thinking. Somewhere in my mind I was convinced he was still fighting. It was a strange feeling, but a strong and compelling one. I couldn't place why I felt so strongly about this man. Someone I had never met, and never even seen.

My mum and Laura looked surprised, but I knew what they were thinking. They believed that I could sympathise with his situation, and would have wanted the same for myself. I decided not to go into details about the real reason I was convinced he should be kept alive. I didn't fully understand it myself, and didn't want to have to explain it.

That moment seemed to act as a trigger for the memories of my unconsciousness to slowly start coming back.

Later that evening I was lying in bed. My mum and Laura had a left a few hours before, and I had spent my time flicking through magazines and daydreaming.

I had recently finished reading an article about Joe Simpson and Simon Yates, the two mountaineers who almost died climbing the Siula Grande in the Peruvian Andes. Simpson fell and broke his leg on the descent and was unable to move. Yates attempted to lower Simpson slowly down the mountain a few hundred feet at a time. When Simpson was accidentally lowered into a crevasse and with no chance of getting out Yates was forced to cut the rope. It is a harrowing story, but somehow Simpson survived the fall and crawled back to base camp.

I was mulling over the events, trying to imagine myself in that situation, what I would do, and whether I would have the passion for life to pull myself through. I doubted it, but you never know until the circumstances are upon you.

I imagined what it would feel like hanging off the edge of the mountain, helpless and knowing that you were probably about to die. Or how it felt to make the decision to cut the rope and condemn your friend to death. As I pictured the mountain scenario the mental image I had created changed. I could see my father casually strolling down the side of the mountain and white light illuminating the sky above the summit.

My mind had wandered off on a tangent. The mountain was no longer a foreboding place. Quite the opposite. I remembered clearly that this was something which happened to me whilst I was unconscious, and I was suddenly aware of how close to death I had come. It was all becoming clear.

I remembered reading stories about people who had suffered near death experiences, and one thing they all had in common was the bright white light, and the feeling of comfort as they accepted their fate.

Medical advances, and specifically cardiac resuscitation, has made these experiences more and more common. I expect that there is a scientific explanation for these experiences, that people who are dying are prone to hallucination, but I didn't feel that this was something that science needed to explain to me. I knew what had happened, and how I felt.

I had always considered myself an atheist, but from that moment on I would be a lot more conscious that there are other forces at work. I am not saying I became a believer in God, although I definitely became a lot less sceptical, but I do now believe there is life after death.

I would later read that people who suffer near death experiences would often report long term after-effects, and changes in worldview, such as increased interest in spirituality, greater appreciation for life, increased interest in the meaning of life, increased empathic understanding, decrease in fear of death, higher self-esteem, greater compassion for others, heightened sense of purpose and self-understanding, desire to learn, greater ecological sensitivity and planetary concern, a feeling of being more intuitive or psychic. To some extent or another I felt that this was happening to me. I was changing for the better. Maybe it would be good for everyone to have a near death experience.

A week later and I was well on the way back to normality. The doctors still wanted me to remain in hospital for observations, and thought that another week or so of progress would lead to me continuing my recuperation at home. I was happy to do whatever I was told.

I even felt well enough to discuss my future with Laura, and promised myself that I would speak to her next time she visited.

I had a feeling that things would be ok, and there was no apprehension when I thought about what I would say. I was filled with positivity and possibilities, and was convinced that our situation would be resolved.

THE FINAL COUNTDOWN

"Somebody should tell us, right at the start of our lives that we are dying. Then we might live life to the limit, every minute of every day. Do it! I say. Whatever you want to do, do it now! There are only so many tomorrows."
(Pope Paul VI)

I spent the rest of that evening in the hospital reading and trying to trigger memories from my dream. I focused on the mountain article to see if anything happened. Nothing did. I frantically flicked through the pile of magazines on my bedside table looking at images, hoping they would trigger something. They didn't.

In the end I gave up, and focused on what I was going to say to Laura when she came to visit the next day. I was going to lay it on the line. Use the accident as a cut off point to forget everything that had happened before, and start anew.

All the signs from Laura had been good. She had been to visit me every day, and I knew her well enough to know that she wasn't the kind of person who would provide false comfort to someone. It wasn't in her nature.

I slept well that evening. I was keen for the next day to arrive so I could move on with my relationship with Laura.

As usual she arrived with my mum the next day and we chatted for an hour or so about nothing in particular. I was glad of the company after spending the night alone. I listened as they talked, and tried to think of a way to get my mum to leave us alone without sounding rude and making everyone uncomfortable.

I don't know whether my mum sensed that I wanted to be alone with Laura, or whether she genuinely needed to 'pop into town quickly'. Either way, it saved me from an awkward moment, and I was grateful for that.

Laura had sensed that something was up. I had been quiet, my mind had been elsewhere. As soon as the door closed behind my mum, she turned to me expectantly. She was smiling, and this gave me the confidence I needed to open the conversation.

"So", I was dithering. This had seemed a hundred times easier when I was running it through in my head the night before.

"How's things?"

What a pathetic question.

"Things are good, thanks", Laura replied.

I could tell that things were getting a little bit awkward. I needed to sort that out, but now I was too aware of the awkwardness. Bollocks.

"Good. Good. Good"

Repeating the word 'good' sounded even more stupid.

There was a magazine on my lap. I pulled it up over my face and asked if I could try again. I composed myself and lowered the magazine. Laura was smiling back at me, I laughed the ice was broken.

"What I really wanted to say was that, the same as before the accident, I want us to work things out." I paused, trying to read her face before continuing, "I don't want this, me in here, to be the reason we sort things out. I don't want to base our future, assuming we have one, on sympathy. I want…"

Laura cut me off from my ramblings. "Trust me, I want the same thing, and I think you know me well enough to know that I would never ever do that."

This was more like the way I had envisioned it the night before. Laura continued;

"I wanted us to get back together even before the accident. I just got a little weirded out by your story, and needed some space to make sure I could deal with it before getting in touch."

Laura paused and looked right into me. I didn't feel uncomfortable, I was happy. She could do whatever she wanted.

"You are over that phase, aren't you?"

I assured her that I felt like a new man, and not just because of the accident. I knew what I wanted before the accident, and now I just wanted it even more.

Laura liked that line, and moved in to kiss me. It felt awesome. I could feel my recovery gathering momentum from that moment and I couldn't wait to leave hospital. Laura had agreed to move back in, and she spent the next week either in the hospital, or sorting out the house ready for my return.

My mum was delighted we had sorted things out. She had always really liked Laura, and saw our break up as another massive reason for the downward spiral in my life.

Every time the doctors came back with test results, I hoped that would be the day I could leave. I was excited to leave, and it seemed like they were prolonging the process.

Eventually, almost two months to the day of my accident, I was allowed to go home. I would need to return once a week for tests, and wasn't allowed to do anything remotely physical for a long time, but I was going home, at last.

I had been in hospital for so long that life felt suspended. I was treading water before getting on with the rest of my life. Going home meant getting back to normality. A fresh start with Laura, and a renewed vigour for life.

I had been told to relax, but I was finding it difficult. Life seemed too short now, and I needed to get as much done as possible.

The final few hours before leaving the hospital dragged on for ages. It was a lovely summer's day and I decided to pass the time in the hospital grounds sitting on a bench and watching the world go by. It didn't make time go any quicker, but it added to my appreciation of being alive.

I watched as different kinds of patients came past. Some in wheelchairs, looking sad. Others with relatives taking a stroll round the gardens. Elderly patients, sitting on benches, staring into space and reminiscing over their lives. The other patients said hello as they passed me. We all had the hospital experience in common which provided us with a connection. When I glanced into their eyes they all had one thing in common, unhappiness. Even though the sun was shining and it was a beautiful day, there was a feeling of melancholy in the garden that day. Apart from me. I was lucky. I was going home.

Locked away in my room I had been immune to the pain and heartache contained in the hospital. Sitting in the hospital on that summer's morning gave me an insight into the pain and suffering of life, and made me realise how lucky I was to get another chance. I vowed to make the most of it.

At 12pm Laura and my mum arrived. I had left the garden and was waiting in my room, thinking about what I had seen that morning. As soon as they entered my room I was on my feet and ready to leave. A quick kiss for Laura, and hug for my mum, and I was ready to leave. I was out of the door before them and leading them down the corridor to reception. To freedom. To life.

The journey home only took twenty minutes, and was one I knew well, but everything seemed new, different. I felt like I was making the journey as a prisoner being released from prison. Enjoying my freedom for the first time in years. Even the slightest normality was pleasing. Seeing someone walking their dog. A couple walking along holding hands. Everything was good. Everything made me happy.

Laura attempted to keep the journey entertaining with light conversation, but I wasn't really in the mood. I was happy to sit in the front seat and watch the world go by.

I was going to enjoy each day from now on. My life had come full circle. Twelve months ago life was getting me down. I hated lots of people, and couldn't handle what I saw as the unfairness of life. Six months ago I had taken a backseat on life, effectively giving up. I had lost faith in people and wanted nothing to do with anyone. I broke up with my girlfriend, lost contact with my friends, and stopped participating in life.

Now I was back to normal I was going to make the most of it. The last time I could remember being this happy I was a child. I had the kind of happiness that you see in children. A happiness that hasn't been broken by the experiences of life. My slate had been wiped clean. The accident meant that I could draw a line under the last twelve months, and get back to living life and enjoying myself.

We got home and everything felt different. The two months since I stumbled out of my front door hammered on vodka, and almost died, had bought some subtle but noticeable changes to the estate. There were neighbours cars I didn't recognise, changes to gardens which made the place feel different. More leaves on the trees. More sunshine. More life. Changes you never notice in the daily routine of life.

My mum parked in our driveway, and scrambled out quickly in order to help me out. I didn't feel like I needed any help, and certainly didn't want any, but let my mum do the 'mothering' thing and help me out of the passenger seat. Walking up the drive to the front door I could feel there were people watching me. Neighbours who had heard about my accident, and were hoping for some kind of horror story to retell at a later date. I strolled confidently to the front door, which Laura had already opened, and entered.

Once inside I began to feel a bit tired, but decided to look round the house and re-familiarise myself with my surroundings. It was like I was visiting a relative, everything was familiar, but not as much as it should be. It would take time for this to start feeling more comfortable again.

Laura had made the place immaculately tidy, almost too tidy, and I was afraid to do anything in case I created a mess. The house still had the memories of being alone, being drunk, and being desperate.

I was upstairs, and could hear Laura and my mum talking in the kitchen. They obviously thought I was out of earshot upstairs as they were discussing their worries about my convalescence. They were worried about what I had been up to before the accident, and how that might affect my recovery.

I had thought my mum was in the dark about that, obviously Laura had told her everything. I let it go, the only way I could prove to everyone that things had changed was to get on with my life and show them.

I went back downstairs, being deliberately noisy so they could end their conversation and there was no awkwardness.

"Any chance of a cup of tea?" I asked as I flopped onto the sofa and slipped my shoes off. This was like old times. I could tell they thought I was being cheeky, but at the same time, both my mum and Laura were pleased to see my cheeky side back again. My quietness in the car on the journey back had worried them.

After the tea, and small talk, my mum made her excuses and left. I think she sensed that we needed to be alone. My mum has highly tuned women's intuition, almost telepathic, I don't know how my dad coped with it.

I thought we might need to have a 'talking session' as well, but wasn't really in the mood. That night in the hospital, when we had decided that we would make things work, had made everything clear to me. I was now happy to move on and up and leave the past in the past. I was running this over in my head, getting prepared to pre-empt any 'chat' that might be coming my way, when Laura suggested we watch a film.

The film started and we both settled down together on the sofa. It felt good. There was no need to talk, life moved on from there and was better than it had ever been before.

Life moved quickly from that point onwards. Being together with Laura again gave me the stability I needed for my new sense of freedom.

My sick leave from work came and went. I spent most of my time reading about anything and everything, watching documentaries, absorbing information, and doing my CV. I was determined to spend as little time as possible wasting my life away in my old job. I didn't want to be like the middle aged men in my department. Killing time until they retired, and then killing time until they died. Life isn't about killing time, it's about doing something.

My convalescence gave me a lot of time to think, and I came to the conclusion that I needed to do a job that returned something to society. My work had paid my wages whilst I was in hospital. Although that would have stopped after six months and I would have been left with nothing. I didn't feel much loyalty towards my employers. They were also still guilty of being a big, fat organisation that was full of idiots, and that was their own fault. During my recuperation I hadn't done much, so my wages had gathered in my account, and now that gave me a certain level of freedom, and time, to weigh up my options for the future.

I returned to work briefly to check on what my liabilities were having been off work for so long. There weren't any, so I set about putting my plan into action and returning to university.

I knew that I was too immature when I first went to university, and had chosen poorly when I decided to do a Media Studies degree. It made me cringe looking back at what a cliché I was, but I was young and the main concern I had was leaving home and meeting girls. Now I was going to return and study to be a doctor.

I wanted to give something back to society. I needed to do a job that meant something to people, and meant something to me. There are enough people in the media, doing marketing, project managing, auditing. These jobs are created by bureaucracy, they aren't really proper jobs, just bureaucratic wastes of life.

Having witnessed my father's death, and despite how painful that had been, I knew that I wanted to work with cancer patients.

I was able to enrol on a five year undergraduate course, but due to my lack of science A' levels I would have to do the pre-course Medical year. I had thoroughly researched this and knew that the government would sponsor me all of the costs. The lack of doctors meant I would even get living expenses. I would be a lot poorer than I had been, and Laura would have to cover a lot more of the household expenses than before, but I had okayed that with her. I had done the sums and it would be tight for a few years, but nothing that we couldn't handle. I could do the course at Bristol University and Bristol Royal Infirmary so there was no need for a massive life changing move.

In the long run it meant that not only would I be doing something that fulfilled me, but also the monetary rewards were very good, and the long hours were not even an issue. If I had to do a fifty or sixty hour week in my current job I would probably cry, but this was different.

I had to work a few more months in my current job before the studies began. I used that time to find an evening job at a local pub in preparation for beginning my new student life. I also needed to show willing to Laura, as she was going to have to make a lot of sacrifices for me.

The moment I handed in my notice ranks as one of the happiest in my life. After years of frustration, watching untalented and annoying people progress their way up through the company. Watching them getting more and more filled up with their own self importance. Spending the majority of my life surrounded by buffoons. I was now able to give the lot of them a metaphorical two fingered salute in the best possible way. Actions speak louder than words, and by handing in my notice I was able to send out a signal to everyone that this workplace was a big pile of crap.

I had looked forward to that moment for the last few years. Before I had plans for exposing the terrible people I worked with. Now I just didn't care. I was happy to leave them to get on with their strange, boring, money focused, stress filled, lifestyles. That was punishment enough. I was just disappointed in myself for taking so long to escape, and the fact that a near death experience had been required to provide me with the motivation and impetus to leave.

The final month was great. Every day at work was another day closer to leaving. Having that finality, knowing that there was something to look forward to, made life at work quite good. Even though all I was doing was making posters and leaflets, time passed quickly and pleasantly.

This was combined with my home life with Laura, which was going better than we both could ever have hoped for. Both of us had been able to write off the weird period, and it seemed that, if anything, it had made us stronger.

It was with this in mind that I had decided to ask Laura to marry me. My life was coming together. I had none of the insecurities about work and my future which had been hanging over me prior to the accident.

Before I had been wound up by karma, I had always firmly believed that things happen for a reason, and they happen when they are meant to happen. I always believed that forcing things to happen, having a life plan, was asking for trouble. This was a principle that had generally been good to me so far in my life. Right now I was more than ready to take the next step with Laura, and, unless I had been seriously misreading the signs, Laura felt the same way, and I wasn't about to completely embarrass myself and ruin everything.

We had been doing a lot more things together recently. Making time for each other during the week, and making sure that we always did things together on the weekends. By something, I mean something other than getting a DVD or going to cinema, which were easy, and lazy ways to pretend to have quality time. So when I suggested a weekend away to the Lake District I knew that Laura wouldn't suspect a thing. I wanted the proposal to be a surprise.

With the Lake District trip looming I began my search for the perfect ring. Laura was like most girlfriends, she had made it blatantly obvious which styles of rings she preferred on many occasions. She would point out rings she liked in catalogues, make me look at her friend's rings that she liked. I knew EXACTLY what she liked. Gradually drilling it into me that she liked white gold, and she liked a plain ring, and she liked small diamonds. How difficult could it be to find one of those, that description sounded like every ring I had ever seen.

It was more difficult than I could ever have imagined. After three hours of ring shopping I was cursing the need for proposals to be a surprise. It would be a whole lot easier if you could bring the good lady down to the shops, get her to choose, and then just stump up the funds. Obviously you would need to clearly define the budget beforehand, otherwise you were asking for trouble.

All the rings looked pretty similar to my untrained eye. The slightly effeminate male shop assistant was confusing me, and trying to get me to spend more money than I wanted to. White gold was really expensive, and the provisional budget I had set myself was looking completely inadequate. Eventually the sheer amount of time it was taking, and the need for the perfect ring, led to some budgetary flexibility. Laura was worth it.

As I left the shop with the ring I started to feel nervous. I questioned what I was doing for the first time. Before I had been carried along by the romanticism of the idea, but having bought the ring, the reality was starting to set in. I was sure of my position, but not as sure as I had been about Laura's.

I had to call on all my newly found optimism to convince myself that I was doing the right thing. Now came the hardest bit, keeping my feelings, and my plans, a secret until our trip to the Lake District the following weekend.

Returning home, and trying to appear normal, was a bit tricky, but I got through the rest of the weekend without Laura suspecting anything. The working week would be easier as we slipped back into the normal daily routine.

Monday evening was the same as usual. We ate, watched some television, and relaxed. I was constantly thinking about the weekend, what to say, how to say it, where and when to say it. I masked my thoughts well, but inside I was excited about starting the next chapter of our lives.

It would all come crashing to an end on Tuesday evening. It was classic 'reap what you sow'. My old life was about to catch up with me, and I should really have seen it coming.

On Tuesday evening I got home at 6pm as usual. I only had three more days left at work. Only three more days of the bullshit. I sat on my sofa at home, contemplating how much better was life was about to become, and generally feeling pretty happy about everything. Friday would be my last day at work, then I was off to the Lake District and I was going to ask Laura to marry me. My whole life seemed to have a renewed purpose and a future that I looked forward to. I don't remember ever actually being as happy as I was that evening. I cast my mind to the ring I had chosen. I hoped she liked it. I had hidden it in a pair of my shoes at the bottom of our wardrobe, she would never find it there.

Laura always came home about twenty minutes after me. It was a routine I had got used to. I started the evening meal, knowing that Laura would join in when she got home.

We didn't have any specific plans for the evening, just relax and plan our activities for the weekend in the Lake District.

After eating and researching the Lake District on the internet, Laura decided to go upstairs and run a bath.

I heard the bath running upstairs, the sound of running water relaxed me, and I settled onto the sofa to watch television until she came back downstairs.

Fifteen minutes later there was a knock at the door. I wasn't expecting anyone, but maybe Laura was. I hauled myself up from the sofa and went to the front door. It was 7:30pm, not an unreasonable time for somebody to call round.

We had a spy hole, but I never remembered to use it. I wish I had remembered it this time. Now I had something to lose. A life I loved. A woman I loved. A future I wanted.

I opened the door.

Straight away I knew it was a bad move. I looked into the eyes of the man at the door and everything started moving in slow motion, especially me. I was frozen to the spot.

I recognised him immediately, even though I had only ever met him once before in my life. His face was permanently etched on my memory, but I had never expected to see him again.

Unfortunately for me, the place I recognised him from was the Viceroy car park in the city centre, and the last time I had seen him he had been lying on the floor suffering from a knife wound inflicted by me.

I could see the scar on his neck. It was a vivid reminder of the depths I had been to just a few months ago. It also reminded me of how far my life had now moved on. That night in the car park no longer seemed real. That part of my life was like a long forgotten dream. I had compartmentalised it into a strange 'other' life, that had nothing to do with me. Now I had collided with that life head on, and I knew it wasn't going to be good.

He didn't say anything. Just looked me up and down to confirm that he had the right person. I could see pure anger in his eyes.

I didn't have time to move. Even though everything was moving in slow motion, I was moving in even slower motion. In fact I wasn't moving at all. Only my eyes moved. I looked down and saw the knife in his hand. He noticed that I had seen the knife, and lunged forward.

Five brutal blows later and I was lying on the floor, blood seeping from my stomach. I looked up in time to see the yardie spit down in my direction and walk off into the darkness.

I couldn't believe it. I couldn't feel any pain. Only shock. After everything I had done and been through, I was finally sorting my life out, and now this. At first I was sure I was going to survive. I felt faint and weak, but Laura must have heard the commotion, and she would soon be down to help.

I waited for what seemed like ages, but she didn't appear. The feeling of faintness was progressing into something more overpowering. The light on the porch was burning into my eyes, but I knew I had to keep them open. Closing my eyes meant giving in. I wanted to cry. My life was seeping out of me.

I tried to shout for Laura, but the only sound that came out was a quiet gasp.

I was holding my stomach trying to stem the flow of blood, but I could see the puddle of blood inching across the floor further and further away from me. Escaping my body and taking my life with it.

I tried again to shout for Laura, this time there was a slightly louder gasp, but it sent a shooting pain up from my stomach that made me convulse. The pain of the convulsion sent a small jet of blood from my mouth which sprayed onto the laminate flooring. I had only ever seen that happen in movies, and when that happened I knew it wasn't a good sign.

Panic set in. The porch light was getting intense. I had to use all my concentration and will power to keep my eyes from closing. Laura must come down at any second. In my delirious state I had forgotten that a Laura bath lasted a long, long time.

The panic began to seep away. Replaced by a remarkable calmness. There was a stillness in the air. No sounds, no movement. The light no longer seemed as bright. I relaxed and closed my eyes anyway.

A WASTED LIFE

"The doors we open and close each day decide the lives we live."
(Flora Whittemore)

Laura had an especially long bath that evening. I guess it was my time to go.

She found me twenty minutes after I had officially died. It wasn't a pretty scene. She called the emergency services, but despite a couple of attempts to revive me, they had to give up.

Laura had been unable to watch, and just sat on the edge of our sofa in the lounge with her head in her hands. She was too numb to think about who might have done it, but later that month she would raise her suspicions about the possibility of yardie retribution with the police. They were unable to do anything. A couple of interviews with local prostitutes yielded nothing, and although the case wasn't officially closed, effectively it was.

Once I had been pronounced dead, Laura phoned my mum to break the news. My mum came over immediately. By then the crime scene investigators were in the process of sealing the house and the local media were outside, so my mum picked Laura up in the back alley and gave Laura a lift to her parent's house.

My mum stayed for a few hours, drinking tea. She didn't want to go home to an empty house. She needed the company to help her forget all the death in her family that year. She was now totally alone. It felt like she no longer had a reason to be around anymore. She would eventually feel ok, and get on with living life, but it would take a long time.

Laura stayed with her parents, she had decided that she could no longer live in the house of my demise, and remained at her parents until she was able to revisit the house to sort everything out. A few weeks after the police had finished with the crime scene, she found the courage to return to get everything sorted out.

She asked a close friend, Kate, to accompany her to the house on a Saturday morning to assess the damage, and try to work out how long the process might take.

The house felt eerie as soon as they entered. It was cold from the lack of human activity, and dust had settled in a way that only happens in unoccupied houses. There were some slight signs that the crime scene team had been there. A couple of fingerprint marks on the wall, some prints left in the dust.

As soon as she got through the door Laura wanted to turn back. Kate sensed this, and gently persuaded her that it needed to be done. She knew that the longer she left it the harder it would be.

They had brought some boxes to pack the things. There were only two main categories for packing, mine and Laura's. I didn't have a will. I had always considered myself too young to have a will. No one wants to think about death in their twenties. No one wants to think about death full stop. It had never occurred to me that I would die. Apart from every time I got on an aeroplane, but that was just an irrational fear.

My mum had told Laura that she could choose to do whatever she saw fit with my things. My mum trusted her wholeheartedly, and couldn't face going through the pain of sorting through my life by herself. She had only just sorted through my dad's and her parent's lives. To do her son's as well would be too much.

The first thing Kate did was put the kettle on to make a cup of tea. Laura sat down at the computer, and switched it on. Once it had loaded up, she logged in and went to our 'My Pictures' file.

Kate poked her head around the kitchen door, found Laura crying at the computer and went to comfort her.

"Look at those another time, Laura. It's not worth putting yourself through that right now".

Laura knew she was right. She was just tormenting herself. She logged off and went through to the kitchen where Kate was finishing making the tea.

Laura drank her tea and gazed out of the kitchen window into the garden, not really thinking anything, just feeling empty.

Kate was trying to be Laura's rock, and finished her tea quickly so she could start the process of sorting things out. She left Laura in the kitchen and went upstairs. She figured that it was best to have a process, and starting from the top down seemed as good as any other method.

Laura eventually joined her, and slowly went about packing her things into the boxes. Laura wanted my things to wait until she had finished hers. There was too much pain attached to my belongings.

It took the best part of the day to pack all Laura's things. By the time they had finished the house felt even more empty and emotionless. Kate thought they had done enough for the day, but Laura was feeling strong and wanted to go on until there were no boxes to fill.

She started on my things in the bedroom. Firstly my clothes, which were going to charity shops, then my shoes, which were due the same fate.

Laura was obviously unaware that I had hidden the engagement ring inside one of my shoes. In her haste, she packed it away, and delivered it to the Samaritans shop. Remaining oblivious to the fact that I had been about to ask her to marry me.

Sadly, she failed to leave any contact details with the lady in the charity shop. The lady who worked in the shop found the ring later that day when she was sorting through the box.

Laura had provided her with some context behind why she was giving away all this man's stuff. She immediately appreciated the importance and sadness of the find, but had no way of getting in touch with Laura. She felt sad that this couple's love had been lost, and that Laura would never know exactly how I felt. Maybe she was better off not knowing. This way would be easier for her to get on with her life.

Still, she kept the ring on the off chance that she might see Laura again.

Laura got on with her life. Eventually meeting someone else about eighteen months later. Trying to get back to normality.

My mum found it a little harder. She used her retirement to throw herself into charity work. She needed to keep her mind occupied and away from the tragedies that had befallen her family. She found someone to replace me and my dad, a little pug called Monty.

Shortly after finding her new man Laura walked past the Samaritans shop. All my belongings were long gone. Adorning different kinds of people in all different walks of life.

The shop was empty and the lady behind the counter was absentmindedly gazing out of the window when Laura walked past.

She wasn't one hundred percent sure it was Laura, but felt compelled to go outside and check. It was so sad that Laura didn't know that her departed boyfriend had loved her so much that he was about to propose.

She had chased someone else she thought was Laura before, but had been embarrassed to find out she had the wrong person. She decided to risk it, and ran outside to stop the woman in the street.

As soon as Laura turned round she knew that it was her.

"Did you visit me about eighteen months ago to deliver your boyfriend's belongings?" she enquired.

"Yes. Yes I did. Why?" Laura asked.

"You accidentally passed on something that belongs to you. I have kept it for you."

Laura was a little surprised. It couldn't have been anything important, or she would have noticed. "You should have sold it".

"Oh, I could never have done that." She paused. "I think you should come inside".

Laura was now very curious and followed the woman into the shop. The woman went into the back room. Laura craned her neck to try and see what she was up to, but there were too many shelves of unwanted things in the way.

The woman returned, and from what Laura could see, she didn't have anything. Then she placed box on the counter, opened it to reveal the ring, and said, "I take it you have never seen this before?"

"No". Laura was shocked, and just stared at the ring in the box. "What is it?" but she knew already.

"It was inside a pair of the shoes that you brought in. He must have been meaning to surprise you before he died."

Laura could feel herself welling up. This opened up too many feelings. Feelings that she had only recently managed to lay to rest. Things had been going so well in the months before I had died that she wasn't surprised I was planning to propose. The waste of my life was all too clear again. It was like those first few weeks all over again.

Her new relationship was in its infancy, and she wasn't convinced that it could ever be as good as the times we had together. She wasn't convinced that she could ever find anything else to compare. She thought of what might have been, and where we could have been now. What a waste.

LEGACY?

"Have the courage to live. Anyone can die."
(Robert Cody)

So what does my life leave behind? What is my legacy? Do I even have one, or does everyone have one to a certain extent? Good or bad…….

If I was being negative, I would say that I had no legacy, that I had wasted my life. But in death I came to realise that every life has some kind of legacy, whether it is an appalling life from whose mistakes we should learn, or a positive life. I believe that even ordinary people leave a legacy for the people around them. Everyone touches the people around them to some extent.

The last twelve months of my life make me think that my legacy should be to stay concerned with your own life. Don't let the actions of other people get you down, even if they are idiots. Even if the majority of people around you are idiots, just worry about your own path.

I became obsessed with the injustices in life when there was nothing I could ever do to stop it. It is human nature to be selfish, and society has created a framework for selfishness to flourish. You can't change human nature. I was fighting a losing battle from day one, and I didn't have the foresight to realise.

I lost all perspective in my life. I no longer realised that I had a good life. I lost the ability to keep things in perspective. All the bullshit and all the insignificant people around me started to influence me too much. They became the focus of my life, and I lost interest in my own life. My irritation escalated out of control, and my life crumbled around me. I didn't notice until it was too late.

So to summarise, don't let the bullshit and the idiots get you down.
Do you think I believe that?
I don't believe that for a second. Bollocks to it, and bollocks to the idiots.

I'm glad I annoyed all those twats. I'm happy that I broke up John Simmonds marriage because he was a cheating asshole. I'm glad I embarrassed Jane Davids by exposing her for the ass kisser she was in front of the rest of the department.

Dave Dickson deserved to have all his worldly possessions 'stolen' from him. He had done the same to countless people in the past without any real consequences, he deserved to feel how every one of his victims must have felt, and he was a dirty little pervert as well.

Michael Masterson needed a kick up the arse, and I was more than happy to be the person who provided it. Brian Cockburn-Emery was born with a silver spoon in his mouth, led a privileged life, held a position which he had no right, or ability to hold, and abused it. He deserved to be found out. They all deserved everything they had coming, and now that I can look back at my life, I am glad I did it.

I guess I am not that bothered after all. Ignore all the previous legacy rubbish. I want my legacy to be 'not accepting all the crap that you see around you'.

I am deeply sorry about Laura. Sorry for the way I hurt my mum. I wish I hadn't hurt them both so much. But, at least I wasn't like the idiots at my work. They might as well be dead. Their lives are pointless. At least I had a point.

I want you all to react to the idiots you come across in your every day life. Next time someone jumps a queue in front of you, tell them to get to the back. If someone does something inconsiderate on the road, make sure you let them know. If a colleague is shamelessly kissing someone's ass, make sure you expose them.

Next time someone comes to your house and pisses on your toilet seat, confront them. Ask them why they didn't feel the need to clear it up, ask them if they would do that in their own house.

If you think someone is skiving off at work, find a way of exposing them. If you know someone is having an affair, find a way to tell their husband or wife. Don't be afraid to make the police earn their money. Report everything to them, even minor offences. If you see someone parking on double yellow lines, blocking the road, find a parking attendant. A child was killed a few months ago because someone had parked on double yellow lines near a school crossing. The children couldn't see cars approaching the crossing, and cars couldn't see the children, until it was too late. If someone had said something to the inconsiderate driver, they would have saved that child's life.

If you can expose someone for being a twat, do it. Make people accountable for their actions. Find a way to make them face the consequences. Don't hold back. You might enjoy it. Maybe, if everyone did take a stand, then life would change for the better. The cumulative effect could change the world. I wish that could happen.

Think about your life. What do you want to do with your life? When you are lying on your deathbed, surrounded by your family, how will you look back on your life? You could look back and say, "I got by". Is that good enough? Is getting by a proper life. It's depressing.

As you go through day to day you never get the chance to think about life. You get by each day at a time. The days pass by slowly, but the years pass you by quickly, and before you know it your entire life will have passed you by. Stop and think about what you want from life. Is working hard, kissing ass and striving to achieve that next promotion really the best use of your time. Just because you can afford a house with one more bedroom, or one more toilet, or a GTE car instead of a GT, does that make you a better person? What does that 'E' mean? Ultimately, it means nothing. Does that really make your life better? Does it make your life more worthwhile? I don't think it does. I think it makes you no better than a worker ant, toiling all day until you die. A slightly wealthier worker ant than your fellow ants, but you are still an ant, you live and die like everyone else, but are you really happy?

Why waste your time. You only get one life, don't squander it. Too many people these days don't do anything. They are unimportant. They have unimportant jobs and live unimportant lives. Idiots. Don't be one of those idiots.

Worker ants scrambling through life, doing whatever it takes to get to the next level, to earn the extra few hundred pounds. Waiting all year for their two week holiday in the sun.

In Winter you spend all the daylight hours inside the office, typing into spreadsheets, managing projects, completing mindless endless admin. Their lives justified by the achievement of promotion from Second Junior Assistant to the Project Administrator to First Junior Assistant to the Project Administrator. Their existence fulfilled by this badge of honour. This sign that they are improving as a human being. Their lives devoted to the sycophantic love of their seniors and perceived betters.

You need to do something more with your life. You shouldn't be spending your life counting down the minutes until the end of the working day. Spending the entire week looking forward to the weekend. Each day you should do something more than wishing your life away. Maybe, probably, I got it wrong. I went too far, but I felt alive. I felt like I was living not dying.

The legal system in this country won't do anything to help. Politicians don't care about society. They just care about taxes, the media and winning elections. It is up to the common man to take a stand, and it starts with not accepting the stupid little things. Zero tolerance for the idiots you see as you go through everyday life. Don't let them rot society from the inside out.

Find a decent set of values, and live by them. If anyone needs a reminder about respecting other people, be the one to give it to them. Don't do anything illegal. Just make these people think about themselves and the way they live their lives. Try to make them realise the consequences of their actions. This philosophy could work if we weren't all so selfish. The total effect of this movement could be greater than the sum of its parts.

We should call it Marshallism in my honour. This isn't a 'shock and awe' campaign, more of an 'annoy and subvert'.

Don't live your life with your head down, trying not to upset people, trying just to get by. Don't sit at your desk for fifty years, taking shit from people you hate. It doesn't take a Ghandi-esque effort to make a difference. All it takes is a little bit of courage to say something or do something when you cross paths with these people and the opportunities arise.

Look at these people and say to yourself, "Listen, you prats, you idiots. Here is someone who would not take it anymore. Someone who stood up against the scum, the unfaithful, the liars, the cheats, the twats. Here is a man who stood up.

Everyone, take a stand.

"I am ready to meet my Maker. Whether my Maker is prepared for the ordeal of meeting me is another matter."
(Winston Churchill)

www.ingramcontent.com/pod-product-compliance
Ingram Content Group UK Ltd.
Pitfield, Milton Keynes, MK11 3LW, UK
UKHW041438180426

11947UKWH00007B/515